The Sense of Being
Vikas Parihar

This is work of fiction. The characters in it are all fictional.

Copyright @2022 by Vikas Parihar

Contents of The Sense of Being   Start Page

1.	Chapter 1	4
2.	Chapter 2	13
3.	Chapter 3	16
4.	Chapter 4	18
5.	Chapter 5	25
6.	Chapter 6	29
7.	Chapter 7	31
8.	Chapter 8	34
9.	Chapter 9	36
10.	Chapter 10	42
11.	Chapter 11	51
12.	Chapter 12	60
13.	Chapter 13	138
14.	Chapter 14	141
15.	Chapter 15	152
16.	Chapter 16	164

The Sense of Being

Chapter 1

Andrea and Vivan fired several gunshots a week apart from each other in the same city of United States, both are captured live and caged into two prison cells, through one of the prison walls they can hear each other clearly. Their cells were next to each other like hate next to an unfulfilled desire. They were able to carry conversations like a realized possibility.

Andrea asked, "Read me something from your work."

Vivan reads The Glass of Wine.

"He was touched by many lips, by the lips of the most beautiful women and men, gods and goddesses, angels and demons, animals and worms and several other magical, non-magical and transcendental entities, by lips of those who were bound by space and time, and by lips of those who were not bound by space and time. Once, time personified ejaculated inside him. His structure contained a unique beauty and creativity. World's best wines were poured inside him and served. He has seen the long history of human existence, a long journey which was filled with struggles and changes, a journey of human imaginations, creativity, and curiosities. He has seen the world's greatest painters making paintings. He has seen poets lost in their imaginations. He has seen writers trying to capture their imaginations into the words. He has seen youths, full of energy, trying to find peace and direction in life. He has lived the most peaceful and the loudest moments of existence and of human society.

When his creator created him, he said to the Glass "You will always be young, full of energy, filled with imaginations and dreams of the youth. You will always have desires, curiosity, search, and restlessness of a youth. "Listening this the glass was delighted but he didn't realize that with all these qualities and boons he will never be able to attain composure, equanimity, and equilibrium. Whoever touched him, liked him, whoever found him, liked him and whatever his creator has given him because of that, long history, its pain, journey, conflicts, and agitations were not able to imprint the wrong impressions and the dust on him. The Glass has seen expansion of sex, lust, and desires among several living entities. He saw sex of men and women, men and men, women and women, animals and humans, gods and goddesses, gods and humans, gods and animals and sex of several other beings. When all those entities fucked, moaned, and ejaculated, he listened those moans, he saw those ejaculations.

He has seen pianists playing piano until their fingers bleed, he has seen the rise and fall of empires, he has seen violinists standing outside in full moon nights, gazing in sky, and playing violins for hours. He has seen some people getting aggressive and some people getting calm after drinking wine from him, but wine

was not a taste for him, he was only a wine container. Wine for him was like persona of a person which others can see and live but he himself cannot enjoy it, cannot see it, and cannot feel it for himself. No wine poured in him was ever able to influence him. In many ways he was self-centered and for many things he was indifferent. Here and there sperms were ejaculated inside him and were served as drinks to women, to slaves and to same sex lovers. Centuries ago a prince of a great and one of the most powerful empire used to spit inside him, twice he urinated inside the glass and made his female mistress drink it , later when that empire decayed , the glass was found by a failed artist from the west ,the artist often put half smoked cigarettes inside the glass and often cried in frustrations of his failures, couple of times he masturbated and ejaculated inside the glass and left the sperms to rotten and turn into a disgust.

***

It was full moon night. The sky was clear, and the flow of wind was at its most comfort. The glass saw a guy with very beautiful fingers. He had a mark on his left forehead and one of his left side front teeth was slightly broken. His fingers were thick and long. He was holding a violin. His clothes were elegant and expensive, they gave the impression that he put them carelessly, his hairs were dark, here and there they gave impressions of an unsolved existential mystery. The guy was served white wine in that glass. He had first sip from the glass. As soon as his lips touched the glass, glass felt a sensation, the sensation that he never felt from anyone's touch, kings, emperors, or the most beautiful gods, angels, goddesses, or other transcendental beings. The glass was unaware of such sensation, something moved inside him, he lost the sense of time, when he was back in time, glass looked at the young guy, his face was filled with composure, but his eyes were full of agitation, the glass saw a contradiction. That guy didn't pay any attention to the glass, he only carelessly glanced at the glass once or twice. The guy was lost in his thoughts and in his being.

The glass of wine looked at his face again and said, "Perhaps it's not composure on his face, perhaps it's concern or anxiety but it doesn't look like discomposure."

The glass couldn't reach any conclusion. Perhaps emotions are the absence of the conclusions. The young guy paid for the wine and left.

From that moment onward, the glass of wine was unable to forget the image of that young guy. The endless remembrances of him began. The glass started desiring sensations and emotions that touch created. In a couple of days, he couldn't like anything in that restaurant and in the space surrounding it. He got disinterested in everything and in everyone.

He thought "That young guy is my master. My creator created me and abandoned me. He told me that I will always have the energy which will never allow me to attain equanimity and it will always keep curiosity alive within me, because of

this energy, the dust of time, the burden and pains of long human history never accumulated on me. He never poured wine inside me and drank from me. I don't know how many more glasses like me he has created, spoken to them the same words and boon them in the same way. I don't know where my creator is and if he remembers me or not, that young guy is my master, I will find him and when he drinks from me, I will feel the same sensations and emotions repeatedly, perhaps endlessly. I will feel the same bliss I felt when his lips touched me for the first time. Perhaps he is one of the greatest violinists. Whenever he will play violin, I will listen. When he will be with his lover or mistress, I will see who attained his love, what that being is like and what's so special about her or him and what's the beauty of that being? With him and around him I will feel at home and perhaps I will never have to move again. or perhaps being with him will be like being at home, perhaps he will outlive me."

The glass of wine decides he will go in search of his master.

He thought "Here every day different types of wines are poured in me and served. Several people appreciate my being and existence, but I want to live with someone whose being and existence I appreciate."

He decided to run away from the restaurant, other wine glasses, windows, doors, tables, chairs, cooking pans, forks, spoons, and several other entities on his request decided to help him.

The glass has seen castles and palaces where he used to live being destroyed in time, yet he searched for the eternal abode. He has seen luxurious and extraordinary mansions decay and reduced to dust in time. Among all these, he was always found by someone, and he was always given a safe and comfortable journey to his next destination. There have been times where he waited in those ruined palaces and castles for centuries to be found, during those times the smallest elements of nature, birds, ants, lightning bugs, and other small lives have been his companions. Here and there in those times, he has seen entities which were not bound by time and space. He struggled to make sense of them and self.

It was the first journey Glass was doing on his own. Fourth night from the day when he saw that young guy, around midnight he left the restaurant. As soon as he walked out, the first thought crossed his mind "What direction he might have gone? East, West, North or south. There is an equal possibility of him going into all these four directions, and what if he is a celestial entity, will I be ever able to find him? Should I go back in the restaurant? Should I not search? Should I not leave? "Thinking all these, his remembrance appeared in his mind. He decided to continue his journey.

Then the glass thought "Maybe I should look for his footprints on the road, but I haven't seen his shoes, I have only seen his face and several people walk on the same road." A confusion started inside him; he looked in all directions. From

where he was standing, all directions were very different and unique. In the east there was an old town, in the west after crossing a small forest a very beautiful and rich town existed, in the north mountains covered with snow were standing and in the south beautiful red valleys were in decay. He decided to travel towards the west. The sky was clear with stars and darkness, the moon was in decay after attaining its peak. The moonlight was pervading most of the parts of that forest. After walking for a while, he came across a narrow spring of water, the moonlight was mixing into the spring, after years he came across such a beautiful scene, the image of that young guy was the strongest in his memory, that beautiful natural scene couldn't subside or subdue that remembrance and the effect of his image and memory. The glass appreciated the scene as much as a preoccupied mind can appreciate the present movement.

The glass stayed there for a while, then started his journey again, after walking for a long time he reached an area of the forest which was filled with dense large trees. The area was filled with darkness, thousands of lightning bugs were flying and playing with each other. One of the lightning bugs flew to the glass and asked him "Dear glass where are you going? Have you lost your way?"

Glass "No, I didn't lose my way. I am searching for my master. Have you seen him? His face has the rarest transcendental charm and beauty, the charm and beauty that I have never seen before, he was holding a violin. I saw him three nights back."

The lightning bug said" I have seen him; he went towards the town on the other side of the river in the west. It seems you have travelled a long journey, if you like you can stay, rest, or play with us."

The glass thought "Years have passed. I haven't played with lightning bugs and spent time with them, I should spend some time with them."

The glass said, "I will play with you."

The glass of wine played for a while with the whole group of lightening bugs, when he got tired he set down under a tree, the lightening bugs started arranging themselves into different shapes, first they arranged themselves into the shape of a violin, then into a wine glass, after that into different stars , later they arranged themselves into shape of magnificent beautiful waterfall , in last they started moving around and inside the glass in such way that it started glittering. All of it delighted him.

In all the joy and play he didn't forget he was in search of his master and among all impressions, images, and remembrances, his master was the best, the strongest, the most captive and the most beautiful.

After spending whole night with those lightning bugs, the glass started his journey early in the morning. After walking the whole day, without a break, he arrived

towards the side of the forest from where that beautiful town of west was visible. A river stood between this side and the other side like a reality between a dream and its realization. The side of the river he was standing on, was filled with beautiful flowers and hundreds of colorful butterflies.

One of the butterflies asked him "O glass, where are you going? Have you lost your way? Are you looking for something or someone?"

The glass "I am searching for my master. I think he lives in the town on the other side. The lightning bugs told me they have seen him going in this direction. "While he was saying this several colorful butterflies gathered around him. That butterfly said "We can help you in finding him. We have been in the gardens of the beautiful home in that town several times and we know the people who live in those houses. Other small creatures who live in that town can help as well."

The glass "Your and other small creatures help will be very helpful to me in finding my master. I want to cross this river and go to the other side but don't know how I will be able to cross such a vast and deep river?"

Butterfly said "Several boats go from this side to another side, maybe you can climb on one of those boats or a bird can pick you up and fly you to the other side. "

The butterflies started thinking about the birds who can carry the glass to the other side. They thought about several of them and concluded that among all the birds found on this side of the river either owl or eagle would be best to carry the glass to the other side, both got the necessary strength and flying capacities.

Then the same butterfly who spoke with him first, asked "What's the name of your master? What does he look like? tell us about him, we will fly to the other side of the river and will start searching for him."

The glass "He has exceptional charisma, he was holding a violin when I saw him, he was dressed up in a black suit with white shirt. He has a mark on his left side of forehead and his left front tooth is slightly broken, both mark and slightly broken tooth add up to his charm."

The butterfly pointed towards an oak tree and told the glass "You can rest under that oak tree, a pair of squirrels live there, they are our friends. Both are humble, respectful, and genuine beings, they will give you good company and will take good care of you."

The group of butterflies flew towards the town on the other side. The river was blue and deep, as if the bluest sky jumped into it with all its depth and mysteries.

The glass sat down under the oak tree. It has been years since he spent this much time with nature. Under the oak tree he saw a group of ants, several of them were dissecting a dead worm and couple of them were taking the dissected parts to their

home. There was another group of ants who were preying on a wounded insect, the insect struggled. The struggle of the insect and the dead worm reminded the glass of several living entities, magical and mystical entities whom he has outlived. The glass thought "To outlive everyone is one of the ways to utter loneliness. "By that time the pair of squirrels came running to him, they introduced themselves, asked about him, they had a conversation where he and them felt belonged and understood.

In the evening the butterflies returned, glass asked them "Did you find my master?"

One of the butterflies said, "Not yet, we are planning to go back tomorrow and look for him, it's a big town, it might take us several days."

The glass thanked them for their efforts and help.

That night one of the owls helped the glass to reach the other side of the river. As butterflies and the glass requested, the owl left the glass on the other side and flew back to his home. It was midnight when glass reached the other side, the town was filled with mesmerizing lights, it gave an impression as if that town might be one of the most beautiful spaces in the whole existence, the glass missed his master and his touch. Couple of lightning bugs flew to him, spoke and they became his friends. Late at night he fell asleep.

Next morning couple of butterflies came to see him from the other side, they told him "If you want, you can go and see the town, we will continue to look for your master, meanwhile if you find your master you can go to him and let any butterfly you meet know, he or she will be able to communicate the news to us. If you don't find him before sunset, come back to the same place, this place is safe. We have requested all the butterflies of this town to help us find your master, they have agreed to help us. If you lose your way in the town, ask any bird, butterfly, or small creature in the town, any of them should be able to lead you back here." After saying this all those butterflies flew inside the town.

After walking for a while glass entered the town. The town was very precise in its structure. All the houses were extremely beautiful and most of the people living there contained a mystical and mesmerizing beauty within themselves. Most of the houses had one or two musical instruments placed in the front yard, each house had at least one musical instrument inside the house. The town was filled with art and people's dressing sense was highly elegant and sophisticated.

Glass thought "Who build this mesmerizing town? It doesn't seem that old. Is the founder of the town alive?"

Glass came across a rabbit; he asked the rabbit "How old is this town?"

Rabbit "Around 300 years old but no one knows exactly how old this town is. I have heard conversations of different people, in different houses and families, here and there they mentioned this town is eternal, it has always been here, and it will always be here. It existed from eternal to eternal. I don't believe it, because how in an eternal town, people die and take birth, they grow old and get dieses. I think people love to have romantic ideas about self and surrounding."

Glass "Who founded this town? Who built it? Who designed it?"

Rabbit "Dibas, his name is Dibas, he is one of the most famous and influential musicians of all the time. Although no one knows the true beginning and end of time."

Glass "Is he alive?"

Rabbit "I don't think so. No one has seen him for decades but there has been no evidence of his death. His music continues to live in this town as if it has been written and played just yesterday. Well, time and the absolute both very mysterious." The rabbit left after saying this.

Glass wandered in the town for the whole day; he found no signs of whom he was looking for. Around midnight he walked out of the town and came back to the same park. By that time the butterflies fell asleep, they gave the message to lightning bugs for the glass that they were not able to find his master, they will continue their search tomorrow. The glass gazed at the town for a while from where he was standing. Later he fell asleep thinking about his master and the beautiful streets of that town.

Next morning those butterflies asked help from all the small creatures living in that town to find his master. Whole day the glass wandered in the town in search of his master. It was almost midnight neither he nor small lives like rabbits or mice or squirrels or ants or other living entities from that town or butterflies from the gardens were able to find his master. At night, on his return to the garden on the river shore he lay down and gazed at the sky, the sky was filled with stars and a moon in decay. He thought "**Why my creator created me and then abandon me?** Why didn't he keep me with him? He might have created several glasses like me and would have left them on similar journeys as mine. If my creator would have kept me with him then the desire to find a master wouldn't have appeared inside me and there is a high possibility that the master, I am searching for has several wine glasses far better, far more beautiful, perhaps much more ancient then me. What will be my significance then? What is my significance now? What has been my significance since I have been created? "

In his long journey he has seen the greatest desires of humans come true, but the simplest one remaining unfulfilled and unrealized. The glass tried to remember the image and being of his creator. The image and being appeared but vague,

unclear, and unrecognizable, then he thought "Where he might be? What he might be doing? Thousands of years have passed. Does he still remember me?" Thinking all these he fell asleep.

On the fourth day he went to some new areas of that town, by end of the day he was exhausted, at that time a butterfly flew to him and said, "We found a young guy who matches the description of your master."

The glass was delighted listening this. The butterfly took him to the home backyard of that guy. One of the other butterflies flew to both and said, "It seems this young person is organizing a party and it seems several guests will be arriving very soon here."

Later a couple of squirrels poured water on the glass to wash the dust accumulated on him, nightingales flipped their feathers around the glass to dry him. From the house windows the glass saw the young guy, he was the one glass was looking far. The glass went into ecstasy seeing him, in that very state of being he thought "Perhaps I will never be able meet my creator and perhaps I will never be able to find him but to whom I have considered my master, from now on I will live with him, I will be able to see him every day, he will pour wine inside me and will drink from me."

Lightning bugs told him "Today when your master comes next to you, we will create light around you in such a way that he will only pick you."

Night started; the town was filled with lights. The young guy put on the same clothes he was wearing when the glass saw him the first time. He was holding the same violin; his hairs were carelessly done. Several elements in him were indicating that he doesn't want to look sophisticated or perfect.

World on of the most expensive wine was poured into that wine glass. The young guy played the violin. Glass thought "My master is such an extraordinary violinist. I love his music." Although he didn't know whether it was his music, or he was playing someone else's music, or he was playing music of Dibas. The young guy completed the sonata. On completion everyone clapped and appreciated him. His equanimity or perhaps the restlessness remained intact.

When the young guy walked where that glass was kept with other glasses which were filled with the same wine, lightning bugs created light around the glass, the glass started glittering. The young guy picked the glass and took a sip of the wine. As soon as his lips touched the glass, the glass felt the same sensation and ecstasy he felt in the restaurant when he had first sip from him. In that sensation and ecstasy, the glass closed his eyes. When the glass opened his eyes the young guy was holding the glass in his right hand and was talking to one of the guest, the very moment an over drunk person lost his balance and end up hitting that young guy, the young guy lost his balance, glass slept out of his hand , when the glass

was falling down on the ground , he shouted " My master ,please help me , please protect me."

The glass fell on the marble floor and broke into multiple pieces. The wine filled in it, spread on the floor; a few drops of wine fell on the black shoes of that young guy. The guy, the guest with whom he was talking and the over drunk man, all three of them moved away from pieces of the glass. The glass of wine died.

That young guy didn't know which wine glass it was, he had no memory that it's the same glass from the restaurant he visited a couple of days back, he didn't know the long and tiring journey the glass went through to find him. He didn't know how and how much the glass longed for him, desired him, and remembered him. When the glass of wine broke and died, butterflies, lightening bugs, squirrels, mice, rabbits, and several other lives present there, who helped the glass in his search cried and wept in immense sorrow. The person whom he considered and desired his master felt nothing.

In couple of minutes a lady picked the pieces of glass and threw them into a nearby trash cane, later she cleaned the space. The space was back to what it was when the glass was alive. Small lives went back to where they came from. The eternal, space, and time continued as they always do.

He wrote "The imaginations of the creator, about whom it was told to me that he is my master. The imaginations of spaces beyond the time. The mesmerizing descriptions of that creator and inclinations those descriptions create. Does he remember me? When I will cross the river of time and go to the other shore, will my master recognize me? Or will I shatter like that glass of wine?"

Vivan said "That's it. It's the end of the story."

Andrea "Is that glass you?"

Vivan "In one sense or another that glass is all of us, perhaps each and every human being or perhaps each and every living entity."

Andrea "You know if you would have continued to write, if you wouldn't have lost your way, if you would have left, you would have been one of the greatest and the best authors."

Vivan "But I lost my way." Tears filled his eyes; from his right eye a tear flew all the way down on the prison floor.

Chapter 2

Several gunshots were fired, an ex- city mayor, an old nun and founder of a multinational company were killed.

***

It was a usual morning; Mathew didn't have to take off Alison's panties because she didn't have it on. He moved his tongue on her vagina for a while, then bit on left side of her vagina, his teeth left an impression, latter he pulled his hard penis out of his pants and pushed it bare into her vagina, she moaned. He gradually started switching his penis in between her vagina and anal.

While he was fucking her, his office phone, his cell phone, and her desk phone started ringing, they rang several times. Annoyed, he picked his desk phone, all the sudden he pulled out his penis, put the phone back, zipped in his hard penis, instructed Alison "Not to pick any calls or response to any press questions "and rushed to his car.

Alison was Mathew's secretary. She agreed to spread her legs for a promotion.

***

On the call, Mathew learned Andrea, his wife fired several gunshots which killed city's ex-mayor James, an old nun Nancy and Lucas, a multinational company founder, along with several other people.

***

The shooting immediately captured huge attention locally and globally. Globally because it happened in the United States.

People of the county and the city found something to talk about, something other than the usual and the obvious. The news flooded about the incident on electronics, social, commercial, and print media. People discussed it over meals and brunches, in gatherings and in casual conversations. Here and there the conversations leaked into professional meetings, as soon as it was realized it might not be professional, the leak was cleaned with mop of a professional statement or a sophisticated professional joke.

An old lady reacted, "The evil in the world has increased and the goodness is dying every day." She reacted as if in the old days there were no evils, and everything was perfect. A secretary after sucking vagina of his boss in lunch break expressed his desire to get into the minds of such people, by such people he meant people like Andrea and find out why they do what they do. His boss instructed him to get inside her, he followed the advice. They fucked while most of the people were chewing their lunch. In couple of minutes, he ejaculated inside her, both her vagina and his penis were wet. He thought, he performed very nice, she was still unsatisfied. She went to restroom and masturbated.

People in the city who had anxieties, depression, obsessive compulsive disorder, and other psychological disorders struggled with images and imaginations in which either they performed similar acts or similar acts were done to them and their loved one. Several of them increased their SSRI medicine doses without asking their prescribers, several of them overdosed and overate.

News anchors spoke with high energy and a minor expression of concern over what happened. It was the first such incident in the city. The news TRP was high, more advertisements were played, more money was made. Every advertisement was about comforting life, securing life, enriching life, about making it more beautiful, full of content, full of colors and joy. It was advertised that it will happen if people buy more stuffs, more gadgets, and more vacation packages. The mass shooting and the idea of comfortable life danced simultaneously, next to each other on several news channels.

***

Mathew picked both of his children Kyle and Kylie from the school and dropped them at his parents' house.

In the car Kyle and Kylie asked "Why are you picking us early? Where is mom?"

Mathew "We are going to grandma's home; your mom will be back soon."

Kyle was six years old, and Kylie was five years old.

Kyle "Where is she?"

Kylie "yes, where is she? She is the one who always picks us up?"

Questions from both children caused tears in his eyes, the only sentence he was able to say was "She will be back soon, sometimes grownups need some time for themselves."

Kylie: "Why she needs some time for herself now, my birthday is around the corner, who will do all the preparations, will she be back by then?"

Kyle and Kylie both continued with their questions, arguments and prediction of the situation, Mathew didn't speak much, his mind was filled with racing thoughts, anxieties, concerns, questions, agitation, anger, and bewilderment. By the time he arrived at his mother's home he almost had an anxiety attack.

His mother was watching the news, Andrea was handcuffed, and two police officers were taking her to the car, Andrea was bleeding on her left forehead, one moment she was crying in grief and another moment she was happy, laughing loud, again she was in tears and again laughing loud, an utter confusion took over her.

The moment Mary realized Mathews' car pulled into the driveway she turned off the TV, wiped off her tears and walked out of the door, towards the car.

Both Kyle and Kylie started shouting" Grandma, grandma."

Mathews helped Kylie in getting out of the car and Mary helped Kyle in getting out of the car.

Both Kyle and Kylie hugged their grandma. Grandma hugged back and kissed both.

Marry "I have both of your favorite cookies on the dining table please help yourself. "

Both Kyle and Kylie rushed inside the home saying, "Thank You Grandma, we love you."

Mary's eyes filled with tears again, she touched Matthew's left arm with her right hand, his eyes filled with tears, she said "Why did she do it, she had been a wonderful mother and a great daughter in law. She is such a sweetheart, what happened?"

Mathew "I don't know Mom, I am shocked, nowadays it's impossible to know what's going on in another person's mind even if one is twenty-four seven next to that person. "

Expressions of anger grew on his face; Mary was unsure if her question made him angry or he was angry at Andrea for what she did.

Mary "Would you like to come inside; I will make you some tea or coffee whatever you like?"

He and Mary walked inside, Kyle was eating his favorite, chocolate chip cookie and Kylie was eating her favorite, oatmeal cookie.

Mathew "I will be right back."

He walked into his room, the room had several memories, several memories of the first time, few of those experiences filled him with pleasure, others filled him with horrors.

He walked into the bathroom, pulled out his penis and started masturbating himself. His first masturbation was in the same bathroom, done by Jerry, one of his babysitters. Apart from Jerry and Mathew no one knows about it. Initially, his first masturbation was a memory of being violated and pleasure, later as parent it became a memory of horror and fear, horror and fear which were almost impossible to get out of. He struggled with those horrors and fears inside and pretended to be well outside.

Chapter 3

Laying down in the prison cell, Andrea's mind was filled with racing thoughts, her heart was beating fast enough to fall off the chest. One moment she felt what she did was right, another moment she felt it's wrong. She became a constant stretch between right and wrong, correct, and incorrect, happiness and distress, what was and what should have been. She thought about Kyle and Kylie, what they might be doing, where they might be, and hoped Mathew didn't drop them to her mother's house, she thought of her mother as "a careless stupid whore, either she over trust someone or doesn't trust at all, a confused childish woman, a woman whose body grew, and mind never did, a filthy and disgusting woman."

Then her thoughts switched from hating her mother to the consequences of what she has done, first consequence that came in her mind was she will either be given a death sentence or will be sentenced for life, the very thought of her children growing without her, her not being around them, the **insecurities world and societies offer to such children gave her a panic attack**. She felt a sharp pain in the chest, she felt as if she couldn't breathe and was about to die. She fell unconscious.

Her mouth was wide open, neck twisted toward the left side of her body, she dreamed. She was called inside his office by Lucas, the city mayor at that time. She was sixteen , young , excited , she believed in every propaganda Lucas and his team did .She believed that by doing a free internship at city mayor's office which included the responsibilities such as taking files from one desk to another, getting coffee for office people , picking up the calls and cleaning up the desks , she is part of something great ,she had been made to believe whatever she is doing will make the world a better place .Wherever she went, she appreciated Lucas, dropped good words about him and sometimes went on saying that she thinks Lucas should be state representative and in future should run for presidency .She believed he is doing something to make earth a better place and leaders such as him can lead the lost humanity to a right path , while she was believing that Lucas was too busy supporting the policies which were helping corporates and institutes to make and retain a lot of money and wealth , while individuals live, celebrate , cherish, buy and survive their lives by either one type of loan or other type of loan. The gap between rich and poor continued to increase, she didn't notice it at that time. She was too busy making world a better place.

 It was lunch time when she was called in by Lucas, he asked her to take a seat, he mentioned, he thinks she have great perspectives, and he very much appreciate what she is doing, he would like some more help from her, he would like her to help him relax, out of politeness she said "I will be more than happy to do that. "

By the time she finished the sentence, Lucas pushed his hard penis on her mouth, when she tried to pull her back, he grabbed her hair tide with one of his hands and

forced his penis with another hand inside her mouth, moved it inside out, outside in several times saying "Take it in, you fucking bone, take it in. "

Andrea didn't know how to respond, she was horrified at that moment, a memory, a fear, a horror popped up from the time when she was six years old. She almost froze.

Lucas pushed his penis deep and deep into her mouth, when she was about to throw up, he pulled it out and slapped her face twice, again calling her "Bone, you fucking degraded bone."

Bowing down on the floor she started throwing up, while she was throwing up, Lucas masturbated and ejaculated, partially on her neck, partially on her hairs, and a few drops of his semen fell on the carpet. He pulled back his penis into his pants, grabbed her hair, pulled her mouth up and told her "Get out of my office, you fucking bone. You are fired." he grabbed her beasts and squeezed them hard, hard enough to hurt.

Horrified, shivering in fear, she noticed an anger on his face, the possibility of a beast hiding under a thin layer of sophistication, manners, politeness and well behavior. She rushed out of his office crying, bewildered, shocked, horrified, she went to ladies' room, wipes off his semen from her hairs and neck, few drops flew into the dress, up to her bra and were absorbed in it.

She rushed to her desk, picked up her purse and rushed out, while rushing out she ran into Angelina, Lucas's secretary, Angelina never liked Andrea for no reasons. Rather than asking what happened Angelina rudely asked her "Where are you going?".

Andrea in tears walked past her without answering.

Dreaming all these, Andrea suddenly works up in the prison cell, her heart was beating fast, he pushed her right hand into her panty, started masturbation thinking about Mathew and her first love making.

One of the evenings when her mother Bernadette arrived home from her second job and Uncle Jack just left, Andrea said to her mother "I don't like Uncle Jack."

Bernadette's face turned red in anger, she grabbed Andrea's both soldiers, held them tight enough to hurt Andrea, pulled her closer to herself and said, "Don't break this family like your filth father did, bastard who couldn't keep his penis inside his pants."

She pushed Andrea and said, "I don't want to hear any complaints about Uncle Jack, he is helping us, you don't know how I am keeping this roof on our head and how much I am working to keep food on our plates."

Andrea "If you would have forgiven dad when he bagged, we all would have been together, and these issues wouldn't have appeared."

Listening to that, Bernadette slapped Andrea. Andrea's eyes filled with tears, seeing that, tired and exhausted Bernadette hugged her and said "I am sorry, I am so sorry. ", they both cried and cried. Andrea for one reason and Bernadette for another.

That day Andrea decided whomever she marries she will forgive all his mistakes and will keep her family together, which helped Mathew into having many out of marriage affairs and yet remain married. Andrea knew about several of them and never mentioned or asked Mathew about them. Her whole goal was to keep her family together, under one roof, Kyle, Kylie, Mathew, and herself.

***

In a couple of months Uncle Jack died in a car accident, he was drunk, when he was supposed to push the brake, he ended up pressing the accelerator. His car merged into a large truck from the back. By that time he had already fucked , kissed , ejaculated in and touched pretty much each and every part of Andrea's body .Six years old Andrea was relieved by Uncle Jack's death .In the severe car accident his body broke into several pieces , on his funeral Andrea relieved and at peace, was thinking about what would have happened to bastard's penis , she imagined it was wounded severally and will be soon be eaten up by worms when the body of the shitty bastard will go inside the ground .

Bernadette Andrea's Mother described him as "A man of dignity, a pure soul and a great help." She put him next to angels.

Just to insult Andrea's father she went on saying about Uncle Jack "He was not like other men who don't know where to put their junk, he knew what is garbage and what isn't? "After saying this she busted into tears and almost collapsed on the stage, a young girl whom Jack was fucking occasionally rushed to her and helped her to get back to her seat.

When all the assigned speaker finished speaking, it was announced if anyone else would like to speak, Andrea's father stood up, walked to stage, spoke about forgiveness, love, mistakes as right of every human being, he went on to saying

doing mistake is not bad, but not recognizing them is sin and not forgiving them is a straight way to hell for eternity. Jack was not mentioned a single time in his speech, Andrea's parents turned Jack's funeral into their fight ground, a place of personal mess. He started being overly affectionate toward his girlfriend and pretty much asked Andrea to call her mom which was interrupted by his girlfriend with a statement "You can call me Linda if you like?"

Towards the end of funeral when Andrea's father noticed Bernadette is paying some attention towards him and Linda, he grabbed Linda and kissed her for long time squeezing her butt with both hands, Linda pulled herself back saying "Honey, we are at a funeral, it's not a valentine party. "

 Soon Linda discovered that he might never be over Bernadette. She broke up with him with a message on a sticky note which she left on the refrigerator door and secretly walked out of his apartment, and never returned to his apartment or his life. That day he fucked his secretary again, and again, and again. They started dating which assured Andrea's mother that she was right; her ex-husband and his secretary were having a love affair and she made the right choice of divorcing him. The incident which was a byproduct of her own action reassured her what she believed is true.

***

Because of what uncle jack did to Andrea, in time, gradually it became impossible for her to feel safe around any man, apart from her father. Michael on whom she had crush asked her out in high school, he was her first boyfriend, when he first started kissing her, it took her a while to allow his tongue inside her mouth, when he first kissed her vagina, a feeling of horror and pleasure filled her, her mind struggled with images of uncle Jacks. In her mind sometimes Michael was there, other times uncle Jack. When Michael pushed his tongue inside her vagina for first time, she pretty much pulled his hairs off his head. After that they were often naked fucking ,either in her bedroom or his bedroom, in her basement or his basement, in his car or in her car .She often insisted bare sex , Michael never hesitated , he continued to fuck her ,she continued to swallow the birth control pills , they broke up after he realized no matter how many times he fucks her , no matter how many times he make her come , it's not sufficient ,it's not enough , she is not satisfied. It created a big hurt on his male ego and he broke up with her , then another guys came , he loved her , he dreamed about playing with their grandchildren together , create many babies with her and so on , in time he realized that he couldn't satisfy her , her dissatisfaction started seeming to him as his weakness , his incompleteness , when they got into break up fight she busted into tears and confessed " It's not him , it's her .It's what circumstances made her , it's what the consequences made her ",he interpreted and listened whatever he wanted rather than whatever she was saying , he left , she rushed to stop him , after that fight she realized that whatever uncle Jack did to her at age of six might have damaged her far deeper than she can realize and that damage and hurt might

never heal , and because of the damage , she might never be happy with anyone and will end up hurting those who fall in love with her , she closed herself for couple of year and didn't have an boyfriend or slept with anyone , those years , she struggled with loneliness , obsessive compulsive disordered , depression , stress and anxieties at a sever level and often swallowed anti depression pills, more than the recommended dosage, she masturbated two to three times a day thinking about the best looking male she saw that day , often uncle Jack popped up during those masturbations and she struggled to erase him , often in masturbations two or three males were present , one she desired , another who pushed him on her Uncle Jack or Mayor Lucas ,sometimes all those psychological clutters made her feel masturbation a mere struggle , other times it felt as if it's a fiasco .She never stopped the struggle and the fiasco , she continued to masturbate .

***

When Mathew first fucked her, he first put her butt on an ice bag and later put his penis inside her mouth and vagina. The discomfort cold ice created took off her mind from Uncle Jack and Lucas, they pretty much disappeared , in an attempt to maximize pleasure Mathew pulled his penis all the way out of her vagina and pushed it back , it made her possible space fully open and close several times, in their first love making she came twice before Mathew ejaculated , lying next to him naked gave her a feeling of comfort , security and at home , she had a deep soundest sleep .Next day at work she started missing his touch , his kiss , several times his smell filled her nostril , her nipple grew tighter and she felt a tickle in her vagina , she rushed to restroom and masturbated on Mathew.

They started seeing each other more often, sometimes their lunch was fornication, other times their dinner and breakfast were fornication. To keep things interesting, they did it everywhere, in public parking lots, in movie theaters, in her and in his office restrooms, in his house backyard, in his living room, kitchen, bedroom, bathroom, closet and basement.

Mathew felt there is something different about Andrea, he didn't know what it was, but that different thing caused him to fall in love with her. She had the same feeling about Mathew. When Andrea fired the gunshots, Mathew and she came to know that they were two damaged people who felt comfort and perhaps love in each other's company but never healed damages and wounds of each other.

He proposed within couple of months of dating. She accepted and got married. Till the last minute she wasn't sure if she would like her mother to be in her marriage. Mathew convinced Andrea to invite her mother, she sent the invitation on text about which her mother complained for years, and Andrea always responded, "Mathew convinced me otherwise I wouldn't have invited you, sick and damaged people like you don't deserve any invitations."

Andrea's mother cried and said, "I was never enough for your father, and I will never be enough for you, what else can one do for both of you?"

Andrea "Dad is dead so please let him go, that's what you can do, let him go and get over him. What he did was not that big of a mistake, your idea of perfect marriage and your idea of institution of marriage made a big issue of a small mistake."

Her mother always ended such arguments with "You fool girl. "

In their last argument Andrea threw a flower flask on her mother when she said "you fool girl ", she busted into tears and said "What kind of mother are you who bullies her own child, shame on you, you filthy, disgusting woman ", she spit on her mother's face and left. In a couple of hours, she fired the gunshots.

Chapter 5

From the other side Andrea asked, "Where did it all start? Any ideas? now since death seems so close and so certain, all the things which seem certain became vague and all the vagueness became so certain."

Vivan "I don't know, I don't have an idea of preciseness, it might have started long time back when the first sign of life showed up in existence or when my grandparents were born or when my parents were born or I was born, or when this whole existence manifested. Maybe it started few years back or trillions of years back, don't ask me for preciseness. Time and preciseness both are stress, anxiety, and horror for me, may be that's the true tragedy, too much desire of preciseness, too much desire of punctuality. Apart from that death has always been certain, it's the matter of time when oneself recognizes it and what oneself does with the realization of certainty of death. So I don't know where it started, in your ideas things might have beginning and end , a well-defined beginning and a well-defined end , in my idea and the place I came from , world , this whole existence is an endless continuum , things don't have a precise definition where they started and where they end , everything is related to everything else ,impacting each other , restructuring , redefining , disturbing and soothing each other .To answer your question , which doesn't hold much value if I answer it or not because when one could see and realizes the certainty of death and that it's few of the only elements which are certain in life , most of the questions and most of the answers become useless and several true curiosities begin."

She said, " Is it possible to never learn how to live?"

He answered, " I don't know, is it possible to never get an opportunity to live?"

For a while she didn't say anything, he didn't say anything.

She said "I wish I can come into your cell and fuck you, leak you, masturbate you and swallow your cum. "

He said "I think , It's before death horniness, it's not uncommon, in India I have seen the market where the goats are sold for meat, somehow they sense the nearness of death and male goats starts jumping on any female goat, and sometimes male goat jumps on male goats as well, may be female goats desires the same at time of death, I have to warn you, I am not that great looking. Be careful imagining me inside you and masturbating on me."

She said, "Do you not desire it? you don't want to come inside me?"

He said, "I recently masturbated, my hands are still sticky and filled with the smell of my semen."

Her "I have been masturbating several times a day, the nearness of death changes many aspects; it takes away many insecurities and gives many others."

Him: "How often did you masturbate when you were outside?"

Her "That's not a question to ask a lady and a gentleman should never ask that."

Him: "I don't think I am a gentle man; would a gentleman shoot and kill several people?"

Her "Well yes so-called gentlemen won't kill people as you did, or I did but they can do worse. You know there is a tale The beauty and the beast, in that tale the beast is ugly, very ugly, but now, in this era the beast is far better looking than beauty herself, the beast is highly sophisticated, well behaved, full of good manners and bad thoughts, the beast will hold the door for you and will say after you."

Him: "Did you kill one of the beasts when you fired the shot?"

Her "I killed two of them and one of their bitches. Coming back to your masturbation question, I masturbated as much as I can when I was outside, and I masturbate as much as I can in prison."

Him: "Why outside, was your husband not good enough?"

Her "He was good, he made me come pretty much every night and sometimes twice or three times in one night , it's more than any average woman in United States would get, but more is not enough , looking back it seems to me I have been wounded and damaged in such a way that no man can satisfy me or perhaps nothing can satisfy me , perhaps these sorts of damages can never be cured ."

Him "It sounds only if divine or the absolute manifest into a male then and then you will be satisfied."

She was annoyed by the comment and said "Why, will he fuck me whole night?"

Him: "Whole night and the whole day, from eternal to eternal."

Her "Do you think He is not doing that with us right now, has He not fucked us up already?"

Him: "You are right, I don't know about you, but I think throughout my life as far as I can remember He has messed me up well, in pretty much everything, I don't remember being happy, is it possible? Is it possible to never feel happy in thirty plus years of life? and only feel horrors, sorrows, pain, displacement, bewilderment, and constant anxiety."

Her "Our perception and realization of the world is based on duality, good and bad, right and wrong, joy and sorrow, love and hate, comfort and discomfort, happiness and distress, and so on. So, if you remember sorrow, you must have known joy and if you remember being distressed, you must have known happiness. There must have been something which made you feel happy, like when you fell in love with someone for the first time. Have you ever fallen in love with someone?"

He didn't reply.

Andrea " My father died when I was 10 years old , he died because of heart attack , he died longing for love and forgiveness from my mother , he hated her for not giving it to him , she went on hating and disliking him, she hated him when he was alive and she hated him when he was dead , most of the time the hate and dislike lower down or disappears for a dead person but my mother's hate and dislike for my father increased when he died , she called him degraded pig , a filthy low grade animal on his funeral day and onwards . She often got angry that he didn't suffer enough, and she often assured herself that he went straight to hell for breaking the law of the institute of marriage, where he will suffer for eternity. Look what the idea of perfection and institutes can do, it can destroy families for no good reason and can make someone hate someone else or self to an unbelievable extent. I always longed for a good mother, a good father, a family, a safe and comfortable home, I am not sure if these desires are my weakness, or these are natural human instinct. My mother was too busy hating my father when he was alive and when he was dead, in that hate she forgot most of the things, including her responsibilities as mother, I searched for a mother figure and I came across sister Nancy, I am not sure if she ever looked at me as a daughter figure, perhaps I was a ticket of heaven to her. Sister Nancy was one of three people on whom I fired gunshots. Perhaps I was one of the puppet sisters Nancy was looking for."

Vivan "Do you think sister Nancy is dead? or might have been saved?"

Andrea " I am pretty sure she is dead , I fired one shot in her head and another on her left chest , in her heart ,even if the bitch is not dead , I don't think they will be able to save her , and even if they will be able to keep her alive , with those sort of injuries she will be in living in hell , that's all I wished and longed for her , living in hell while living and when dead ."

Vivan "Why her?"

Andrea " Uncle Jack was the first man who molested me at age of 6 , he died in few months , Lucas was second man who molested in at age of 16 , in his office, where I was an unpaid intern , he pushed his penis inside my mouth , grabbed my hairs and force a blow job on me , he pushed his penis fast and deep , it made me throw up , while I was throwing up he masturbated on me and ejaculated on my head , filthy bastard . I knew I couldn't go to my mother; I knew she worshiped him as a perfect family man."

She stopped; a sound of silence fell in between them. Neither she spoke nor he spoke for a while. Then she spoke again "I don't want to go through the whole stupid episode of it, I know for certain, either I will get the life prison or a death sentence, first will be worst then second, I want to commit suicide, but these bastards didn't leave a single sharp object, we don't even have freedom of death, freedom of suicide. To me all other freedoms talked seem like phony nonsense, only true freedom is freedom to live and freedom to die. When asshole uncle jack

died my mother kept Jack's photo inside her room, like someone keeps a filthy thought inside one's mind.

Chapter 6

Andrea's mother kept Uncle Jacks photo in her room, referred him as man of dignity, integrity, an honest and a great soul, whenever Andrea didn't like over glorification of Uncle Jack and disagreed, her mother called her stupid girl who doesn't like good, and often mentioned she is like her father is those regards, in return Andrea referred her mother as stupid woman, who doesn't even know what is good and what is bad, who is good and who isn't. Till her last day she referred her mother as stupid woman. On every mistake her mother called her stupid girl, even when Andrea appeared on TV, hand cuffed, being dragged to police car, her mother in tears watching the TV called Andrea "Stupid girl."

In prison when Andrea spoke about her mother to Vivan, she referred to her as "A woman too worried about mundane and ignorant about profound."

Vivan said "Aren't we all, most of the people don't even talk or want to realize that one day all of us will die, leaving pretty much every material possession, body and skin color, see the cling of humans, the fools, pathetic jerks who are too eager to jerk, jerk off, fuck and fuck off."

Days went by, as they always do, Andrea and Vivan didn't speak to each other, both had some presumed idea of what might be happening outside, about them, for them and so on, if it happened or not, they didn't know, all their assumptions and imaginations were like ideas of the world in human mind, a perception, several confusions, many imaginations, and some reality.

***

For several days Andrea and Vivan heard each other urinating, flushing the toilet, crying. laughing, speaking bad and good words to self.

After several days, she asked "Why it happen?"

Vivan "I don't know for sure. The origin is deeper, far -far away, hidden in the darkness, mostly unknown and well protected."

Andrea "I wish we could have met outside of prison. "

Vivan "You are funny, if we would have met outside of prison you wouldn't have exchanged more than two sentences with me. Even those two sentences would have been very superficial or very professional."

Andrea" I don't think so. I think you have too many thoughts, too many prejudices and too many judgements."

Vivan "I don't remember ever being happy, is it possible?"

Andrea "It's not possible, look back you might find few moments of happiness. Close your eyes and look back at farthest points, take a walk in the past."

Vivan "What am I in this part of the world? an outsider, sometimes I wonder which journey is the worst, starting as outsider and after many years ending as outsider, or starting as an outsider and ending as a murderer? "

Chapter 7

Andrea rushed out from Lucas's office and drove to sister Nancy. Weeping heavily, she told Nancy about what happened, sister Nancy first consoled her by hugging, then offered warm green tea and said, " Don't degrade yourself by hating him, a degraded person like him doesn't deserve even your hate. "

Andrea " Should I call 911?"

Sister Nancy at once said " No "her pitch for "no" was very high. She lowered down the pitch , regained her sophistication and politeness and said " Don't degrade yourself to his level by calling police ,forgiveness and love are virtues of God , hold these virtues ,if you forgive him , you will be above him , higher than him and you know God will love you more than he loves him , you know he already loves you more than he loves him .Let it go my sweetheart, let it go ."

Andrea have always seen Lucas as a father figure, that was one of the reasons she was fascinated by all the propagandas Lucas and on the behalf of Lucas were done. When Lucas molested her, she felt she lost a father figure second time, first she lost her father at age of 10 and now at age of 16 she lost another father figure. The absence of father figure and what happened to her in the absence of father figure created a fascination towards father and father figure ,she thought all those people who have father alive and in their life are the most fortunate ones , the luckiest ,with perfect life , she often imagined what her life would have been if her parents wouldn't have divorced , if her father wouldn't have died and so on , many what ifs often cluttered her mind. She was fascinated by Lucas because several times on local news and in other ceremonies, festivals Lucas and his family appeared perfect. Lucas' love for his wife and family seemed perfect. He often made lengthy and lovely speeches about the importance of family, institute of marriage and how much he loves his family and appreciates his wife for being the soul and the strength of the family. He often placed her pretty much next to goddesses and angels from the sky.

***

In the evening Lucas arrived home, his wife already received a call about what he did to Andrea. Her face was red in anger and eyes filled with tears.

Her " You need to stop treating the girls, in your office like whores. "

Him" So someone called you, who was it? that fucking lesbo Nancy or my low graded secretary because tomorrow I will push my penis inside both of their mouths and will push it deep enough to chock them."

He grabbed her soldiers tight with both of his hands. He grabbed her tight enough to hurt her.

He pushed her on the bed, she shouted " Stop it, Lucas. "

He shouted " You, fucking bone. "

He forcefully pulled her underwear down, moved her hips up, pulled down his pants and pushed his bare penis inside her anal, and started moving inside out, shouting " You fucking useless, lifeless bone, you fucking useless, lifeless bone.", she busted into tears, he ejaculated inside her, pulled out his penis, two drops of his semen dripped from his penis hole on the bedsheet.

While putting back his penis inside pants, he spoke in anger " Get ready on time for the evening party at James's house and ask that low graded Mexican filth (by that he meant their maidservant Maria) to wash this bedsheet."

He walked out and smoked couple of cigarettes, a memory from his childhood popped up, his stepfather started hitting his mother calling her a lifeless bone, fucking bone, he hit her several times and later fucked her in anal. Eight years old Lucas, shaking in fear and anger, hiding inside the bathroom often masturbated while all this was happening, sometimes he masturbated twice in the row, sometimes four times and sometimes until he was exhausted passes out. He often fell asleep on the bathroom floor while his stepfather was forcefully fornicating his mother. This memory invoked a rage inside him, and he started shouting "fucking bone, fucking bone." And started trembling in anger.

He started looking at his stepfather as a strong, powerful, and confident figure rather than an abusive maniac. He started seeing his mother as a powerless entity and gradually developed a deep dislike which turned into hate and superiority complex towards women in general. More his stepfather abused his mother, more Lucas hated her. In deep psychological spaces he started idealizing him. Here and there he mentioned his stepfather as " He always got what he wanted" and deep down in the spaces where he desired power, that's what he wanted to be, someone who always gets what he wants.

His stepfather often slapped him, punched him, sometimes pushed him on the door and in the walls. He often twisted Lucas's ears for no good reason. Lucas followed his stepfather's footsteps, called, and thought most of the woman as bone, a lifeless entity, after reaching where he did, a person of power and influence, he abused his power, and pushed his penis on many women, few accepted and took it inside, others rushed away like Andrea to people like Nancy who manipulated them not to report the issue. Lucas continued with such support, women who took him in, remained in his office little bit longer compared to those who rejected.

While his wife was still crying in the bed, with her naked, fornicated anal hole, while pulling up his pants back and zipping up the zipper, he said rudely " Get ready on time for Lucas's birthday party, I don't want to be late. "

He went outside and started smoking cigarettes. She went into the bathroom and showered, on application of the shower gel and the burning sensation it created

she realized where the hurts are, there were some red bruises just below the neck and on the shoulder where he grabbed her very tight while penetrating.

The dress she originally planned to put on would have exposed those bruises, so she decided to put on something else, something that covers the reality and adds a little bit glamour on it.

They arrived at James's party, they looked like a perfect couple, their photos were taken together which appeared in the local city newspaper next day, they looked perfect and loving in the photo. In the party Lucas spoke about her, in his words he pretty much put her on a pedestal where he worshiped her, in his mind she was a bone, a lifeless entity to exploit. While they faked a picture-perfect smile, she all the sudden felt a pain in her anal area and a burning sensation, she managed to repress the true emotions the pain caused and continued her picture-perfect smile, she appreciated Lucas as loving, caring father and husband, tears appeared in her eyes, Lucas kissed her in the act, while kissing he held her like a princess. She spoke and did what Lucas instructed her to do on such occasions, for this event they rehearsed the act for almost a week.

Over the time she perfected how to suck in the abuse and the desire to fight it pretty much vanquished as time passed. A glimpse of Lucas and her wife on a local TV channel, an act of such love and care created dreams of a perfect family in many teens, girls, boys and in youth who were going through broken family situations such as Andrea, they wished to have a father like Lucas and mother like his wife. The truth was hiding behind the curtains, behind the walls and deep inside the hearts. Lucas continued to carry the psychology of his stepfather to always get what he needs from his family, to do so he manipulated his family, up to any extent. He often referred his mother as stupid and a low life.

Chapter 8

When Andrea rushed out from Lucas's office, he made a call to sister Nancy. Sister Nancy was the woman in which Andrea put the faith which she always wanted to put in her mother. Sister Nancy was the one who referred Andrea to Lucas's office. Sister Nancy was the first woman who spoke to Andrea about heaven and the kingdom of God. She was the first person who pushed the thoughts in Andrea's mind that human existence on the earth is a byproduct of sin and disobedience.

Church phone rang Nancy picked; Lucas was on the other side. He mentioned he is planning to double his donation to her church this year, and how things got little bit off hand with Andrea, Nancy should talk to her and make sure the matter doesn't go to press or police, he continued how much he and his family appreciate what Nancy and her church is doing for the community, the donation amount to church will depend on how she handles the issue with Andrea, and he hung up. Between donation, power, and true morality, Nancy picked the donation and power.

Andrea rushed to sister Nancy with tears flooding out of her eyes. Sister Nancy hugged her and tried to console her by rubbing her hand gently on Andrea's back, she asked "My dear child what happened?" She already knew what happened and she kind of planned and thought through what she would say to Andrea, so Andrea keeps silent on this matter and never discuss this with anyone else, she already plotted a plan to manipulate and silence Andrea.

Nancy had cookies, warm tea, and hot coffee ready, she offered a warm cup of tea and cookies to Andrea, Andrea said "No", but she gently forced those on Andrea with statement "My sweetheart, please have one cookie and have some warm tea, it will make you feel better "Andrea did what Nancy said. Sister Nancy throughout her nun life have been using cookies, tea, and coffee to repressed her sexual desires, whenever her vagina whispered, " I need a penis inside me ", she pushed several cookies, a cup of tea or coffee inside her mouth, that quenched her desires of penis and kept putting additional pounds on her body. From a thin girl, she became an overweight, from an overweight she became an obese. Later her dresses, her shoes, her shocks, and her whole body started shouting that she was obese among the obese. She stopped fitting into most of the church chairs.

That day, just after Lucas hung up the phone on her, she created her own version of "out of hand situation" , in that version Lucas's penis popped up in front of her eyes although she have never seen it in reality, her vagina whispered " I need it inside me , I need his penis inside me " , she pushed more than usual cookies inside her throat , and two cups of coffee , that didn't help her much , her hands almost reached her vagina to masturbate , she somehow pulled them back.

Gradually her mind became a war field of what she desired and what she should be desiring.

In time, Sister Nancy developed her own theory about cookies, tea and coffee, her theory was if cookies, tea, and coffee can help her to stop sinful activity by sinful activity she meant fornication, masturbation, and penis imagination then cookies, coffee and tea can help and prevent any sinful activities, including the negative emotions such as anger, stress, lust, anxiety etc. Her theory made her serve cookies, coffee, and tea where she shouldn't have, her theory made her speak about cookies, coffee, and tea where she shouldn't have. Despite a lot of cookies eating, coffee and tea drinking, she had all the mischief of a sexually repressed woman, what she denounced in day, she longed in the night.

Chapter 9

Third or perhaps fourth time Andrea asked, "Where did it all start, Vivan?"

Vivan " I don't know , sometimes I think preciseness is a tragedy ,a mere stress , or perhaps an anxiety .It might have started when the very first element of this existence manifested or perhaps it might have started when very first sign of life began on the earth ,or perhaps when I was born , or perhaps when my parents were born , or perhaps when my grandparents were born or perhaps when my first ancestor was born , why do you like preciseness so much , look what the idea of preciseness did to us ,it spoiled us , it bewildered us, perhaps idea of preciseness pushed us where we are right now ,locked here in this prison cell, waiting to be killed , in return of killings we did ,among many uncertainties and unsure things I am pretty sure it's one of the hardest things to grow out of is the unhappy childhood , especially if oneself search for a home and is not allowed to find one and is constantly displaced from one place to another , kicked around from one company to another like a filthy disgusting dog, like myself, live in a constant fear of being send against once will where he came from , and not allowed to know what the stability or certainty look like .I was born and raised in a small village , a village of population 3000 or perhaps a little bit more. My parents and grandparents were not able to get along, my paternal aunts both being in the same street constantly fueled up the misunderstanding between my grandparents and my parents, they constantly portrayed my parents as horrible people. A constant bickering and arguments were in the home , my grandpa often announced loud, it's his home and he can and will throw us out any day and anytime he wants, from childhood I didn't find a comfortable place to live , as grown up I asked my father why didn't he and my mother purchased another home and moved out , someday in their old age my grandparents would have come back to them ,and he would have been able to provide a good home to them and to all of us , my father replied "By not leaving them , he was fulfilling his responsibility of a son." In my early age it didn't make much sense but, in my thirties, it started making sense.

I always had several complaints against my parents like they didn't give me a good home, they didn't give me a comfortable life, a good extended family or sometimes I complained they didn't give me a good society, how foolish I was. I continued to blame them for several things, for several years, the things they were not responsible for. I guess one of the easiest things in the world is to hate and blame parents, to hate and blame those who gave birth to us and to hate those who raised us. As far as I can remember my grandma had been sick, she had asthma and some other diseases. My grandpa and my mother were busy working in the farm , and my father was busy at his job .I don't know how old was I ,perhaps 5 or 6 ,one of my far cousin about 10 years older than me tried to convince me to put his penis inside my mouth , when I didn't agree, he tried to convince me by saying

it will taste great, I still disagreed, he didn't force me to do it ,at that age I thought he wants to urinate into my mouth. He lay down on the bed, pulled off his pants, pulled out his penis from underwear, put a thin cloth on his genital area and made me sit on his penis. I don't remember if my pants were on or off, or if he came or not. I am sure I did not get penetrated; I know it for sure because in later part of my life I learned what anal penetration feels like. I only remember one or two of such encounters with him, I don't know how it ended .I think that was my first sexual encounter , or that's was the first one I remember, scientist say till age of three we don't create memories ,around age of 10 when I was in fifth grade ,I had my second encounter , this time a guy who was around 3 to 4 years older than me got interested in me , Often in late evenings we didn't have electricity in the village, I was walking to my home from village temple ,he called me to talk ,I knew him from my childhood , we both grew up in the same street , after some talk he asked me "Let's go for a walk ".

I agreed , we entered into a narrow street , he grabbed me , pushed me to wall ,and started kissing me ,I don't know when I recovered from the initial shock and started liking his kissing , he pushed one of my hands in his underwear, that was the first time I touched someone else's penis and balls , all of the sudden we realized a motorcycle is coming in that direction , I pulled off my hands and he stopped kissing , we immediately resumed a condition of normal walk , my heart was beating fast ,I didn't brush that night to keep taste of his mouth alive in my mouth ,as far as I remember he was the one who masturbated me first time or taught me how to masturbate , I remember having only couple more encounters with him , once he took off his shirt and my t shirt and made me feel the warmth of his body , I felt a great comfort , third time again our encounter was in the same narrow dark street when there was no electricity in the village , this time he pushed my right hand into his underwear ,made me grab his penis ,holding my hand with his hand , he started moving my hand on his penis , up and down , he kissed me and whispered in my ears , keep doing it , he pushed his hands in my underwear and started doing the same while kissing me on my lips ,he pushed his tongue in my mouth couple of times during masturbation ,first he ejaculated and then I ejaculated , I remember my hands being sticky and my underwear being wet. He wiped his hands and my hands with his handkerchief and asked me to kiss his penis. He pulled his pants down, I set down on my knees and kissed his penis from side, he pushed the tip of his penis inside my mouth, a drop or two of his semen flew inside my mouth that moment I tasted semen for first time in life and smelled them. Our encounter was over and was undisturbed. He instructed me not to mention what happen between us to anyone. He kissed me, I went home and slept with wet underwear. My grandpa's home was pretty much a large living room, with only one room, which was being used as kitchen, my grandpa used to own couple of farm animals, two bullocks to help with farming activities, two buffalo's and one cow for milk, the animal barn was all the way back in the house, the animals used to go through the house to reach the end of house, there was no back door entry or exit for them. Around the same time when I tasted and smelled semen first time my father started building a bathroom and a restroom, before that there was no bathroom in the house, men of the house used to shower

in the veranda, which was in the middle of the house and women used to take bath all the way back of the house , there was a big piece of flat stone, surrounded by three walls .I remember my mother and grandma taking bath there.

My grandpa didn't like construction of the restroom and the bathroom , he got angry and upset , there was a huge argument between my parents and my grandpa, he threatened to kick us out if any further constructions, changes or improvements are done in the house, for years the house remained the same , there were no further constructions or improvements or enhancements, even if my father and grandfather both were financially capable of doing several of them, it never happened .The house continued to be what it was. Often arguments broke between my grandparents and my parents on trivial things, for no good reasons, a constant bickering occupied the space of the house. Both of my paternal aunts continued to put bad thoughts about my parents in my grandparents' heads, they continued to create misunderstandings, my grandparents trusted them more than they trusted my parents. Things continued the same way, whenever my grandpa used to bring anything to eat from the market, fruits, cookies, chocolates, or sweets, he used to send me to give some of those things to my younger maternal aunt's home. I can't eat before that, what a nonsense. My fourth encounter with the same guy was at his home , he called me at his parents' home when no one was home, his home was also pretty much a big living room , as most of the homes in the village were, my grandpa's and his parents' home were in same street, his parents' home had two rooms , one of the room was kitchen in middle of the house and another room was at end of the house ,next to the last room there was a swing ,we were on it , the house door was almost closed , after few kisses ,he turned me around , pulled my pants down in few seconds I felt his hard penis on my anal hole. He was about to push it inside me, we heard the door noise, it was his elder brother. He immediately pulled up his pants and zipped it, I did the same, I rushed out of the house, the only thing I heard was his brother shouting at him "What were you doing?". His elder brother was no angel, in later part of my life I learned he was fornicating his first cousin. She was a couple of years older to him. I am still not sure why he didn't close the door fully and why he picked the swing for our encounter; I think it was intimacy, perhaps we both got carried away with it. That day I learned; intimacy can expose. After that incident once or twice I ran into him in the same narrow street, he kissed me, made me touch his penis and ejaculated in his underwear. In Later part of my life, I learned he was doing the same things with many other guys of my age, younger and guys of his own age, his older brother was caught fornicating with his cousin, she was 6 years older to him. Their father was beaten twice for forcing himself on two *Adivasi* (tribal) women.

I don't know why we stopped seeing each other. Later one of his cousins got interested in me. He was not good looking. I didn't take any interest in him. He once grabbed my hand and tried to push it inside his underwear. I pulled my hand off, he tried to convince me, several times on several occasions, I didn't agree, he gave up.

Before age of 14 I had three more sexual encounters, one of them was inside the village temple ,the temple had stairs to go all the way up to the roof, the stairs had a twist to right side , where it merged into the roof, that area was mostly dark ,with or without electricity, much light never reached that area like a sense of equal opportunity never reaches to a racially biased mind , this guy was of my age , he was son of my far cousin, he is still alive and have two children , a daughter and a son .He suggested we should go on the roof , I walked upstairs with him, he touched my hand and said "Let's play a game ".I said " which one . He said *'Chumma chati*" (kissing and leaking). He continued " In this game, I kiss you and you kiss me back on the same space of my body. "

I asked, " Where will we do that?"

He holding my hand took me to the area where it was mostly dark, he first kissed me on my lips, I kissed him back, then he kissed me on my neck, I did the same, we continued and pretty much kissed every part of each other's body, including fingers and toes, People came and left from temple, our encounter continued undisturbed, we finished with kissing each other's penis and balls, we both were necked by then. Me and him dressed up and left, that was our first and last encounter, none of us tried to have another, we ran into each other several times over the years but never discussed or mentioned what happened between us. We spoke and behaved as if we never kissed, as if we never touched each other, we talked about other things.

Next one was with a guy who lived next to the narrow street where I had the sexual encounters, while I was walking by his home, he called me , he told me he want to show me something , and asked me to come upstairs ,I followed him ,we arrived in his room, he asked me to check his penis, if its large and thick enough , it was not hard when he initially pulled it out, I touched it , it started getting thicker and longer , I continued to move my hands on it for a while ,it attained it's the full length and thickness ,I bent down on my knees , and took his penis inside my mouth , and started sucking it. He started moaning in pleasure. I continued, in a few minutes, he came inside my mouth, his ejaculation was warm, I swallowed it. His face lit up in joy, perhaps he didn't expect what he got, before I left, I told him " Your penis has a perfect length and thickness." His joy doubled. I left, that was the first and last such encounter between us.

My last encounter before I was sent to a boarding school, was in one of my cousins' marriages. I caught the eyes of a guy who was a distant relative of my elder cousin's wife. In such busyness of marriage, so many people, dancing, and music he found a quiet place to take me to and do things he desired. I guess desires have their own mysterious ways. He was couple of years older than me , may be 4 years or 6 years older .Downstairs people were dancing , joking , socializing , upstairs he was undressing me and himself, in few minutes we were naked , he kissed me on my lips for a very long time, pressed his tongue deep inside my mouth , while kissing on my neck , he told me "You are so beautiful." , he was the first person to say it, he sucked my nipples , that pretty much made me come, when he was sucking them I felt whole another level of sensation in my

body ,he kissed me on my belly button and moved his tongue around it ,he kissed me on my back , I did the same and little bit more , I kissed his balls and started sucking his penis, his penis was salty and had smell of his urine. He started moaning in the pleasure. After a while he asked me to stop, again kissed me long on my lips, lay me down with my back facing up, he kissed my back and kissed my hips. He spit on my anal, the spit was luck warm, he lay down on me, grabbed his penis with his hand, put it on my anal and pushed it inside, for a moment it felt as if a sharp weapon was pushed inside me, I said " ah, it's hurting me. pull it out. "He whispered in my ears " First time it feels like that, little bit of pain, gradually it will go away, trust me." He moved my face on the left side, pressed his mouth on mine, started kissing and moving inside out of me. Every time he moved inside out of me it felt as if a sharp arrow is moving through me, he continued to move his penis in a way that gave him maximum pleasure, and continued to kiss me, perhaps he kissed me to sooth me or perhaps to make sure that I don't make loud noises due to pain his moving penis was causing me, he ejaculated inside me in couple minutes. Tears came out of my eyes, I was agitated, bewildered and angry.

I said, " you are a bastard", and pressed my nails hard on his soldier to hurt him ,he moved his thumb on my lower lip and said 'You are beautiful, very beautiful." and started kissing me on my lips ,for a while I didn't kiss him back ,then I participated back, he started sucking my nipples again, I started filling pleasure but said " Stop it ".He said " Tell me you are not upset or angry with me for penetrating you ", smiling I said " I am not ", I further added " Maybe we should go down stairs now. "He grabbed me tight and said, " No I don't want you to go, please stay. "

I said "why? Do you want to penetrate me again?"

He grabbed me harder and said, "yes I do, I want to fuck you whole night."

He looked into my eyes and said, "Someday I want to marry a girl who looks like you."

Why he didn't say, someday he would like to marry me or a guy who looks like me? I don't know.

I didn't say anything, he fell asleep, I continued to look at his face, and kissed his nose, he was my first, to whom I lost my virginity. I was not sure if he was virgin or well experience, I didn't bother to ask, now here waiting for death, I am making the list of the questions which I should have asked when I was out of prison, it's one of the questions. I want to know if my first penetrator penetrated someone else before me and was, he ever penetrated by someone else, I know it will not change anything, but we are not always curious for reasons of change, being curious is our nature like fornicating or being penetrated or like a desire to ejaculate and masturbate. The marriage was five days long ,in next four days he penetrated me 16 times ,sometimes he was inside me for 7 minutes , sometimes 10 minutes and other times it felt even longer , every time he got inside me , he grew intense and intense ,it was almost impossible to keep my moaning down but I kept it lowest ,I don't think he left any position unused, sometimes he was on

top of me, other times I was on the top of his penis , the most used pose was doggy style . I am getting harder, and my nipples are getting tide just by revisiting those memories. Towards the end of every intercourse, we both pretty much showered in the sweat, and sometimes I forgot what my smell is vs his, our smells mixed into each other, in those moments it felt to me as if he melted inside me and I melted inside him, as if we are one being not two.

In those four days my whole sense of being transformed. I didn't keep count how many times I came in those four days. I clearly remember sometimes I can in pleasure and other times because of the pain his penetrating penis caused me. In those ejaculations I realized I am a pleasure-seeking entity; we all are pleasure seekers. By age of 14 I had several penetrations, ejaculations, masturbations, and sexual encounters, I was fucked, leaked, loved, penetrated, and kissed.

The marriage ended the sixth day, before he left, he told me " I will miss you and will always remember you. ``After that he penetrated me sixteenth and last time. I never saw him again, sometimes I wonder if he would have thought about me, if he would have desired me, if he would have masturbated on me, if he would have made love to someone else thinking about me. I thought about him several times over several years and masturbated on him. It's impossible to forget the first. Isn't it?

His penis was long and thick, after him I only encountered three more such long and thick penises. I still remember his penis, his balls, his smell, and his touch. Sometimes I miss it. The taste of his semen just came into my mouth, I still remember it so clearly, so vividly, with its texture, thickness, stickiness, and warmth.

Vivan pulled out his penis and started masturbating, the guy from the front prison cell gave Vivan the fuck finger and shouted at Vivan " You pervert ". He threw spit with a very strong force with a hope it will reach to Vivan, it did not, he tried it couple of times, Vivan shouted " You are unnecessary tiring yourself ", gave him the fuck finger with his left hand to the prison in other cell while continuing to jerk off his penis with his right hand.

Vivan fell asleep on ejaculation, when he woke up, it felt as if several hours had passed. The cell had no clock, the flowing time was undisturbed by this fact.

He thought to ask the time from the prison guard, but the guard was too far and Vivan didn't know how the guard would respond. He didn't ask the time and resumed his story. He didn't know if Andrea was awake, or alive or fell asleep or died. He didn't care.

Chapter 10

Vivan continued "After that I was sent to the boarding school in ninth grade. It was a boys only boarding school. Initially I didn't like it. I hated it, the food was bad, from one large living room, my grandpa's home, I moved to another living room, smaller and worse. The room I was assigned had 24 beds, 24 students from 8th and 9th grade living together. There were other better rooms where only 10 to 12 students were living, the room I was put in was a mess. In evening after dinner most of the people used to go out for walk, In those hours the boarding house used to give an impression as if no one lives there , initially I didn't like going for walk , one of those evenings I was taking evening nap, someone came , lay on top of me and started kissing me , it woke me up, he grabbed my hands tight .I wasn't able to move, initially I didn't participate , struggled for a while , then gave up , I started kissing him back ,opened my mouth to allow his tongue inside , his lips were thick ,he bit me on my lower lip. He tried to take off my T-shirt, I resisted and said" What if someone come? "He said " Don't worry, everyone is gone for a long walk or to market, no one will be back at least for an hour."

He started sucking my nipples, I moaned in pleasure , he started kissing me on my stomach , and unzipped my pant, pulled it down , took off my T shirt , pant and underwear , I was naked , he was still fully dressed, he kissed me for a while ,unzipped his pant , pulled his penis out , took saliva from his mouth , applied it on his penis and pushed it inside me , after pushing it inside me , he took off his T shirt , whenever he pushed and pulled inside out of me fast , it caused a pain to me , the pain appeared on my face, in my eyes , he looked at my face, in my eyes and smiled , just before ejaculation , while kissing he bit my lower lip hard enough to bleed it. I pushed my lip inside my mouth and drank the drops of the blood. On ejaculation he pulled out his penis , lay down next to me for couple of minutes then dressed up, picked up my clothes from the floor and gave back to me , he looked very happy as if he nailed a score or got something everyone wanted and wasn't getting , I didn't know who he was until next day , he was one of my classmates, and all of the sudden from that day onward he was meanest to me , he tried his best to make my life as miserable as possible, as of now I don't know why he did it . He was not the only one who bullied me, several of my classmates and my seniors did it. I didn't want to stay in the boarding house, I suffered bullying throughout my high school ,It was a terrible experience , that was the first time I remember heavily suppressing my emotions, I wanted to shout but didn't , I wanted to slap people who were bullying me but I didn't , all I did was cry and repressed my emotions , I was unable to do anything , they were so many , I told my father I don't want to stay , once I ran away from my boarding school, in that small town I was easily found, my father hit me very hard on my head and slapped me several times, I cried hard and loud, the hits were strong, for a movement it felt to me I will faint but I didn't, my father said " What will people of the village say if you come back , they will bully you ,look he is back to the village from the town , he couldn't even survive in town , they will judge you , will try to make your life miserable and full of guilt.", sometimes I think I came

from a very self-shamed place where people think living in a village is shame and failure. Those who live in urban areas seem to them in excellent joy and living a superior life, I know that's not true, especially the way in which the crime rate increased in urban areas of India in the last decade. Those who moved to cities and found a good life in cities mostly started looking down on villages where they are born and on its people. This attitude towards the people of the village further increased self-hate and inferiority complex in a life full of hardship and struggle. I stayed in the boarding house, the bullying and repression of my emotions continued. I think those repressed emotions also have something to do with my gun shooting , now it seems I was trying to release those emotions, perhaps bullets were my expression or perhaps they weren't, that's one of the things about self-imposed psychological repressions , after sometime one doesn't know what oneself want or need , in my head ,everything is a confusion , sometimes I feel joy for what I did and other times I feel sorrow , sometimes I feel light and other times I feel burdened, especially when I think about what my parents and sisters might have been going through , and anyone else who loves me or hold true appreciation for me might be going through after what I did. Thoughts started racing into his mind, among many thoughts one of them were " Earth will be far better and in an excellent order and harmony without human race, human race is one of the most degraded, the filthiest among all species, it's a mere nonsense.". He slapped himself twice on right side of face. The slaps were hard and left marks on his chick.

Another memory popped up in his head, in the same boarding house, in the evening hours when no one was in the room he was walking around in the room, one of his seniors popped up, he grabbed Vivan, Vivan struggled to set him free, his senior overpowered him and pushed him on a bed, held both of his arms tight and started kissing him, while kissing he pushed Vivan's hand in his underwear. He was hard. He bit on Vivan's nipples, Vivan tried to push him back saying " Stop it, I don't want to do it".

He didn't stop, he dragged Vivan's lower down, forcefully turned him around, pulled out his penis from his pants and pushed it inside Vivan. In a couple of minutes, he ejaculated inside Vivan and left. That night Vivan cried and cried and cried, the memory brought tears in his eyes in the prison cell.

Vivan resumed his description "After what my father said I stayed in the boarding house, against my will, I still struggle to forgive my father, sometimes I want to kill him, other times I wanted to hit him, once or twice I desired immense pain and suffering for him, but never wished him dead, strange I wanted to kill him but doesn't want him to die. Before I jump into further description of what happened and why I did it , I have a correction, I ran into total six penises I liked the most , they all were long ,thick and beautiful, the correction is necessary because I earlier told you I liked four penises , I don't want to falsify the information , not that it hold much relevance to you or someone else , but they hold a lot of importance to me, as far as my experiences with penises goes I think beautiful penises and beautiful balls goes hand on hand. Second large and lovely penis I

had was one of my juniors, he was in 9th grade, and I was in 10th grade at that time. He had always been nice to me since beginning, he was first person I remember being polite, respectful, and caring to me in the school, once we were talking laying down in beds next to each other, he asked me to kiss him, I kissed him on his right cheek, we continued the conversation afterwards. By the early of my 10th grade, I started liking him. I started finding excuses to be around him or keep him around me. One evening when the sky was clear and stars were twinkling in the sky, we went for a walk towards the school playground.

We set down on a rock and talked for a while, all the sudden I asked him to kiss me, he did a quick kiss on my right cheek, I held one of his hands in both of my hands and asked him "kiss me on my lips." He said, " Not here, what if some sees us."

I said, " Let's go in the dark. "

I started walking. He followed me, in few minutes we arrived at the back of school admin building, it was dark, from that place whole town was visible, my school and boarding house were on a valley surrounded by several valleys. Sometimes I used to go for a very long walk on the valleys on the other side of my school. He was about six inches taller than me , I put my right hand on his neck, moved my head up , he started kissing me ,I opened my mouth , he pushed his tongue inside my mouth , while kissing he gradually moved me close to the wall, in few seconds I was leaning on the wall, I was able to hear the whisper of small lives .I saw twinkling stars in the sky when he started kissing me on my neck , he pulled up my t-shirt , and sucked my nipples , he moved down further , kissed the areas around my belly button and moved his tongue on the area just above my penis , I couldn't describe what I felt. He pulled off my lower , took my penis into his mouth and started sucking, it was my first blow job , he was strong and masculine build , **I think he sucked** me because he wanted to make sure I receive some pleasure, he stopped in couple of minutes , I kissed him again , I pulled up his t-shirt , sucked his nipples, moved down, pulled down his lower and underwear together, I touched his penis, it was large and thick , larger than the penis which penetrated me as my first ,I sucked it for couple of minutes, he moaned in pleasure, I stopped , turned around, pressured his penis on my anal area , he holding his penis ready to penetrated asked me " Are you sure ?"

I said " Yes, this is the only thing I am sure about at this moment?"

He pushed his penis inside me, it has thin lubrication of my saliva. The penetration and his moves were full of energy and were intense, couple of times he almost pulled out his penis and pushed it back inside me, from the moaning coming from him, it was easy for me to understand, all of it was giving him a lot of pleasure, intense pleasure. His intense energy, fast and sharp moves for few movements felt impossible to withstand but the way he helped me was so cute and lovely, he held me as if he never wants to let me go, for first time **I felt a feeling of forever,** I moved my head back, rested it on his soldier, started looking at the

sky and twinkling stars. I grabbed my penis in my right hand and started masturbating.

It was first time when I masturbated while being penetrated, when he ejaculated inside me, it was intense, a huge load of semen flew inside me. I ejaculated almost around the same time, I showered in the sweat, he didn't sweat that much, while ejaculating he said," I love you", I said it back.

I am not sure if he meant it or not, and I don't know if I meant it or not but among all the people who penetrated me, I liked him a lot, his name was Ethen, originally, he and his parents were Adivasis (tribal people), more specifically from schedule caste, I was considered an upper caste compared to him, I never cared about caste, upper or lower or race or ethnicity or nationality. The penetration under open sky, with twinkling stars and cool breeze was an amazing experience, after that night he penetrated me five more times. Once in the hostel restroom and rest four times in my room on one the night , that night all my roommates were out of town ,I was alone , we slept whole night naked next to each other , he penetrated me four times that night , twice in doggy style ,once I set on his penis and in last penetration I was under him, my butt facing the roof ,that year he failed in one of the subject in 9th grade and got kicked out of the school .

Twice he came to visit the Boarding house, but I never saw any sexual interest in him for me. I tried to kiss him, he didn't kiss me back, only thing he did was kissing my hands and leave.

I asked him a couple of times " Did I do anything wrong?"

He said " No, you didn't?"

Third person who got interested in me in high school was one of my classmates who was also my roommate at that time, he had good height and good personality, and a large penis, almost as large as Ethen's. From 10th onward, we were assigned to share one room with four people, in a different building. The building was meant for students from class 10th to class 12th. That night my other two roommates went to visit their parents, he was shy on initial approach , he asked me if he can lay down next to me , I said yes , gradually he courage to put his one of the hand on me , then inside my t shirt , first he touched my stomach , the slowly moved it up to my right nipple and then to left , he touched both nipples gently and moved his fuck finger of both of them. I pushed my hands inside his underwear, pulled it down, moved down and started sucking his penis, he moaned in pleasure and ejaculated in couple minutes, I swallowed his semen's. Before falling to sleep I kissed him on lips. When we were done kissing, he started taking off all my clothes. I asked him ' Why now?", he replied he wants to sleep necked next to me. The same night I woke up from his kissing, he started kissing me on my neck and sucked my nipples past midnight. He gradually moved down and kissed my belly button, I was totally seduced, he kissed on my lips and pushed his tongue inside me, then he whispered in my ears ``Can I penetrate you? "I said "yes", before he penetrated me, he applied coconut oil on his penis, and then

pushed his long and thick penis inside me, the penetration was smoothest and most pleasurable to me and him. After ejaculating he said " *mene kabhi nahi socha tha ki tu itni jaldi de dega* "(I never thought you will convince for penetration so quickly and easily) .

I told him "I have always liked you since I saw you first time. ", that was not the case. I never thought of him like that until he approached me. He was one of the guys who bullied me extremely for almost a year in 9th grade. After our first sexual encounter he never bullied me again, his name was Mukesh. That year he pretty much penetrated me every night and sometimes twice, the only day I was unpenetrated when I was at my parents or he was away from the boarding house, sometimes we did it in the restroom , sometimes in bathroom , sometimes on the boarding house roof , couple of times in the dark nights in the valleys, couple of times in the school bathroom and twice at a place where Ethen fucked me , sometimes he used coconut oil as lubricant , other times his spit and sometimes he pushed his unlubricated *lund* inside me, *lund* means dick or penis, while most of the boys were masturbating and ejaculating ,Mukesh was fornicating me and was ejaculating inside me, he was not the only one with whom I had sexual encounters that year , there we four more guys but those were short lived affairs.

***

I had an encounter with Aakil around the same time , he was a dark skin ,average build and with a very attractive face, his penis was average .We had sexual encounters twice , in both I sucked his penis and later he fornicated me .Both times he ejaculated very quickly , I didn't like it , and perhaps these quick ejaculations filled him with some kind of guilt or shame, sometimes I am surprised , how much burden man as a male entity decided to carry, I myself was little bit upset after every short lived ejaculation, we ended without any discussion and never spoke to each other again, not even on graduation.

Around the same time, two other guys got interested in me Neel and Yash, we had small encounters that year, next year both grew into serious and more frequent encounters.

Yash was a great kisser, I still remember our first kiss, his lips were thick. After our first kiss, I remembered it for several days, the very memory of it got me hard several times in my classes, I don't know what was in that kiss, but I ejaculated twice in my underwear thinking about it, once in math's class and another time in English class while my teacher was explaining a metaphysical poem. Both times I was scared that my semen will flow out through my underwear into my pants ,it happen but the spot they create were not large enough to be noticed , as soon as the school was over ,I rushed into bathroom to take the shower ,since there were no water heaters all of us were taking shower with cold water, after shower I went into Yash's room to see if he is there , he wasn't , I looked around for Mukesh he wasn't there , that time Neel came into my room , looking for one of my roommate , I was alone in the room, my hormones were hitting sky high , at that movement I could have slept with anyone , even a dog , a horse , a rabbit or a pig

or an ugliest looking male. Throughout my life since my earliest masturbations at age of 7 or perhaps 8 or 10 , I often thought about animal sex ,most of the times it was a bitch being fucked by a dog, sometimes it was a bitch being fucked by a dog and several dogs were surrounding her, other times it was sex between two sparrows , sometimes between a female water buffalo and a bull , other times sex between male and female goats, at age of 10 or perhaps 11 I tried to have sex with a baby water buffalo , it was a failure, I ejaculated around her vagina ,I never tried to have sex with another animal ever. I felt and I still feel a terrible guilt for what I tried to do with that baby water buffalo. When I was going through a horrible dark time of loneliness and displacement, I did couple of masturbations thinking about cats and dogs being penetrated by their owners. I know it seems abnormal to you, may be sick and perverted but its normal to me, I guess we all have our own definition of normal, abnormal, creepy, weird and pervert, that's how we judge and that's how we define if something is fucked up or fine. don't we? We all are self-centered bastards, self-centered assholes. I walked close to Neel and started kissing him, he immediately started kissing me back, perhaps this would have been at the back of mind, or this was something he always wanted to do, he grabbed me and pushed me on Mukesh's bed, and jumped on me. I didn't realize that the room doors were open until I was almost necked and he was half necked, when I noticed , I asked him to close the room door , he rushed and closed them, pulled off the last piece of cloth my underwear from my body , pulled down his pant and underwear together , turned me around and pushed his penis inside me , I moaned ,he whispered in my ears to keep it low but the intensity with which he moved inside me made it impossible to keep it down, to control my moans sounds, he pressed his lips on mine and pushed his tongue inside my mouth ,he started moving faster, I ejaculated in couple of minutes , after I ejaculated it grew harder for me to withstand his intensity , he held me strong enough that I couldn't move, finally he ejaculated inside me , his ejaculation was an relief , when I looked at his face , he looked delighted and was smiling , as if he achieved something great, as if he nailed on to something, I was upset with him , very upset . I didn't like him being inside me once I ejaculated. I stood up and started dressing myself and said, " It was a terrible mistake. "

He said, " I loved it. ", I said " Of Course you did? It was all pleasure for you? "

He dressed up, grabbed me , moved me closer to wall , grabbed my face with both of his hands and kissed me , I didn't kiss him back and grew reluctant to open my mount, somehow he managed to make me open it ,and pushed his tongue inside my mouth , I tried to push it out with my tongue ,when he was done , he said " Don't be upset , *tuze chodane me bahut maja aaya* (it was a great pleasure fucking you.)" and I will do it again." He left after saying that.

I ejaculated on Mukesh's bedsheet while Neel was fornicating me, first I went to restroom and cleaned Neels mess, his semen dripped down from my anal hole, after that I washed Mukesh's bedsheet, hang it up to dry. I put another bedsheet on Mukesh's bed. That day I already had two ejaculations, I was tired, after dinner I fell asleep, my other two roommates went to sleep at one of my teachers houses

because the teacher and his family went to visit his in laws, around midnight I realized someone started kissing me, it was Mukesh, I said " Can we please not do it today? I want to sleep ." while I was saying it , he pulled up my T shirt and started sucking my nipples, by that time I was little awake , I remember him pulling down my underwear, he started kissing my thigh , I started moaning in pleasure , he asked me to sit on his penis , in few second I was on top of him and his penis was inside me ,I was worried that few semen's of Neel might still be inside me , what if Mukesh finds out ,it didn't happen , Neel's semen sort of worked as lubricant for me , towards the end I ejaculated on Mukesh's stomach around the same time he ejaculated inside me , he used his underwear to wipe my semen off .He didn't put his underwear back . In every fornication I pretty much showered in sweat, I always felt very satisfied with every penetration Mukesh did, he satisfied me pretty much every time, in 10th grade I had three more short sexual encounter, couple of lip-to-lip kisses by two of my classmates. I gave a blowjob to Ansh one of the juniors a 9th grader, next year Ansh transferred to another school, I am not sure if it had something to do with our small sexual encounter.

I think most of the guys, pretty much all of them were straight but given the boys only school, easy availability of me and hardness to get into relationships with girls due to restrictions from society, made them easily available to me.

In 11th grade , Yash penetrated me first time in one of the restroom, later it turned out an regular encounter, every day after school when pretty much everyone else went to play ground or somewhere else, he used to come to my room, our kissing used to start with him pressing his lips on mine, after a long lip to lip kiss, he used to kiss me on my neck ,stomach and later suck my nipple ,after that I used to pull his lower down ,kiss on his underwear , then pull down his underwear, put his penis inside my mouth and suck it for some time , after that he used to turn me around , pull down my lower and underwear together and push his bare penis inside me, it pretty much became an every evening ritual for us , sometimes he fucked me in his room , sometimes in the bathroom , other times in my room, couple of times we did it on the boarding house (hostel) roof. I was always scared what if someone see us, he was never. On the hostel roof, he often fully undressed me and him. On the roof he always penetrated me in the doggy style. In India most of the building roofs are flat and have access via stairs, in case if you are wondering, how me and him can get into a doggy style on my boarding house roof.

Mukesh was my companion of the night; he always fucked me at nighttime. Neel and I often made love just after school, the hours after school and the hours after dinner were the quietest one in boarding house. Before dinner Neel used to fuck me, after dinner Yash and in night Mukesh. My anal hole was constantly lubricated by semen. Neel either penetrate me in his room or my room, he only fornicated me twice in the restroom and once when I was taking shower, there were many days when all three of them fucked me, after every fuck I set down in the restroom as if I am doing potty, rather than stool the fornicators semen's

dropped out of my anal hole, towards end of the year I lost the count who fucked me more, Neel or Yash or Mukesh. I made sure each of them thinks he is the only one having sex with me, I managed it well with my penetrations, after ejaculation cleaning, and schedules of penetrations.

In 12th grade, Mukesh got into a romantic relationship with a girl and started fornicating her, our relationship ended without any discussion, Yash was a year senior to me, he graduated and left, I never heard back from him, Neel continued to fuck me.

In one of the intimate moments between us Neels roommate Charan who was always mean to me and bullied me heavily in the first two years of school, walked on us, in return of keeping quiet and not telling anyone he demanded I should let him fuck me as well, Neel immediately agreed in fear of being expose, I was reluctant and didn't agree.

I said, "My ass is not a public toilet where anyone can urinate, masturbate and ejaculate."

Neel somehow convinced me, the very movement Charan penetrated me, Infront of Neel, while Neel was standing Infront of me with his unejaculated hard penis. Charan has always been mean to me, and he was mean to me while fornicating me. Neel and Charan were only two people living in four people's room. As soon as Charan ejaculated and pulled his penis out of me, Neel pushed his in. Charan dressed himself up, walked to me and spoke with his usual mean tone, he always had for me *"ab se tuze roj chodunga."* (From now on, I will penetrate you every day). While Charan was saying it, Neel ejaculated inside me. I felt violated, insulated, and disrespected by both. I dressed up, and walked out of the room, with a desire to never walk back in. I had some water, went into restroom, set down in potty pose, their semen flew out of my anal hole.

Gradually they both started penetrating me together, it turned out to be an all-time threesome, sometimes when Neels penis was moving inside out of my anal, Charan's penis was moving inside out of my mouth, gradually both turned into mean bastards, they fucked me whenever they want, on Sundays, they fucked me in the noon, in afternoon and in evening. Twice they double penetration me, several times they both pushed their penises inside my mouth together, it was too much to take in. Sometimes I cried. I think all those ideas were coming from Charan. I prayed for the year to be over soon, but it didn't, couple of times I resisted, they both were strong enough to overpower me. Charan often commented "We already fucked you so many times, now why you want to resist and reject us." Several times he bullied me while moving inside out of me. Sometimes I desired to cut his penis, I wish I should have.

In seeking comfort, I slept with my three other classmates and one junior. The comfort I got was only momentary. I graduated from high school with many bareback penetrations, several blow jobs, and no STD. You know one of the terms used for blowjobs in India is Colgate, if someone wants to tease someone else for a blow job they say "Colgate *karna he kya?*" (Would you like to do Colgate,

means would he or she be interested in giving a blow job?). Desires always find ways to express them, don't they?

In high school we used to bring pirated Hollywood and pornographic movies. I first saw porn in 9th grade, I was 14 years old at that time, now it might sound too late, but around 20 years ago it was early to watch a porn at the age of 14. I remember once me, my classmates and seniors watched porn movies for almost seven hours, in one of them a girl was being fucked by a horse, in another porn a dog was penetrating a young girl and in an Indian porn a guy fucked his girlfriend's friend, while fucking he told her "I thought about it several times.", she smiled and said "why did you wait so long?", he said " I was being a pussy.", she said " Be a dick now and fuck me harder." , his moves got intense , she started moaning loud , making horny sounds.

Most of the people fell asleep after couple of hours, I guess everything have a limit, even watching porn, that night while watching porn me and Mukesh had a public sexual encounter, he pulled up the blanket on his short, grabbed my right hand, pushed it into his underwear, and started moving it on his penis, in couple of minutes he ejaculated.

From my description you might get an impression that throughout my high school I was only having sex, that's not true, I spend on an average less than two hours every day on sexual pleasures. I was very hard working in academics. I was a good student and a good human being. I never bullied anyone or looked down on anyone. I never preferred anyone for sexual encounters based on their skin color or caste or social and economic background. I was penetrated by various shades and colors. I allowed people of all castes, races, and ethnicities to fuck me. I am not sure if I was, or I am equal opportunity in other measures of life but in sexual encounters I was and still am.

Chapter 11

At age of eighteen I started my engineering, I decided not to lead the same way of sex life as I did in my high school ,for two or three months I tried my best not to show any sexual interest in anyone, during that time whenever I saw a good looking guy I used to get hard, I repressed my desires and try to focus the energy in study , pretending to be same as others , that was my definition of normal at that time or perhaps that's the definition of normal for most of the people ,whether they accept it or not is whole another thing. I learned in time, whether it's a sophisticated or unsophisticated society, developed, developing or decaying, we all lie to ourselves in many subject matters, unfortunately we are timid and dull enough that we couldn't live without lying to self and to others.

In college most of us were taking the college bus to go to college because it was outside of the city, driving on personal motorcycles means dealing with pollution and ugly city traffic. That evening I sat down next to one of my senior Manan, he was a year ahead of me, he told me " I will be alone home tonight, my parents will be out of town to attend a marriage, come to my home after dinner, it will be fun." After that he saved his numbers on my phone, he told me "Give me call, if you want, I can pick you up." I didn't answer but wasn't able to stop thinking about it ,all sexual encounters from my high school started rushing in my mind, by the time I stepped out of the bus I was hard , I started walking towards the home where I rented a room , I changed my clothes, I was hard, I had my dinner, I was hard , that evening I was only able to eat less than half of what I used to eat , a memory of me giving blow job to Mukesh popped up in my mind and retained for long time , then first kiss with Yash popped up , I felt the taste of his mouth in my mouth, the memories of me being fornicated by Ethen under open sky ,Neel and Charan's double penetration memory felt as if it happened to me couple of minutes back , vivid images of my first penetration rushed into my mind with extraordinary details ,in couple of minutes memories of all my sexual intercourses and encounters flooded in my mind .

I grew restless and immediately called Manan and asked him to pick me up, he sounded immensely happy on the phone, in less than 20 minutes he picked me upon on his motorcycle, it was almost 8 pm, sunlight started fading away after, the city lights struggled against the darkness of night, his parents' home was not that far, about 15 minutes walking from the home where I was renting a room. We arrived at his parents' home in less than 5 minutes, he parked the motorcycle, fyi in India most of the people use motorcycle for general commute, he unlocked the door, we went inside, my heart was beating fast, it happens to me pretty much every time whenever the possibility of a sexual encounter is created, especially the new one, my heart starts beating faster and faster.

He asked me to have a seat on the living room sofa and sat down next to me. He started playing a porn clip on his phone, we watched it together, the clip had two

guys and a girl, all three of them were white, clean and fit , their body gave an impression as if none of them have any hairs apart for eyebrows, Eyelashes and head hairs, first few minutes one of the guys sucked her vagina and another guy sucked penis of the vagina sucker, then they replaced each other, in third move the girl sucked both of their penises. Later, one of the guys penetrated the girl's vagina and another guy penetrated the vagina penetrator from the back. Manan stopped the video and looked at me, I saw desire and lust in his eyes. He grabbed my face and started kissing on my lips , I kissed him back, he reminded me of Yash little bit, he started undressing me and himself , he sucked my nipples , I sucked his penis and kissed his balls, when we both were almost necked he asked me "Let's go in my room." , holding me from back he took me to his room, he kissed me for a little bit and asked me " Have you done it before ?" , I said " No ". I knew I was lying and still I did it, I think that's the morality of modern man, he knows what's wrong and what's right, what is true and what is false, yet he does wrong and yet he speaks the untruth. The answer changed his mood, he kissed me as if he was kissing an angel, I asked him " How about you?", he didn't reply. I knew what that silent meant, it was not his first time, in couple of minutes he penetrated me in the doggy pose, with the pleasure sounds he was making it felt to me as if I am having sex with a dog, as if he is a dog and I am a bitch. I liked it, thinking of him as "*kutta* " (dog) and thinking of me as "*kutti*" (bitch). He ejaculated in couple of minutes. He asked me to stay for the night, I did. **He fucked me three more times that night, second time I asked him to do it on the** living room sofa, he did it, third time we did it in the kitchen and fourth time in the bathroom. In between penetrations we slept next to each other, holding each other, in a deep and sound sleep. That day, in the bathroom for the first time I saw myself being penetrated. My penetrator was standing behind me, moving inside out of me. I liked being necked, being fucked and being desired. Next two days, Saturday and Sunday were holidays, he dropped me back to my room on Saturday morning, I showered, had my average tasting lunch, and took a long nap, I wasn't sure if he will ever call me back, but he did, the same evening and asked me if I would like to join him for dinner at his home, I said "Yes". He picked me up, before dinner he fucked me once.

It was an instant fuck, like an instant coffee, as soon as we walked in, he pulled down my pants then his, pushed his unlubricated penis inside, I moaned "*ahh,* maybe we should have done after dinner, I am hungry." He didn't respond, continued to fuck me, I started feeling violated, he moved my face towards him and started kissing me, the kiss was comforting, it took him little longer to ejaculate, we had two beers, it was first time I tasted alcohol, at age of 18. I think I have been late, if I would have been open and courageous, I would have tasted it at age of 14 or 15, that night apart from alcohol something else happened for the first time. Manan invited three more people two of them were from my college, my seniors and one of them was his cousin, son of his maternal uncle. I stopped on the third beer, the kick was high, they had couple of more beers, Manan's cousin looked at me and asked Manan " *Muze bhi iski lena he.* " (I also want to fuck him), Manan said "*Le le , muze koi problem nahi he , mene pehle hi paach bar le li , ek dam tight he, ekdam maja dene wala. Muhart mene hi kiya he.* "

(Fuck him, I don't have any problem, I have already done it five times, his ass is tide, and gives a lot of pleasure. I was his first.)"

His cousin " Lucky bastard ".

His cousin looked at me and said " *Lene dega.* " (would you let me fuck?)

All four of them were looking at me, from their expressions I kind of guessed that Manan had shared all the details from last night with them, I said " It will be too much for me."

He said, " I promise I will be gentle. you are too beautiful to hurt."

He moved closer to me, moved his right thumb on my lips, and said " *Tuze chudne ke pese lena ho to me de sakta hu?*" (If you want money to let me fuck you, I can pay you.).

I said " No, I don't need any money?"

He started moving his hand on my right chick, gradually moved it to my chest and moved it on one of my breasts, he started moving it down, I held his hand with mine. He said, " Your hand is so soft. " And he kissed my hand.

Manan who was next to me told me " *Le le iska bhi, bahut maja aayega.* " (You should let him fuck you, you will get beyond imagination pleasure.)

I stood up, held his cousins' hand, and said, "Let's go, only one time, okay?"

He said "Yes, of course, only one time?"

We went inside one of the bedrooms, he closed the door, grabbed me, and started kissing me intensely, he pushed his tongue inside my mouth. His mouth and my mouth both were filled with the taste of beer.

Gradually he pretty much took off all my clothes, but he was still fully dressed, I pulled off his T- shirt, kissed him on his neck, I set down on my knees, unzipped his pants and started sucking his penis, he started making sounds in pleasure, and said " *Bhenchod Manan* (Sister fucker Manan), how did he convinced you to let him fuck you, he looks like a monkey and you look like an Angele. Lucky asshole."

He moved his hands in my hairs and indicated me to stop, I stood up, he kissed me, turned me around, used his spit as lubricant for his penis and pushed it inside me, he was as intense as Ethen, his penis was close to Eithne 's in length and in thickness. He and I both showered into sweat by the time he ejaculated, it reminded me of my first penetration, as soon as he ejaculated, we fell on the bed.

He laughed and said, " It was great ", I didn't say anything, just kissed his smiling lips. Outside I heard Mahesh and Karan complaining , how much time Prakash(Manan's Cousin) will take?, I heard whisper *" Kitna time aur chodega ye , hum kya hila kar nikale ?"(* How long will Prakash fuck , do we masturbated and ejaculate ?).Prakash also overheard it , he dressed up ,did a long kiss on my lips

and walked out .I didn't expect to be fornicated by four guys in the same night and wasn't willing to accept it, but after Prakash I sort of gave up, I decided not to ejaculate until the remaining two are done penetrating me, when Mahesh walked in , I was already necked and on the bed , he undressed and jumped on me ,kissed me , pulled my legs up on his soldiers and pushed his penis inside me , I moaned, he asked me to look at him , into his eyes, I did .He said ,he want to see expressions on my face while his penis is moving inside out of me, several times he pulled his penis pretty much all the way out and pushed it back inside me , he moaned *" Bhechod maja aa gaya ."* (Fuck, it feels amazing.), my whole focus was on not ejaculating, couple of times I came very close to it but managed to stop is by thinking about something else, about me being in library, me being in a farm, me reading a spiritual book, I tried to think about the objects with which I had no sexual memories attached, toward end I held my penis very tight , pressing it , it was my most aggressive attempt to stop my ejaculation , he ejaculated, I again showered in the sweat, I was tired and didn't kiss him.

In couple of minutes, he walked out, Karan walked in, he was tallest among all and the most well-built, he was dark skin, his skin reminded me of Ethen, he quickly undressed himself and stood necked in front of me, his penis was longest and thickest among all the penises I encountered by then.

I stood up from the bed, touched his penis, kissed him, he kissed me back, I sat down on my knees and started sucking his penis, I sucked it for a while, whenever I closed my eyes, an image of me sucking penis of Ethen popped up in front of my eyes. My outdoor fornication with Ethen created sexual memories with dark sky, twinkling stars and moon, whenever I looked at them, I used to get seduced and hard. I opened my eyes to be where I am, in couple of minutes I stopped, I posed to have a doggy style fornication, Karan pushed his penis inside me, I moaned, every push and pull forced me to moan, outside I heard Mahesh, Manan and Prakash joking " What is Karan doing to make Vivan moan so much?"

Manan replied " *Uska bahut bada he, lagata he lapak ke chod raha he*?" (It seems he is fucking intensely with his big and thick cock.)

Mahesh" *Kya tune sabke lund dekh rakhe he?"* (Have you seen every' s dick?)

The movement Karan was about to come, his penis was hardest and thickest, he pushed it inside me with highest intensity and power, it became impossible for me to hold my semen's inside me, I ejaculated on the bedsheet, he ejaculated inside me, I fell on the bed, and he fell on me, in couple of minutes he fell sleep necked. I moved him and went to restroom, set down on the toilet seat in potty pose, from my penis yellow urine flew out and from my anal hole semen's of Manan, Mahesh, Prakash, and Karan started dripping down. I washed my anal area with water first then applied some coconut oil, that night I learned semen which is sometimes called cum is one of the best anal lubricants.

I have swallowed semen of couple of my fuckers, couple of times, I learned that everyone's semen has a unique taste, smell, and texture, just like everyone's penis has a unique smell, taste, texture, and shape. I like salty penis.

I dressed up and went outside in the living room where Manan, Mahesh and Prakash were still drinking, and smoking. Prakash asked me to sit down next to him and asked me If I need anything? and I said water. He passed me a water bottle; I drank it all then he asked me" Do you need anything else? "

I said, " Some more alcohol?" He got me a chilled beer from the refrigerator, I took a few sips, Prakash held one of my hands, kissed it and said, " You are so beautiful." I didn't respond, after finishing up the beer, I expressed my desire to sleep. Manan told me I can sleep in his parents' bedroom, he went to show me the bedroom, and he gave me a blanket and pillow.

I lay down, he got necked and lay down on top of me, started kissing me and said " *Ek aur bar chodne ka mann hai mera ,drink karne ke baad tu aur bhi sexy lag raha he ?*" (I want to fuck you one more time, after drinking you are looking sexier than ever.)"

He got necked, took off my clothes and penetrated me, after ejaculation he fell asleep next to me necked, I didn't put on my clothes either, I fell asleep necked, that night I was fucked four more times, twice by Prakash, once by Karan and once by Mahesh. I came one more time that night again when Karan penetrated me, after that night I didn't pick any call from any of those guys for a week and didn't get involved with anyone sexually but after some time I started missing penis in general, so I called Manan, he picked me.

We had a threesome. it was me , Manan and Prakash, I asked them to kiss each other , they did, I asked them to suck each other , they did, in return they pushed both of their penis inside my mouth together , I sucked those, they double penetrated me , I somehow managed to go through it, two penis inside my anal hole .In second round of fornication one of them pushed his penis inside my mouth and another inside my anal, our threesomes, double penetrations and one on one encounters lasted for three months .In these three months I was fornicated by Karan only twice , I tried to convince him for a long term or more frequent sexual encounters , he didn't show any interest ,in both encounters somehow he singled that since girls are not taking much interest in him and they are not available that's why he is penetrating me. Mahesh and I had around four to six more encounters and gradually stopped seeing each other, in one of my threesome encounters with Manan and Prakash, I asked them to penetrate each other. It shocked them, they said " We are first cousins."

I said, " You sucked each other's penis, what difference penetrating each other will make?"

Initially they disagreed, I sucked both and gently spoke "Please do it for me, if you both like me, you will do it. Please for me."

Gradually their shyness and reluctance disappeared. They penetrated each other, I assisted them in the whole act. Prakash was disgusted by the whole act; Manan didn't feel any shame.

Next time when Prakash stopped by, I called him "Brother fucker."

He said, "Don't remind me of that, since that incident I haven't spoken to Manan."

To wipe off his guilt and shame, he fucked me with immense intensity. For couple of months. Manan did the same, when we saw each other next time, he fucked me with great intensity as well. I continued to see Manan and Prakash both separately, they never spoke about each other.

In one of the encounters between me and Manan at his home, his younger brother who was in 9th grade at that time and was around 14 years old end up walking on us when Manan was about to ejaculate inside me. Manan and I both were necked, and he was penetrating me in banana split pose, he immediately pulled out of me seeing his younger brother in his room. The pull out, shame and shock didn't prevent his ejaculation, he ejaculated outside of me, few drops of him semen fell on mt thighs and some of his bed. When he suddenly pulled out of me, it caused a pain inside me. I said "Auch, please don't pull out so fast next time.", I turned around and saw his younger brother, I immediately covered my genitals, my penis, and balls with both of my hands. I saw Manan's ejaculation Infront of his brother, while ejaculation Manan said "shit, shit, shit", that all he was able to say. I saw a terrible shame on his face. First sentence Manan said to his brother was "please don't tell mom and dad about it." His younger brother said, "I won't but you let me fuck him."

Manan looked at me and said, "Please let him."

I said "Seriously."

Manan "Please for me. I don't want my parents to know.*Ye maadarchod bol dega* (This mother fucker will tell my parents) "

It was not Manan's request because of which I agreed, I kind of got vibes that Manan's brother might be virgin.

I said "Yes ". Manan dressed up and walked out of the room. His younger brother called him "Maadarchod*(mother fucker)* ", Manan called him " Maadarchod *(mother fucker)* ". I guess both brothers were not able to get along. He undressed, I sucked his penis, I didn't bother to wipe off Manan's semen from my thighs. I asked, "Is it your first time?", he said "yes". For some reason I wanted to believe he was not lying, although I had no proof of his honesty or dishonesty.

He unzipped himself and pulled out his penis. I grabbed his young, adolescent penis and started sucking it. When I was sucking him, he moaned "Oh, it feels so good, keep sucking me ", he came inside my mouth saying "Oh my god, oh my god, I am coming, I am coming ". I swallowed all his semen. He pulled up his pants, kissed me and said, "You are so beautiful" and left.

I dressed up, asked Manan to drop me back to my rented room. He did. We didn't speak. In next encounter with his brother, I let him penetrate me. He ejaculated inside me saying "Oh it feels so great, ahh, ahh, I am coming, ahh I am coming.". Next time when Manan took me to his home, his younger brother was there. We

kind of got into threesome, all three got necked, kissed each other, sucked each other, then I asked both brothers to kiss each other. Manan grabbed his younger brothers face and kissed him with great intensity, he kissed back. In couple of minutes Manan was inside his younger brother, penetrating him. Manan's younger brother called him " *Madharchod (mother fucker)" ,* Manan while moving inside out of him said " Don't call me *Madharchod* call me *bhaichod (brother fucker) , tuze abhi chod to raha hu* (I am fucking you right now) . "

His younger brother smiled and kissed Manan. I felt like an outsider. Manan intensely fucked his brother, his brother moaned. They both were biological brothers from same parents. After this incident for almost a year, I didn't get involved in any sexual activities. The whole incident of a biological brothers fucking each other turned me off. I don't know why.

I started reading books, that was the year, I was fascinated by Camus and Kafka. The same year I have written three short stories " The Glass of Wine" , "The Son of Music " and " The Peace Finder", my creativity was at its peak , I have written several other stories ,maybe I never told you or maybe I told you but once upon a time I fell in love with short stories and short story writing , I started noticing the smallest elements of nature like an ant walking with sugar Crystal, a new leaf on a plant or a twinkle in the sky, I used to be mesmerized by the smallest elements, it was the same time when for the first time I read Franz Kafka , Albert Camus , Sartre , Herman Hesse , teaching of Buddha and learned couple of Zen Meditation .For almost a year I didn't do any sexual activities, not even jerking off. At that time, I could have qualified as a celibate monk. Couple of times I had erections while I was sleeping and woke up with wet and sticky underwear.

I read, meditated, wrote short stories, and kept a notebook of all the good things I read, realized, and noticed, that year I felt self-sufficient and content. I used to go my university regularly , paid attention in the classes and spoke very little to pretty much every one , in the evenings when the stars were visible I gazed at them for hours, my room was on the third floor, exit from it led to the flat large bordered roof, in the days on summer I slept on the roof, sometimes I miss being self-contented ,after that year , for years and till now I think I am distracted , discontented, stressed out, in constant agitation and in a constant anxiety.

Andrea woke up, she had been sleeping and dreaming till now. Perhaps that's what happens, few of the most important aspects and events of once life are never heard or recognized or seen. She woke up and put her head next to the wall. Vivan continued to speak "One of the days, when I was in library, I think it was towards the end of second year or perhaps first semester of third year when I noticed him, before that I didn't even knew his name or who he is? There was something about him or something in him, when I noticed him first time something happened inside me, from that moment onward I remembered the structure of his nose, lips, his forehead, his neck, and his fingers, perhaps his whole being with an extra ordinary detail. His forehead had a mark on the left side, one of his front teeth, left side one was slightly broken with a small gap in between the two front teeth, to me everything about him was perfect and adorable. His fingers were thick. I

liked the structure of his fingers, nails, and loved the smell of his body. I only smelled him couple of times, maybe two or three times. If I close my eyes and think of him, his smell fills my nostrils as if I am smelling him right now. His remembrance is one of my senses of beauty. Among all the features, his nose, mark on the left side of forehead and the structure of his neck attracted me the most. I still remember them in the excessive detail. I never made love to him, he never made love to me. I loved him in my thoughts, emotions, and imaginations. I guess that's easy, or I guess I chose it to be that way after everything I have been through sexually before I came across him, or perhaps I was not prepared to receive love, I was not prepared to be loved. It's strange, isn't it to be afraid of love and to be loved. The only touch I remember of him was handshakes and twice I held his hands in mine for no good reason, just to fill his touch."

Andrea " Do you sometimes regret not making love to him?"

Vivan: " Yes, very much. I regret it every day, perhaps every moment."

Andrea " Why?"

Vivan " I think keeping him alive in imaginations and thoughts after I graduated made me lose context of the reality and of him. After him, I was not able to love anyone else, years passed, almost a decade, I am still in love with him more than ever, stupid me. ``While speaking the last sentence tears busted out of his eyes, he started wiping them off with both of his hands. The moments grew full of silence until they were disturbed by a thought, by an imagination and by a desire.

Vivan said "Love is the greatest strength when realized and love is the worst weakness when lost. When I first fell in love, just thinking about him used to fill me with composure, contentment, and ecstasy, but in later years whenever I thought about him it gave me migraines, headaches, regrets, anxieties, perplexities and pain, perhaps it was the beginning of realization that I am too far from him, I began to regret that I never kissed him, never expressed my feelings towards him and never made love to him or allowed him to love me. When I will be given death sentence, I will die with regrets, with incomplete desires, I will die filled with discontent and lamentations, I think that's the worst way of dying and perhaps that's the worst way of living. I am a fool, the only person I should have made love to, I didn't. I should have killed myself, instead I ended up killing several other people. I guess the absence of one can't be fulfilled by hundreds of others. I lived incomplete and I will die incomplete." Tears continue to flow from his eyes.

Andrea " Do you think people who die a natural death , laying on hospital bed at age of 90 or 90 plus dies without regrets or with fulfilled desires or full of content , or live a complete life .You know rare people die without unfulfilled desires and without lamentations .In these matters me or you shouldn't regret , I don't think if I have lived longer I would have died with all my desires fulfilled, human desires are endless and they never get fulfilled , since they never get fulfilled we never grow out of regrets and lamentations ,we never attain contentment , I don't think you should fill sorry or lament in these matters ."

Vivan " Do you think I don't know what you said, but to know is one thing, to realize is another and to implement is whole another."

Andrea " Did you ever tell him; you love him, that you love him so much?"

Vivan " No"

Andrea" Would you like to tell him if given the opportunity?"

Vivan " People move on so quickly, people are not like me who are stuck in the past or who are stuck on one person."

Andrea " In that regard me and you are pretty much the same, look at me, I couldn't move on, the memories and experiences of the past constantly troubled me and finally I ended up shooting several people. Anyways, isn't it important that you express your feelings? I know how and how much burdens unexpressed feelings and emotions can cause. Why do you want to carry that burden, especially now? Use the courage that nearness of death gives and express everything that you have desired and desire."

Vivan " I called him after moving to the United States, he didn't even remember me or my name. Imagine how can I express my love towards someone who even doesn't remember me."

Andrea " I know .I have never seen you and I wish someday I do .As much as I can imagine and think of you , it's not possible someone know you and can forget you but I guess you are right , people move on so quickly and look at us we are still stuck in the memories ,in the guilts , in the past , in the shame , in the regrets and we are lost in the emotions .Can I ask you one more question ?"

Tears were still bursting out of his eyes, he said " Yes."

Chapter 12

Andrea " In all these years, here in the United States, did no one approach you? did anyone make love to you? or desired you?"

Vivan " Couple of people did, first time a guy in a Manhattan club approached me, it was my first visit to Manhattan, I don't remember the name of the club. The club was great and was very busy, holding my drink I was looking at the people on the dance floor, one guy, a white guy with blond hairs and blue eyes approached me."

He said "You are cute. "

I said " Thank You"

He asked me to dance with him, I did. He was a great dancer, in couple of minutes he kissed me, I kissed him back, I don't know when and how we moved next to a wall, I leaned on the wall and he continue to kiss me, he kissed me on my lips, he kissed me on neck, he pulled up my t shirt and sucked my nipples, I moaned, it was my first time of public making out. **Initially I felt some shyness, gradually I started enjoying it. We** weren't the only one doing it. In that club there were several others like us. I pushed my hands in his pants, he was hard, his penis was long and thick, I would say 6 plus inches. I gradually moved down on him and started kissing the area around his penis. He gently pulled me up and said, " We can't do it here." I remember a dislike rose on my face, he noticed it, he grabbed my right hand and said, " Let's have a drink" and pulled me to the bar. I was upset, he asked me "What would you like to drink?" I didn't answer, he moved his hand in my hair and said " Not all desires can come true at all the places, now don't be upset, please have a drink and or two with me and I will do whatever you want, and I will show you whatever you want to see? I am all your tonight. I promise."

I smiled and said " Where? Where will you show me?"

He said, " You can come to my apartment, it's only two blocks away."

I said, " I will have a drink if you come to my hotel room."

He smiled and said, " Done deal. Now tell me what you would like to have?"

I said " Martini, Cucumber martini".

He ordered a beer for him and a Martini for me. He found a chair for me and in few minutes chair next to me was available for him, we set their talking about him and about me.

We were several times for several minutes lip locked, either he was pushing his tongue inside my mouth, or I was pushing my tongue inside his mouth, when the

kiss was over, we resumed our conversation, I don't remember how many drinks I had may be 6 or 8 or more. It was one of the best conversations I ever had, we were the last one to leave the club, we took a taxi to my hotel, we reach my room, as soon as we walked inside the room, I started kissing him, soon we were on the bed, high on alcohol, kissing each other and helping each other in getting necked. He sucked my nipples, I moaned, he started kissing me on neck, I was full of pleasure, he pulled off the last piece of cloth from my body, my underwear and pressed his mouth on my thighs and started kissing there, I moaned loudly. loud enough to be heard in the hallway. I moved my hands up and grabbed the pillow below my head, I grabbed it hard. The pleasure was too much to absorb and withstand.

In few minutes, I took the turn, I kissed his neck for a while, pulled off the last piece of cloth remaining on his body his underwear, started kissing his balls, in few minutes his penis was inside my mouth, I started sucking it, he started moving his hands on my head hairs and started saying " Oh, it feels so good , oh that's the way to do , please keep doing it." He had perfect 6 packs or perhaps 6 plus packs, I didn't have and still don't have a single gram of extra fat on my body, I don't have any packs, I never desired them. After sucking his penis for a while, I moved on kissing his packs, I kissed each of them, he pulled me up and turned. I was laying under him, he looked into my eyes and said "You are so beautiful, one of the most beautiful person I have ever seen ", We kissed again ,lip to lip , he pushed his tongue inside my mouth , I pushed my tongue inside his mouth, our kissing , exploring each other's body with hands and cuddling each other lasted for a while ,when it was over , he grabbed a pillow and pushed it under the lowest of my back ,rested my lags on his soldiers , rolled over a condom on his penis and push his penis inside me , looking into his eyes I moaned " *Ahh*". He asked me if I was alright. I said "yes", as usual, and as always. He started moving inside out of me, I asked him to kiss me, and he did, the penetration lasted for a while, towards the end I was showered in my sweat, he didn't sweat that much. He came first and later helped me to come, that night he penetrated me two more time, both time he woke me up from the sleep, first time by kissing me and second time by direct penetration, it felt very romantic to me, I felt desired, I often found male aggression romantic, I don't know if it's normal, but it's normal to me. I guess we all have our own normal and perhaps that's what our conflicts and contradictions are. Next morning, we both slept till late. When I woke up it was almost 10 am. Being next to him, in a hotel room, few blocks away from Times Square gave me the feeling of being at home. Can you imagine what my idea of home is?

I felt at home in the hotel room, there is something very tragic about me. I never found a comfortable place to live, or a place called home. I think there is something very tragic about idea of home in general, people like me who never find it always imagine what it might meant to have a home, a comfortable place where oneself feel un-displaced , belonged, where things are how you want them to be, where shades and colors are of one's own imaginations, where imaginations manifested into the realities in a way oneself desired, that is the imagination of

home for me, but I think people who find homes or who own homes , sometimes seeing them , it's hard to say if they own the house or the house own them, if they live inside the house or house live inside them.

Andrea "People like us, even if we find home, we don't find comfort in it. If we don't find the home, we don't find comfort in it, the idea of home is destroyed or wounded for us, idea of comfort and belonging is pushed away from us far far away, perhaps stolen. We can see where it is, but we can't reach it, we can't reach it. Often it feels to me as if I can see it, but I can't reach it, I will never be able to reach it. Reach a place of comfort, a place of composure. " Tears busted out of her eyes.

Vivan " Is it possible to be wounded psychologically in such a way that healing is impossible, and death is the only relief?"

She said " Yes " and wiped off her tears, for a while silence stood in between the two, later she said, " continue your story, I would like to hear more."

He continued " In the hotel room, laying next to him necked, I continued to look at his face for a while, I moved my right-hand fingers from his forehead to his nose through his lips, to his chin. It woke him up, he smiled gently, opened his eyes, and said, ' Good morning, Sunshine " and kissed me. I said, " Good morning handsome."

The morning was filled with a lot of great things, he expressed his desire to shower together, and we jumped into shower a few minutes later. Till then I was penetrated by several males, but never got an opportunity to explore their bodies enough, to look at their body in great detail, to touch it all and to remember it in detail, when we jumped into shower, it was my opportunity, to explore something I love, I have and I am attracted to, a male body. I moved my hands all over his body, as I moved on my hands and eyes on his body, I started remembering him in images, in touch and in his existence. He was also moving his hands on me .I put soap on his body and started rubbing his skin , he did the same, when soap was washed away from both of our body , I washed his penis ,once it was clean , I set on my knees and started sucking it while a hot water shower was flowing on his back , his penis grew hard, I continued to suck it, for a while I moved my tongue on upper part of his penis , on his glans, he moaned in pleasure, his penis grew hardest, I knew he will be coming soon, I took it in deep, he ejaculated inside my mouth, I swallowed his cum, all of them ,he realized it , and said " Oh ,honey " , pulled me up, and kissed me , some of his semen , their smell , their taste and texture went into his mouth from my mouth, after that kiss was over , he washed his penis and walked out .I said " I need couple of more minutes in the shower" , he said "You got it. " And he walked out of the bathroom.

After he left, I washed my mouth and cleaned up my un- circumcised penis. After shower I dried myself, brushed my teeth, and walked out with a towel wrapped around my waist, he was dressed up.

His name was Matt Van Harts, he was from North Carolina and had been living in Manhattan from the past 6 years, that's what he told me. He was working for a financial firm as an investment advisor. He was almost 6 years older to me. Seeing him all dressed up I thought that's it, he will say goodbye and will walk away, I have heard stories about one night hook ups in Manhattan, most of the time that's what happens, either people say goodbye or secretly walk out on each other and never contact each other, if coincidently they run into each other, they pretend they don't know each other or try their best to ignore each other, That didn't happen, he said " I am feeling a little bit hungry, there is a great restaurant two blocks away, would you like to join me? "

I said, " Yes I will be more than happy too, I am feeling a little bit hungry as well."

He nervously said, " It's a date. "

I smiled and said " Yes, it's a date. "

We went and ate food. I shared his beer, I insisted we should pay half and half, but he didn't accept and paid for lunch, later he asked me " Would you like to see where I live? I have to change my clothes."

I said " Sure. I would love to see your place."

We walked two blocks, he held my hand, it was an strange feeling, till now most of my sexual encounters have been secrete, in private spaces, no one held my hands in public and neither did I, his apartment was on 8th floor, a studio apartment in a nice building in Manhattan, we walked in, he said " Would you like to have something to drink? "

I said " Water, water will be great. "

He grabbed a water bottle from the refrigerator and gave it to me. His apartment was something, small but very well organized and decorated with an excellent artistic touch, very clean and neat, clean, and neat like his body, he got necked and started changing the clothes, while his apartment windows were open.

I said " You know I never felt the level of comfort with my body that you seem to feel necked and dressed up. To feel comfort and confidence within self is such an excellent gift or perhaps a courage, sometimes I wish to know how that feels. "

Him: " In time, you will get there, it takes some time to get there, especially to accept yourself when most of the eyes would like to judge what we are."

I said, "What if I never feel comfortable in my skin, in my body, do I continue to live with discomfort, with this lack of confidence, with lack of self-acceptance?"

Him " If you ever feel that way, stand in front of mirror and look into your eyes, to me they are ocean of innocence, dive into them, look at your face and stillness will begin."

I said, " Is it a confidence building exercise you learned somewhere?"

Him " That's what your eyes are and that's what your face is, I can spend hours and days, laying next to you naked, watching you, loving you, smelling you, kissing you and ejaculating inside you."

I " No one desired me like that. "

Him " I am pretty sure, several have, they might not have told you. "

He was almost dressed up, he put on a white underwear first, then a blue jeans and black T shirt, he was good looking enough that any pair of clothes or any version of nudity can suit him and looks good on him. Sometimes I wonder what it means to be him. Seeing him dressed up like that, I wanted to kiss him, and desired him, one more time inside me. I walked up to him, put my left hand on back of his head while still holding water bottle in my right hand and started kissing him, he kissed me back, and we didn't stop, I don't know when the water bottle fell of my hands and when both of my hands got busy exploring his body once again, we quickly helped each other in getting necked, a part of me told me to ask him to shut down the windows and another asked me not to, I didn't ask him to shut down windows, he penetrated me in the doggy style, I was able to see outside, windows in next building apartments were open as well.

After he ejaculated, he sucked my penis, I ejaculated inside his mouth, this time he swallowed my semen's and kissed me, I tasted my semen, they were mixed in his saliva and warmth of his mouth. We slept till late afternoon. He and I woke up around 3 pm, he said " Lets jump in the shower, get dressed and go out for a walk". We showered each other. I put on the same clothes; he did the same. We went out in the streets of Manhattan holding each other's hands, he occasionally kissed me while walking in the streets, we went to couple of small art galleries and later he took me to a café where we had coffee.

In evening we set on a bench in Liberty State Park holding each other's hands, looking at statue of liberty. We set there till sunset, we talked, he told me couple of things about him like when he moved to New York? what he does for living? where he works? where he was born? Where he went to high school? where he went to college? what major he studied, his favorite music and couple of things he did with his family and friends growing up, I told him couple of things about me like when I moved to United States? What did I study? Where do I live? I told him where my parents live in India? and little bit about my childhood. Whatever he told me based on that it seemed to me his life so far has been a life of comfort and belonging, on the other hand most of my life have been of an outsider in one way or another, of struggles and discomforts.

Sitting next to him gave me psychological safety and hope that falling in love again is one of the possibilities for me.

We sat there till sunset, we saw boats going from Manhattan to Brooklyn and coming back, people going from Manhattan to Brooklyn and coming back from Brooklyn to Manhattan, towards the end of the sunset we jumped on a boat which took us to Brooklyn from Manhattan.

He kissed me on the boat and in Brooklyn, for a while we walked in Brooklyn on the side facing Manhattan, from the other side I saw the beauty of sunset falling on Manhattan, later Manhattan got absorbed in it.

We took the same boat and went back to Manhattan, for couple of hours we sat at Times Square, it was crowded, I loved it, lighting, people, energy, and a lot of advertisements. After that we went to a nearby restaurant, had a lot of drinks and dinner. I was able to finish only half of my dinner and he finished a little bit more than half.

He insisted on paying, I denied and paid for everything that evening. I walked two blocks holding him, we both were drunk, I was a little bit more drunk than him. We took the elevator and arrived at my room. He went to the bathroom and urinated, when he was done, I went to the bathroom and urinated. We both took off our shoes and socks, kissed each other and fell in the bed. Holding each other we fell asleep. We left all lights on. I guess Manhattan walks make people tired or perhaps it was several drinks we had or may be both.

Midnight, pass I woke up from thirst, I drank a whole bottle of water, went to urinate again, walked back from restroom, turned off all lights except one in the room, he was in deep sleep, combination of mild light and darkness on his face and body made him look much sexier and more desirable than daytime. I took off all my clothes, lay next to him necked and started kissing him, it woke him up. He did half awake, half sleep kiss to me, and said" What time is it?". I was aroused and filled with lust, I said "fuck me". I grabbed one of his hands and moved it on one of my hips. He pushed his lips on mine, his mouth had smell of all the drinks and what he ate, my mouth also had all those smells, kiss between us was intense, like a high school kiss, within few minutes he was necked and hard, I expressed my desire to be on top, I meant on top of his penis, till then I haven't penetrated him. He agreed, in intimacy I pushed his bare penis inside me, I loved its bare touch, from his pleasurable moans it was easy to understand the bare touch gave him far more pleasure than with protection on. His last few pushes were strong enough to make me come, while he was ejaculating inside me, I came on his stomach. When he was done. I slowly pulled out his penis and asked him not to move. I drank all my semen from his stomach, I used my tongue for final clean up. He said" I loved your touch, and I loved what you did to your semen, semen are precious things we shouldn't waste them. "Listening this I kissed him, we exchanged some more saliva, he held me in his arms, I slept with my head on his chest. He kissed my forehead and said, "I am so luck to find you."

I said, "Me too."

We both fell asleep, necked, in each other's arms.

**

Next morning, I expressed my desire to take a walk on Brooklyn Bridge and to see Brooklyn. I showered in my hotel, after that we went to his apartment where he showered and changed his clothes. We took the subway which took us next to Brooklyn Bridge. We walked on the bridge, he clicked two photos of us, in one of them he was kissing me on my right chick and in another we kissed lip to lip. Later he WhatsApp me both photos.

We walked to Brooklyn through the Brooklyn bridge; he took me to a café he loved. We had breakfast there. I had two cups of coffee, for some reason I like black coffee and its bitterness, it reminds me of the filth and disgust I went through in my life. In Brooklyn we went to see a couple of art galleries. I liked murals in Brooklyn. He told me some history of them and a couple of things about Brooklyn. what it was, what it is and what it will possibly be if things continue the way they are, he expressed some concerns around the new changes. I don't know why but I liked Brooklyn a little bit more than Manhattan, strange isn't it? but again I know very little about both places so it's hard to make any choice and even if I do, my choices hold no value or significance, they don't and often it feels like they never did, because most of my choices are mere subjective nonsense. The day in Brooklyn with him was one of the best days I had.

In the evening we came back to the same spot from where I saw the sunset on Manhattan. While we were walking, I pulled him pretty much on me, and started kissing him, I was able to feel his hardness, feeling his hardness my nipples grew tide, and I got hard, sunset was pretty much at its end, I whispered in his ears, I want to feel you inside me right now, he asked " Right now, right now?"

I said " Yes, I want you inside me while I see Manhattan standing here."

He asked me to take off my jacket, I did. He wrapped it around his waist, moved me next to railing against the East River, by then the atmosphere was a good mixture of light and darkness, he unzipped my pant, pulled it down from back, pulled it up from front and zipped it back, my hips were necked and exposed to his penis then he unzipped his jeans, pulled his jeans and underwear down from front. My heart was racing, I was being penetrated publicly for the first time in my life.

He whispered in my ear " Are you sure?"

I said " Yes"

He pushed his bare and unlubricated penis inside me.

I moan " Oh, honey ", if anyone would have seen my expressions it wouldn't have been difficult to guess that I am being penetrated.

He said " Hold the railings hard " I did .He did his usual things like pulling his penis almost out and then pushing it in with great intensity, in those movements it was impossible not to moan loud, I tried my best, but here and there it was impossible to keep it inside what I was feeling, I moaned in few of the intense moments, thank god other pedestrians were far away or perhaps they just ignored

it, he said " kiss me and don't stop kissing me until we are done" , I turned my head , and started kissing him, I pressed my tongue inside him and later he pressed his, his moves got intense and fast, his penis felt harder and thicker .I continued to kiss him, and started moving my right hand in his blond hairs. I started moving my left hand on my jeans where my penis was getting hard, thick, and ready to ejaculate. He ejaculated inside me ,it was intense, while he was ejaculating inside me, I bit on his lips , hard enough that his right-side lower lip started bleeding, the moment his ejaculation completed inside me, I had my ejaculation, my underwear got wet in front, few drops of my semen's leaked out of my underwear all the way on my jeans , they created a semen spot on my jeans, he continued to move inside out of me after ejaculation ,his penis was still hard, as usual I pretty much showered in sweat .He continued to move inside out of me until his penis grew soft enough where it can't penetrate me anymore.

He pulled up my underwear and jeans, and zipped his penis back into his jeans, a drop of sweat flew from my forehead all the way to my right chick and fell on the ground, I turned toward him, my jacket was still wrapped around his hips, I touched his lips where I bit him, and said " I am sorry, I lost control. "

Him: " It's alright, I kind of liked it."

Later he put my jacket back on me and hugged me from behind. From Brooklyn we saw Manhattan getting filled with lights and darkness, he whispered in my ears " I loved what we did today, we should try it at some other places, like Central Park.", I whispered back, " I am up for it." We had a long kiss. We took the subway to Manhattan, he took me to a very nice, perhaps an upscale Italian restaurant, I had several martinis, he had several glasses of wine, I think he drank a whole bottle of wine or a little bit more.

By the time we walked out of the restaurant, we were very drunk and were pretty much shaking, we held each other's hands and walked in the streets of Manhattan. We arrived at my hotel room, undressed ourselves, went to the restroom to urinate, most of our urine fell out of the toilet bowl on the bathroom floor, some of his urine spelled out on me and some of my urine spelled out on him.

I said, "I am sorry, it's very hard to hold my dick straight."

He said, "No worries, anyways straight guys should hold their dicks straight we have no obligation of it."

We both laughed.

We didn't bother to clean the urine spilled on us and on the bathroom floor. I didn't bother to drip out his semen from my anal hole, I decided to keep them there whole night, my anal area was sticky from his semen and my underwear was sticky from my semen. I was wet in front and in back both.

We managed to get to bed helping each other and fell asleep as soon as we touched the bed.

Bathroom and room lights were on.

***

Next morning, we woke up around 8 am. When we woke up, he grabbed and pulled me under him and said, "How about I make today's breakfast at my apartment?"

I said, "Sounds like a plan."

I showered first and later he showered. When he walked out wrapped up in white hotel towel. I told him "I am all clean. I just want to tell you because."

He said, "I am all clean as well, don't worry about sex we had without protection. I loved being bare inside you."

That statement made me feel good, good about myself.

We went to his apartment; he cooked breakfast for both of us. The breakfast was alright, but I loved it, because it was first time in my life someone who fucked me and cooked for me, someone who fucked me showed that level of care for me, most of the people I have been with were too eager to penetrate me, enjoyed the pleasure of fornication, ejaculated, and left.

After breakfast he mentioned he must go to work for half day, from noon to evening, he told me "You can stay here if you like, I have an extra pair of keys, in evening we can go for movie or plan something, if you want to do something else this afternoon that's fine."

I said, "I want to do some shopping on 5th avenue and later take a walk-in central park."

He said, "Sounds like a plan, my office is close to 5th avenue, call me if you need anything or need any help."

I didn't want to say no about his apartment key but didn't want to accept it either, so I said, "I won't feel good without you in the apartment, if I want to take a rest, I will go to my hotel room "I kissed him for long and then asked, "Will that be, okay?"

He said, "That's fine, whatever works best for you."

Then he whispered, "We better leave soon, because I am getting hard and I don't think if we stay for a few more minutes, I will be able to control myself."

I said, "I have a solution ". I sat down on my knees, unzipped his jeans, sucked him until ejaculation and swallowed his semen. While putting on his professional attire he said, "I am so grateful I found you." When he was fully dressed up, I said "You look very sexy in this attire.", he pulled me towards him and said "You always look sexy, all the time, I mean it. "And gave me a short soft kiss on my lips.

He went to his office, I took a long walk on 5th avenue, it was crowded, filled with a lot of people, I loved it. Sometimes one need a crowd to not feel lonely. I ate in a restaurant, had two martinis with my lunch, for some reason, I don't know why I dislike beer. After lunch I went to central park. I sat down under a tree for a while, then took a long walk, after that came back to 5th avenue, and shopped for a winter jacket and a hoodie. All that time Matt, his images, his smell, the taste of his mouth and smell of his semen were racing in my mind, I got hard and soft several times. When I went to Starbucks while paying for coffee I got hard, that movement I realized I fought too much against my desire to ejaculate. I asked cashier for restroom key, he handed it over to me with the receipt after writing my name on the cup, which he misspelled as *"Wewon "*, I think it was intentionally misspelled. I went to restroom and started jerking me off, in middle of it, I got a text from Matt, "Hey Sunshine I will be leaving office in 10 minutes, where are you?". I stopped masturbation, pushed back my unejaculated hard penis inside my underwear, texted him the Starbucks address.

He replied, "See you soon."

I replied, " See you."

I got him the same coffee I had without asking him, he appreciated it. I finished my coffee; he finished his coffee. We went to my hotel room. As soon as we entered the hotel room, I started kissing him and said, "I missed you a lot, the only thing I was able to think about the whole day was you. You were my only memory."

Kissing each other we undressed, when we got necked, he asked "Would you like to penetrate me?"

I said, "Yes, I will love too."

He posed for a doggy style penetration, I put a lot of my spit, my saliva on my penis, lubricated it well with spit and pushed it inside his anal, the pleasure of penetration was immense, I moaned in pleasure, and moved in such a way which creates maximum pleasure for me, he was first male I have penetrated. I moaned "It feels so great, your ass is so beautiful, tide and so on."

When I was moving inside out of him the only thing, I was carried over was my pleasure, I didn't think for a moment what he might be feeling, strange isn't it? Are we all inherently selfish and pleasure-seeking rascals?

Andrea "Most of the time yes."

Vivan "I came inside him. He was the first male I penetrated."

On ejaculation, I fell next to him and kissed him. After the kiss I told him he is my first.

He said, "Oh honey, you should have told me, I could have made it special, would have done some decoration, would have made the space a little bit more romantic."

I said, "Every moment I spend with you feels special to me."

He kissed me on my forehead and said "I feel the same way about you "but around the same time I saw a concern, an anxiety in his eyes. I asked him "what is it?"

He said "Nothing". He closed his eyes. We both fell asleep.

Later I came to know what it was. It broke my heart.

***

We woke up in an hour, I showered, changed my clothes, and we went to his apartment where he took shower and changed his clothes. I picked up a book from his bookshelf, it was Siddhartha from Herman Hesse. I always loved that book, first time I read it I was in my early 20s, I was mesmerized by it almost to an extent of my first love.

His face appeared in my mind, the face of my first love. Matt walked out of the bathroom, I looked at him, my first love's face disappeared.

We went out to a bar, had a couple of drinks and dinner, I loved that space and its energy. It was busy, a lot of conversations were happening, all of them collectively converted into a bunch of sounds, I liked those sounds. We stayed there for couple of hours, then he took me to same club we met first time , we had couple of more drinks ,danced , and danced and danced , whenever we realized alcohol is running low in our body , we went to bar and had few more shots , I don't know how many drinks I had that night , and how much and how many hours I danced, but it was great , it was one of the best club night I had, he turned out to be a great dancer. We danced until the floor was closed, we were the last one to walk out of the club.

Holding each other's hands, we started walking towards my hotel. We arrived at one of the corners of central park, he said " Central park is here, let's go inside" , I walked with him , we walked few feet's inside it, he started kissing me, then he pulled me behind a tree , the tree was surrounded by couple of bushes, we started kissing, I pushed my hands in his pants , I have always been very quick , very fast in pushing my hands in the pants, whether the penis inside the pants be familiar or unfamiliar, whether I have touched it , tasted it , smelled it , sucked it or all those yet to happen. He started kissing me on my neck , pulled up my T-shirt and started sucking my nipples, he continue to move down on me, he kissed me on my belly button, and continued his way down, he pulled down my jeans and underwear ,sucked my penis, I started moving my hands in his blond hairs, and gradually started controlling his moves in such a way that creates the most pleasure for me, in couple of minutes I started reaching my climax, I started moaning " Oh, oh honey , I am coming, you are so sweet , oh you are an Angel" I ejaculated inside his mouth, I think he swallowed all my semen, I can't say it for sure, I was too busy in my own pleasure. He stood up, kissed me again, I tasted my semen mixed with his salvia.

He turned me around facing the tree, pulled off my jacket and T shirt, pulled up his T shirt, pulled down his jeans and pushed his penis inside me, that intense move of his hard penis inside me reminded me that we are in a park , that we are in an open space, while he was moving inside me attaining pleasure ,anxieties started triggering inside me ,I said " What if someone come here and catch us having sex in public place like this ,you and me are pretty much necked, what if cops come and arrest us."

He whispered in ears ,don't worry , this area is mostly quiet, and then he moaned "I want to kiss you " , I leaned my head on one of his shoulders , my lips became accessible to his lips ,he started kissing me , we started tasting each other's tongue .Pleasure the kiss created and his intense moves inside out of me didn't help much with my anxieties, those anxieties remined me of the anxieties I was having in my high school days while being fornicated in the hostel restrooms which were accessible to everyone, I used to go through sever anxieties while persons who stood behind me , who was inside me were in intense and in one of the greatest pleasure human society have known , the pleasure of fornication, the pleasure of penetration , the pleasure of fuck .My anxieties used to sooth down when the person inside me ejaculated , pulled up his shorts or lowers or jeans or pants back and exits of the bathroom or restroom unseen, while most of the time I stayed back to let the fuckers semen flow out of my anal hole into toilet, so if I get penetrated by another fucker later , in couple of hours or sometimes in couple of minutes , he wouldn't know some else's is also fucking me , although I have learned in time that semen are one of the best lubricant and perhaps one of the most nutrition drink.

In Central Park, he was still inside me, moving faster and faster, my anxieties continued, it was a struggle between pleasure of the kiss, a penetrating penis, and my anxieties, I moved my lips away from his, his moves got intense, in pleasure he started moaning " Oh, it feels so good, your ass is amazing. "I put both of my hands on the tree In Front of me, and leaned towards it, trying to hold on to it.

My high school anxieties came back, the same anxieties which I had when Ethen fucked me under the twinkling stars and shining moon, when Yash fornicated me on the boarding house roof, when Mukesh penetrated me and I realized the room door was open, I told Mukesh " The door is open, stop, let me close it first " he grabbed me tight and said, " It's okay, everyone is sleeping, don't worry.
" Mukesh didn't lose his grip on me until he ejaculated inside me. Fortunately, no one walked in from the open door.

In Central Park, Matt continued to fuck me until his ejaculation. Whenever I got fucked, in back of my head I had this anxieties what if someone sees me , what if someone catch me getting fucked, what if someone walks on me while being fornicated, I don't know what this fear implies or why I have this fear or these anxieties and why I am not able to get rid of these .Why it continued and where did it start? perhaps it started in my early days of fornications. I still carry what started all those years back.

In central park in couple of minutes Matt ejaculated inside me, while ejaculation he moaned loud enough, I suspect it was loud enough to be heard several feet's away, my body and mind got further filled with more anxieties.

I always liked the stickiness of semen in my anal area, while ejaculation he moaned "Oh god, it feels so great. Oh my god, it feels amazing. I am coming, I am coming. I am coming "and he came. Fucker.

He pulled out his penis on ejaculation, I felt the pull. I turned around and started kissing him, he kissed me back, first he intensely focused on my lower lip and then intensely focused on my upper lip, he was such a great kisser, my stress and anxiety soothed down, I and him both dressed back, we set down, it was mostly dark, small lives were making sounds.

He held my hand, kissed it. He lay down and pulled me over him, we both fell asleep, when I woke up it was almost 2 am, I was lying next to him. I woke him up, we walked back to my hotel room, the city was still alive and was young.

In my hotel room, I urinated, had a glass of water, then he went to urinate. He got necked and jumped into bed, I turned off the lights, took off my clothes and sneaked in bed next to him, I told him " You know it's amazing how comfortable you are with your body, dressed up, necked and getting necked, I don't remember ever feeling such a comfort, feeling so relaxed in my skin."

He said, " Shyness isn't bad, actually it's kind of beautiful."

It was one of the best things any American white male said to me. I fell asleep. Next to him, holding his hand.

Now I look back and see my discomforts in my body, it seems to me they are my existential discomforts which reflect into my psychological spaces and physical spaces.

The existential discomfort that I will never be accepted fully in this society even if I live here for decades and crimeless. The existential discomfort that I will never be fully accepted in the society I was born in because of my sexuality. I think this was one of the reasons I picked up a gun and shot several people. I was not killing them; I was just arranging my own death because I don't have courage of committing suicide. Although in the society I live and, in the society, I was born in, no one seems to be fully accepted, strange, isn't it? Everyone wants everyone else to change and improve.

Necked ,next to each other in that hotel , Me and Matt fell asleep, I woke up around 10 am, took shower , walked to him with towel wrapped around my waist, he was awake, he smiled at me and said " Good morning sunshine" ,he held my right hand , pulled me in the bed, and jumped on me , I said " I just took shower ".He started kissing me on neck , grabbed my both hands with his and whispered in my ears" You always smell great, showered or not showered " and started sucking my nipples, I was aroused, he pulled off my towel, sucked my penis for a while , moved up on me and kissed me , his mouth was full of odor and his touch

was full of pleasure, he turned me, facing my ass to his penis ,and pushed his penis inside me, I moaned as loud as I wanted and as free as I desire , there was no repression inside me at that movement and for first time in my life I didn't feel any anxiety. I decided not to shower after we were done, I wanted to keep the memory, smell, and stickiness of that fornication alive as long as possible, he showered afterwards, we went out for breakfast, he asked me to check out of the hotel and stay with him in his apartment. He asked me if it was possible to extend my vacations, I said "yes", I extended my vacations for one week, rescheduled my flight and stayed at his apartment.

He took the week off, all we did was eat, drink and fuck, by end of the week, we pretty much touched and kissed each and every inch of each other's body, we tried all possible sex positions, I swallowed glasses of his semen and he swallowed glasses of my semen, he ejaculated glasses of semen inside me, and I ejaculated glasses of semen inside him, towards the last two days we pretty much lost the counts how many times we fucked and how. In those hours, in those days , a new way of living ,a new possibility , a sense of belonging seemed possible but for some of us joy, love , happiness and even sense of belonging is a temporary thing, it doesn't last long, it was 6th day in his apartment, we showered after two days, and went out for breakfast ,when we got back, he took me inside the bathroom, sort of pushed me on the sink , first he pulled down my jeans and then pulled down his , pushed his unlubricated penis inside me, I saw me being penetrated in the mirror, I saw my penetrators expressions, it was intense, he kissed me as if he wants to eat my lips away, I moved my lips away from his and said " Calm down please, calm down." his intensity went down, he ejaculated in a couple of minutes ,his face was filled with anxiety , I asked him what it .

He said " I am moving out of Manhattan, back to North Carolina. I am getting married?"

My heart sank, I can't describe what I felt. All the dreams and possibilities I imagined in that week shattered down in a few seconds, I guess that's the weaknesses of dreams and possibilities next to the realities, my eyes filled with tears, I asked " What's his name?"

He replied, " Her, she is my high school girlfriend."

I said " Wow, I can't believe it. Whatever happened between us in the last several days, what was it? A hookup or something from your wish list that you can check out before you start your happily ever after married life."

He said, " No, no don't think like that, I like you very much and how my last couple of days went by, I want my life to be like that with you forever but it's not that simple. Please try to understand."

I was angry, very angry, pushing him back, I said " It's a lame excuse." Silence fell between us. My eyes filled with tears, his eyes were red, some water appeared in them.

After couple of seconds I said, " I want to leave " and started packing my stuff, while packing I felt the stickiness of his semen inside me.

He said, " Please don't rush, you can stay here as long as you want."

I said " why? so you don't get bored, so that your penetrations continue. "

Him: " I won't touch you until you want."

I packed my luggage, booked the flight back for the same evening, called the Uber and started leaving.

He said, " At least can I drop you to the airport?"

I said, " You don't need to worry about it."

I left his apartment, tears were bursting out of my eyes, I put my luggage in the Uber and left for the airport, it was around 10 am, the uber driver was an African American lady, in her mid-40s or may be early 50s, she asked me " Are you alright honey?"

I said, " I will be alright once I arrive home", now when I think back about what I answered, I can say I will never be alright , I don't have a place which I can call a home, I never had one ,and I don't know how to find it , sometimes not finding a comfortable space , psychologically or otherwise can shatter down the idea of home and oneself begins to fade up , get exhausted .

By the time I arrived the airport all bad memories , bullying , forceful sex, pains of penetrations and forceful blow jobs ,the constant displacements , uncertainties , rejections , losses, spaces of annoyances and spaces of discomfort all started feeling up my psychological spaces, gradually they started reflecting in my physical space, by the time I arrived airport , anxieties, nervousness , stress all were dancing inside my body, I took some deep breathes, they helped me to navigate all the ways to my flight door , but after that deep breathing wasn't able to do much, by the time I arrived on my seat , I pretty much lost the sense of space and time I was in, I pushed the laptop bag under the front chair , and somehow put my carryon bag on cabinet with help of the one of the co-passenger, set down on my seat and plugged my seat belt and closed my eyes . In those moments, sometimes in my psychological space I was at my birthplace seeing the bickering between my parents and my grandparents, other times I was in my high school being heavy bullied, then I arrived in my college where I didn't say I love you to person whom I fell in love with, his name is Aryan and perhaps I am still in love with him. These filthy regrets of the past, when will they leave me? Will they ever leave me? Can I ever be truly free from them, oh this burden of the past, it always gives me migraines and anxieties. When I opened my eyes, I saw Aryan in my next seat, I was in my college, I touched his forehead and said " I love you , I have always loved you and I will always love you ."A minor flight turbulence brought me back into the real space, I was touching forehead of passenger next to me , he was young guy, perhaps in his mid-20s, I immediately pulled my hands

back, and said " I am sorry , I didn't mean to touch you , I forgot what space and time I am in and with whom."

He replied " No worries, I didn't mind you touching me. Would you like to get a blanket and some hot beverage, it might help?"

I said " yes"

He called an air hostage and helped me with the order. I had a couple of sips of coffee and put the blanket on me. Hot dark coffee , blanket , his help and my resume of deep and shuttle breathing helped me, in around two and half hours of flight , several times I have lost the sense of space and time I was in , I travelled back to same space over and over , to my college days , in the days when I was about to reach my early 20s , Aryan constantly showed up, perhaps he was and still is my greatest unfulfilled desire, in those moments I learned , maybe I will never be able to stop loving him, and in those movements I learned what incomplete desires do , they never leave, whenever the opportunity comes they reappear, his smell filled my nostrils several times, what I felt being around him in those days , I started feeling it again.

By the time we landed, I realized that I fell in love with only one person in this life and will never be out of it and will never be able to love someone else in that way, and in those movements, I realized I lost him and will never be able to find again, the flight landed, I was in my early 20s in psychological space being in my early 30s physically.

The guy in my next seat helped me to carry my luggage, I vaguely remember he only had one backpack, on arrival outside of the airport, I struggled to unlock my iPhone and open the Uber app.

He said, " I can drop you; my car is in the airport parking lot. "

I followed him, with that psychological state and with those anxieties I don't think I would have been able to open uber or get into taxi and tell taxi driver where I want to go, he opened his car door for me, put my luggage bag into his car trunk, I handed him my phone, and told on google maps use home. I don't jump into strangers' cars but whatever happened in Manhattan turned my rational power upside down.

In around 15 minutes we arrived next to my apartment complex, I turned around and I saw Aryan in driver's seat, in my desperation to hold on to something, I end up kissing him, he was not Aryan, he was Liam, he kissed me back, I unzipped his jeans, pull out his penis from his underwear, he supported and helped me in it. I started sucking his penis, he started moving his hands in my hairs and started moaning "Oh that feels so great and so on", he controlled my move for a while to create maximum pleasure for him and then let me do things according to my will, I kissed his balls and sucked them for a while like sugar candy, it pushed him on pleasure mountain, I restarted sucking his penis.

Sometimes I felt I am sucking Aryan, another times I felt I am sucking Liam, the confusions and actions continued, he ejaculated inside my mouth, I swallowed all his semen, all these experiences taught me, every man's semen have its own taste, like a unique order of body, like a unique taste of lips, like a unique personality. When I was done, I closed my eyes, leaned my head back on the seat for a while. He pushed his penis inside his underwear and zipped his jeans. My mind started filling with bad memories, anger started rising inside me, I got upset and told him " Can I get my luggage?"

Him " sure"

He unlocked the truck, I stepped out of the car, he handed me my laptop bag and cabin bag. He introduced him very politely and lovingly, " I am Liam."

I didn't reply, he insisted " Are you not going to tell me your name? Believe me I am not a serial killer."

In anger, I responded, " Don't you have a wife or girlfriend to go to? Nothing is free, isn't it? I don't know how much a gigolo or a prostitute charge for penis sucking but it must be higher than what driving from airport to here might cost."

His face filled with anger, he grabbed one of my hands, pulled me towards him, and said " I didn't ask you to kiss me or suck me alright. I hope someday I meet you again and can show you that not everyone is selfish and sometimes things can be without a price tag, just for humanity."

My eyes were filled with tears, a tear dropped down from my right eye, all the way to my chick and down on the earth, I said " Vivan, my name is Vivan ".

He let me go and said "I am sorry. I didn't mean to hurt you."

I picked up my cabin bag and laptop bag, went inside the apartment building, had some water, cried a lot, and fell asleep while crying. I didn't even thank him for driving me back to my apartment, I think that's what anger does, it doesn't allow us to appreciate what is worth the appreciation.

Life brought us back together, me and Liam Infront of each other in a strange situation , when I shot several people in the company I was working, the police officer who arrested me was Liam , second time we came across each other I was holding a gun on him and he was holding a gun on me , he could have shot me dead there , it would have made things easy for me but he didn't , his emotions got in, the emotions one blow job I gave him and a kiss we had raised inside him , or perhaps seeing me so lost and confused in flight were the reasons of his sympathy. Neither I was able to shoot him, nor he was able to do so. Who was more stuck in memories either him or I is hard to say.

***

After coming back from New York ,I woke up next day morning and went to work, I was off, wasn't able pay much attention in meetings and wasn't able to do much work, I was constantly aroused and agitated , when I walked to get water

,with any attention it was easy to see I am hard, I rushed to farthest restroom from my desk and masturbated, I masturbated twice in rows, I was exhausted , in an hour I left the work with an email , I am feeling sick and going to emergency room, I went back to my apartment masturbated one more time and fell asleep . All three times I have been thinking about Aryan, my first and perhaps last love. All three times I imagined he stood behind me , he used a lot of his spit as lubricant on his penis and push it bare inside me , while penetrating he kissed me and I kissed him back, he moved faster inside out of me and I moaned, he started masturbating me and I moaned loud in pleasure, he ejaculated inside me , and I ejaculated outside of me ,he was covered in sweat and so was I .We fell in the bed .He kissed me and I kissed him back.

He said, "I love you "Something that I was waiting to hear from him, I said "I love you too", life felt perfect as if I don't need anything else, we both fell asleep necked, in each other's arms. I imagined all that happened in a space and in a time in India. I felt an extraordinary comfort thinking about all those and masturbating on it. I am not sure was it being in India or was it being with him or perhaps both, which gave me such an extraordinary comfort.

I don't think I will ever forget his smell and the structure of his neck. I took one more week off from my work, I hated my work, not the very nature of work but the people I was surrounded by, they were a disgust, a filth, clumsy nonsenses, they were merely a pollution in human society, I have no regrets of killing most of them, absolutely no regret. "

While saying this Vivan's whole body was filled with anger and agitation. He started shaking.

Vivan continued " I went into one of the bars and that night picked a black guy, my apartment was walking distance from the bar .His penis was one of the most beautiful and the most handsome penis I ever came across, things were intense and pleasurable, he undressed me while pushing his tongue inside my mouth, he got an art of seduction and undressing that I never came across in past, I sucked his penis for a while, it was large and thick , largest and thickest I encountered, later I started kissing it , sucked his balls and kissed them , I told him " Your penis is so beautiful, the best one I ever came across, can I have some time with it ?"

He replied, " Take as long as you want, it's all yours and I am all yours tonight."

I played with his penis for almost 30 minutes, explored it in all possible ways, I moved my tongue on it and touched each inch of it. I loved its taste, texture, and smell. Before he penetrated, I pushed tones of lubricant inside my anal hole and on his penis. He gently pushed his penis inside me opening my possible space physically and psychologically, he was second black guy I slept with. His first few moves were soft and gentle , gradually things heated, I was under him ,facing the mattress, he was on top of me holding most of the control, he started moving faster and faster inside out , outside in of me , I moaned, perhaps I moaned loudest, he started kissing my lips and pushed his tongue inside my mouth for a

while, this experience reminded me of my first penetration when I was around 14 years old in an upstairs room inside a marriage home.

 I liked the repetition of the similar experience, I liked the feeling of not having much control, he pulled out his tongue from my mouth after a while , he was an excellent kisser , one of the best one, he was still hard and moving fast, I moaned " Oh baby , oh honey, oh sweety, fuck me , fuck me faster , oh baby " I continued to moan, he continued to penetrate and fornicate me, I showered in the sweat and so did he , he ejaculated, by that time the condom he was wearing on his penis broke, his semen flew inside me ,after ejaculation he stayed inside me until his penis came out naturally , when he realized his condom broke , his response was " Oh shit, the condom broke. "

I said, " Don't worry, I am all clean. " And I kissed him, he said " Me too."

He went to the bathroom, I heard his urination, and flush of the toilet, he flushed the broken condom with his urine, I had some water, when he got back from the restroom, he gave me a long kiss and jumped back in the bed.

 I walk toward the restroom , while walking I felt the stickiness of his semen in my anal area, I was aroused, I was hard , I tried to urinate but it didn't work .His semen started dripping off from where he ejaculated them, I wiped my anal area and flush the toilet papers, I urinated afterwards, I was still hard , I walked into the room , he noticed I am still hard, he spoke with surprise " You didn't come."

I said " No "

He pulled me next to him and said, " Let me help you " and started sucking my penis, at that movement he turned out to be a great fucker, a great sucker and a great kisser , what else someone can ask from a man .I ejaculated in couple of minutes, inside his mouth, he held my semen in his mouth, pushed his lips on mine, pushed half of my semen in my mouth and kept another half in his own, we both swallowed them. I slept next to him, he slept holding me from back, that night he penetrated me three more times , second time I was moving on his penis , he pushed me high enough to pull his penis almost out of me and when it was almost out , he push it back inside me, such an opening and closing of my possible space almost bewildered me , I withstood the bewilderment, this time I ejaculated without any efforts. When he ejaculated inside me, I moaned " Oh god, oh my god " it was loud and intense. I fell asleep next to him, next fornication was 3 am, he fucked me in doggy style, my favorite pose, fourth time I was leaning on a wall, and he was leaning on me. By morning I was exhausted and pleased by the intensity I went through. When he woke up, I told him where to make coffee and requested him to get a cup to me in the bed, he pulled up his white underwear and blue jeans on, his T shirt was still on the floor, made coffee for me and him, poured the coffee in two cups and brought them to me, handed one to me and started sipping coffee from another and asked me" Are you tired?"

I said, " A little bit, last night someone woke me up several times." And winked at him.

He smiled and said, " I know who he is." and moved his right hand on his penis, holding coffee cup in his left hand.

I smiled and said, " I am planning on sleeping necked whole day in this bed, dreaming, thinking, desiring and masturbating on a handsome guy."

He said, " In that case you should not be left alone.", he winked at me, and I smiled.

We finished our coffee, I expressed my desire to see him urinating, he fulfilled it. He told me I can hold his penis while he urinates if I like, I did it and I loved it.

We jumped into bed and fell asleep again.

***

In couple of hours, I woke up from his kissing, we were back to our knotty act, he sucked my nipples, moved his tongue around my belly button, started kissing me on thighs, I was aroused, I started moaning, I was bewildered in seduction like a fish out of water. He started kissing my lips and pushing his tongue inside my mouth, then he whispered in my ears which one is your favorite pose, I whispered " Doggy". He whispered, " Mine too."

In a couple of minutes, we were in doggy style.

He left after fucking me, he saved his numbers on my phone, and saved mine on his, before leaving he said, " Call me or at least pick up my call, I don't want it to be a one-night hook up, okay?"

I said, " I will call you?"

In evening I called him, he stopped by with some Panera sandwiches and soup, we ate, watched a movie, I fucked him in doggy style in my living room. The pleasure of ejaculating inside him was immense. He stayed for the night, we talked a little bit, he told me where he lives, what he does for living, where he went to high school and college, I did the same. I don't know when we both fell asleep on the living room sofa. **When I** woke up, I turned off the TV, asked him to go into the bedroom and sleep, he did it after having some water. I had some water as well, then urinated, got necked and slept next to him on the bed, I pulled up the blanket on both of us. That night we didn't do anything apart from sleeping next to each other. That morning he left early, he told me he must go to work and will pick me up for dinner.

In the evening we went out to eat. I sucked him a little bit in the restaurant parking lot, not enough to ejaculate but enough to keep him hard throughout the dinner and drinks. When we drove back, he fucked me in his car in my apartment parking lot where it was quite and dark. The sex was intense and undisturbed. He didn't stay that night. I liked being fucked in the car. We started seeing each other pretty much every day, for weeks it went on, I almost forgot what happened in New York and missed my first love Aryan very little, only occasionally.

Couple of days went by, **Friday arrived,** he invited me to his apartment. I went there, his apartment was beautiful, well furnished, one of the best and most decorated apartments I have ever seen, he invited 3 more of his friends, all were well behaved and polite, one of them was Marcos, a first-generation Latino, another was George a Caucasian guy and third was Joseph, a second-generation Chinese.

I learned Adrian, the black guy who was fornicating me, have been in United States from couple of generations, his ancestors have been through a lot in past, when I heard those stories from him, I wanted to give him immediately a blowjob and let him fuck me any way he wants. I desired to compensate all the sufferings his ancestors went through by giving all possible sexual pleasures to him.

We started drinking, talking, they shared couple of things , in few hours I was very comfortable around all of them, we all drank a lot of alcohol , someone had several beers, someone had several shots of Vodka, I had several glasses of cocktails, Adrian started kissing me and I kissed him back, rest three were watching , gradually he pulled me under him , I was laying on the wooden floor and he was on top of me . He started undressing me and I started undressing him, he undressed me fully while being half necked, he started sucking my nipples, I moaned, rest three joined Adrian, someone was kissing my lips, someone was kissing my hands, and someone pushed his mouth on my thighs. I moaned and was again restless like a fish outside of water, in couple of minutes they all were necked, Adrian lifted me in his arm and took me to his bedroom, he was strong and almost 6 plus packs. He put me gently on his large custom-made mattress, they followed him in the bedroom, he pulled me in the doggy pose and pushed his penis inside me. George pushed his penis inside my mouth and started moving it inside out of me, while Marcos started kissing my back and Joseph first started sucking my nipple, and then moved on to kissing my balls and sucking my penis.

I never had such an intense and excessive encounter; it was too much to conceived. I wasn't able to hold on to anything , including ideas and the existing model of the world inside my head, I gave up and the moment I gave up , all the anxieties, stress and my troubles with the world disappeared, I started participating in best possible way, I sucked Georges penis ,at the same time I focus on penetration of Adrian , at the same times I tried to enjoy the pleasure Joseph's sucking and Marcos kissing **was creating.**

Adrian ejaculated inside me, I vaguely remember him saying to George " He is all clean, you can go bare. "And George responding in happiness " Bingo", next was George to penetrate me, he pushed his penis inside me while Joseph pushed his penis inside my mouth, and Marco moved down to suck my penis.

George moaned " Oh it feels so good ", he ejaculated inside, pulled out his penis and walked out of the room, Marcos pushed me up on his penis, I was moving up and down on his penis, Joseph moving his hand on his penis and balls ,pleasuring himself and was waiting for his turn, Marcos ejaculated and left the room, Joseph started kissing me , he sucked my nipples, for a while I sucked his penis ,

he made me lay down facing the mattress and penetrated me, Josephs penetration lasted for a while , I think it was one of the longest penetration I had , I ejaculated twice throughout the whole encounter with four of them, the bedsheet had spots my semen created, Joseph ejaculated and left the room, I fell asleep necked , when I work up I had blanket on me . Adrian and George were sleeping on both side of me. I went to restroom, set on the toilet to urinate, a glassful of semen poured out of my anal hole into the toilet seat, I wiped my anal, flushed the toilet and washed my hands, went to kitchen had some water , Marco and Joseph were sleeping on the living room Sofa, my thighs were hurting little bit. I walked to Marcos and kissed him , he woke up and said " Hey Sunshine", I said " Kiss me " , he started kissing me, pulled me next to him on sofa, I touched his penis ,he got hard in couple of seconds, I asked him " fuck me " , he pushed his penis inside me , after ejaculation, he fell as sleep, I walked back in the room, lay down next to Adrian and started kissing him , started moving my hands on his penis, he woke up and started kissing me back , in couple of minutes he was inside me, with thickest , longest and the most beautiful penis among all four or I should say all five including me, I moaned which woke up George , as soon as Adrian ejaculated , George pushed his penis inside me again, he ejaculated , I went to Joseph , he made me stood against wall and fucked me , after his ejaculation I went back and fell asleep, I was fucked one more times that night by each of them, I went to restroom three times that night , every time almost a glassful of semen poured out of my anal.

Next morning apart from Adrian the three said goodbyes to me with a lip-to-lip kiss, they called me sunshine. Adrian was lying next to me, he woke up, held me in his arms, asked me " Was last night too much?"

I replied, " It was unexpected."

He replied, " Too much alcohol I guess."

I didn't say anything, he brought me coffee and breakfast in bed later , gave me a long kiss and jumped into shower , I fell asleep after having breakfast and woke up around the noon, I found a note from him that he will be back around 1 pm ,he is going to get some groceries , he left a towel and a new toothbrush for me, I freshen up and took a long hot water shower, I applied some lubricant to sooth up my anal area, it didn't bleed but there were signs it had too much, and need some rest. After shower I drank a lot of water, my urine was yellow which gave me signs that I have some dehydration. By that time Adrian was back, he asked me how I am doing? I said " Fine, I am little bit tired."

He replied, " I totally understand, I think you might need a couple of days of rest after what happened last night."

I didn't say anything, he put the groceries in the kitchen, got a glass of water and started drinking it. I set on my knees, in Front of him, and started kissing on his jeans zip , I expressing my desire to suck him ,he put down the glass, I unzipped his jeans , pulled out his penis from his white underwear , it was semi hard ,I started sucking him, his penis got hard and thick , in pleasure he moaned " Oh

baby , you know what I need "he started moving his fingers in my hairs , on my head. I held his penis with my right hand and moved my left hand on his balls, his pleasure intensified, I continued sucking, in couple of minutes he ejaculated inside my mouth, I swallowed his cum, each drop of it, he bowed down and kissed me with immense intensity, I kissed him back, it lasted a while, I would say 5 to 6 minutes, I changed clothes back to mine and left. He never tried to contact me, and I never tried to contact him again, I think we ended with no complains to each other, having four lovers and group sex such as that night would have been too much more me, there was a high possibility that number of my penetrators would have increased in time, perhaps would have doubled to eight, with that my anal would have bleed like vagina of a woman in their period.

In following days, so many penetrations done that night, created some sensations in my anal area, I loved those sensations, sometimes I was hard on my work desk, sometimes in meetings, once I ejaculated in the morning team meeting, a spot of my semen popped up on blue jeans, I was afraid that my semen will flow all the way through my underwear into my socks, thank God that didn't happen.

 I had the whole day to go with my sticky and wet underwear, after lunch I went to the restroom to masturbate. I saw a hippy looking long curly haired guy in the bathroom, I desired to suck him but didn't approach him, instead I masturbated on sucking him. I executed a part of modern human conscience.

Sleeping with Adrian, a night with him and his friends took away the feeling of loneliness from me for few days. The moment I stopped sleeping with anyone the feeling of loneliness was back. To skip my loneliness, I went to a bar, had several drinks, approached a Caucasian guy who was in suits and tie. He was tall and handsome. I was direct and asked" Would you like to fuck me?". He said "Sure, let's go to my car". I walked with him; we went to back of his car seat. After one short kiss, he pulled me on his penis, if anyone would have passed by, he or she would have seen me being fornicated. He was on the middle back seat, and I was seating on his penis, I was clearly exposed through his car front glass. He pushed his penis inside me and started moving it inside out of me. My mind started filling with multiple anxieties what if someone sees me getting fucked in the car, what if someone call 911, and police arrest me for having sex in public space, what if someone who knows me from work, or a friend catch me getting fornicated in car. When he pulled me on his penis, my penis was hard, and my balls were dangling. He was moving in and out of me faster and faster. I was moving up and down little bit, he pushed his hands inside my T shirt and squished my nipples , I moaned, I tried to kiss him but he playfully moved his head away and pushed his penis harder inside me .I moaned loud, he smiled, it felt to me he was very much enjoying fucking me and the whole act around it, he pulled his hands out of my T shirt while moving inside out of me, moved my head towards him and started kissing me lip to lip, he pushed his tongue inside my mouth, that moment I got one of the best kiss of my life , he was a handsome white guy , blue eyes blond hairs with a large and thick penis . **I haven't seen it or sucked it,** but I felt its existence inside me. I thought Adrian's penis was the largest and thickest, but this

guy proved me wrong. My fucker in the car was intense, it didn't feel to me that he had any anxieties or concerns around the public fornication, he was enjoying it as if he is doing it in his bedroom .**He held my** waist with both of his hands and started moving me up and down fast, twice he almost pulled his penis out and pushed it back inside me, I moaned " Oh god, oh my god. "I was sweating heavy, third time he went inside me in such a way his penis was hardest, thickest, I felt one of the most intense penetrations, that movement I knew it's time for him to ejaculate and he did, he moaned loud while ejaculating " Oh, that feels so good, oh god, oh god, oh my god, fuck, fuck, fuck. "

I **don't understand** why in the most intense movement of sex " Oh god or Oh my god " comes out of the throats of most of the people including me, and I don't know why most of the guys like to pull their penis all the way out and then pushes it inside, I have noticed this pattern in many males, may be that's what give them the most pleasure or perhaps they all knew that's what will cause me to moan the loudest.

He ejaculated, when I and him both pulled up our underwear and pants, he took 600 dollars out of his pocket and tried to hand it over to me, I pushed it back saying, " I didn't do it for money, I am not a gigolo. "

He said, "I know you are not, take it, for me please. "

He added few more hundred-dollar bills and pushed it towards me " Here take $1000, I am giving you less, you know, you are far more worth than that " I pushed it back. The whole act of giving money made me very upset.

I said " It seems you know how to disrespect. It seems you have perfected the art of insult. I don't need your money. I am not sure why you thought I did it for money, are you a pimp?"

He said " No, no, I am not, don't think along those lines, I am so sorry, I didn't mean to hurt your feelings. "

He put his money back in his wallet. Anger rushed into my body, I grabbed him and kissed him, while kissing I bit his lower right lip, hard enough to bleed it.

He wiped off his blood, strangely enough he was not upset, or angry. He touched his lip with his right-hand thumb, a small drop of blood came up on his fingers, he said " I get it, first I was so rough penetrating you and then I treated you as if you are a prostitute, please accept my apology, can I buy you a drink?"

I said, " I can buy a drink myself, why should I accept a drink from you?"

He said "Please, allow me to do at least something for you."

I agreed, I walked back in restaurant with my sticky and wet anal area, he ordered the drink I wanted. He tried to carry conversation, I didn't respond much, I quickly finished the drink and said, " If I have satisfied your ego of doing something for me can I leave now?"

He said, " Only if you tell me how to find you and only if you promise to see me again. "

I replied " Alright, save my numbers. "

He said, " Will you be able to drive?"

I said, " I live close by, I will walk, and will pick up my car tomorrow morning."

He said, " How about I drop you?"

I said "Sure. I don't see any issues with it."

I punched in my address on his phone, we arrived at my apartment building, before I stepped out, he said " Can I use the restroom?"

I " Yes, why not?"

I took him inside my apartment, while he was urinating in my restroom, I changed my clothes to a relaxed pair of lower and T shirt, had some water, he flushed the toilet and walked out, I sat down on a sofa of the living room of my one-bedroom garden floor apartment. He said, " You only kept the most essentials in the apartment, it's a very wise choice, no clutter."

I said, "You can be honest and direct, you can say I don't have that many things, it won't offend me, there are few things I am very clear about, I am not things and things are not me."

He said, " Well said, are you going to be fine by yourself?"

I said " Again, why are you being so indirect? If you want to stay for the night, just say it."

He smiled and said " Yes, that's what I want. I want to stay for the night."

I said " Okay then, you already know where restroom is, water bottles are in kitchen and if you need juice or milk they are in freeze, next room is bedroom, I don't have any clothes that might fit you "

He said, " No worries, I am planning on sleeping necked. That's what I do every night."

I smiled, he winked at me with his right eye.

I took two water bottles in the bedroom, put them on a table next to the bed, he walked in, took off all his clothes, I took off all my clothes. The room lights were on.

He said " Wow, you don't have a single gram of extra fat on your body, God made you so perfect."

Listening this I jumped on him , he held me up and started kissing me, when he put me on the bed I said your body is like a photoshopped 6 pack version, he started kissing me on the neck and whispered "I am so glad I found you", then

what he did , how he played with my body I have no words to describe, I was moaning and making noises in pleasure for almost an hour, he moved his tongue on my balls and around the belly button, oh I think I am going to ejaculated just thinking about it , thinking about him. While stating this Vivan pulled his penis out of his underwear and started masturbating, rethinking the whole encounter, desiring it to happen again, imagining it happening in the very moment. Andrea on the other side, in another prison cell, pushed her right hand inside her panty and started masturbating thinking about Mathew, her husband. On their first date, she excused herself to the restroom, he followed her, she walked inside the restroom, he walked in and locked it.

It surprised her, she asked " Mathew, what are you doing here?"

Mathew " I am here to do what I am supposed to do. Make love and fuck."

He grabbed her, pulled her towards him and started kissing her before she started kissing him back his tongue was inside her mouth. He made her sit was on bathroom sink and his hands were on her thighs progressing towards her panty, he grabbed her vagina with his right hand and squeezed it as if someone squeezes lemon with hands to get juice out of it. Later he gently masturbated her. She moaned, he pulled her panty down, it lingered in her shoes like an unfulfilled desire in one's mind, from kissing her lips, he moved to her breasts, he pulled them out and started sucking them, she started moving her hands into his hairs, he was dressed up in a suit, he quickly pulled down his pant and underwear both together, grabbed his already hard and thick penis with right hand and pushed it bare inside her vagina, she started moaning in pleasure, he started moaning in pleasure , he continued to move inside out of her vagina, inside out of her possible space. In the past she came in the restroom and in the present, she came inside the prison cell, thinking about the same event, both orgasms happened simultaneously in psychology and in reality.

When Vivan ejaculated he collected his semen in his left hand and swallowed them, then he smelled his hand, he continued to take deep breath out of it. The smell gave him a sense of peace, a sense of familiarity, stillness and belonging.

Vivan fell asleep after that, when he woke up it was almost 3 am, he felt an intense thirst, he drank the water from his cell fountain, he urinated and lay down on the mattress, the mattress, the sheet on it and blanket were neither dirty nor clean, like things which are neither clear nor vague.

Laying down in that prison cell, gazing into the darkness and into the light he thought " So that's it, this is the end, end of all, all education I have received, all the hard work my parents did. The displacement, loneliness, isolation, stress, anxiety, depression, and sexual violence that I went through, all of it, where did it lead me or where did I lead myself among all of it, in excessive fornications and penetrations, in excessive masturbations, in drinking glasses and glasses of semen and alcohol, in killing people and in being jailed, waiting for death or perhaps life sentence which will be worst then the death. "

Over and over, the same thoughts crossed his mind like an endless repetition, the very thoughts exhausted him more than several consecutive masturbations, and he fell asleep.

Next morning breakfast was pushed in Vivan's and in Andrea's cell. There was nothing good about the breakfast, he ate more than half of it, and pushed away the plate.

Andrea from the other side of the wall " Did you have a nice sleep?"

Vivan " Sort of, too much is going on in my head. It still makes me sad that I am an utter failure, can you imagine how stupid I am, when I can see a death penalty or perhaps life sentence for me, I am thinking about failures and success, how foolish, what a disgusting psychological conditioning I have."

Andrea " Believe me you are not alone and apart from that there is nothing wrong in evaluating life even if it seems it's about to end. You never know, you might end up finding something that will take away all your regrets, remorse, and hankering. I am searching for something like that from the past several days or perhaps from past several years or perhaps from eternity. Did I find it? I don't think so. In time it seems I am just walking away and away from it, every moment I am being dragged away, being pulled away, being pushed away from that point of regretless existence."

She was frustrated and pushed her right-hand nails into her left-hand arm, they left five marks. She pushed them hard enough to pop the blood out of skin for 3 pushes out of 5, she pressed her teeth against each other while doing it, later she bit her left arm, the bite left deep red marks on her skin, then she pulled her hairs for a while and stopped. She hit her head twice, very hard on the wall. Vivan was next to the wall. He didn't bother to ask what she was doing.

Some time passed, as it always does, Andrea spoke "Tell me what happened next with that guy, the guy you were telling me about."

Vivan " He undressed and started kissing me, I started kissing him back, he played with me being extraordinarily detailed in touching and exploring all possible pleasure points of my body, I came even before he penetrated me, he didn't bother that I came, that my ejaculation has happened. He wiped off my semen from my belly, balls, penis, and thighs where most of them fell on my ejaculation, in couple of minutes of my ejaculation he pulled me in a doggy pose and penetrated me, initially it was too much to handle since I recently had second ejaculation of the night, but I sustained him, his penis and his moves. He grew faster and faster, deeper, and deeper, he pulled his penis all the way out, spit his saliva on it and pushed it back inside me, I moaned "Oh my god, oh honey, oh my fucking god." I moaned the same words over and over, I should have said, honey slow down, honey please be gentle, or honey please stop I need break, when life

starts fucking anyone in the world, they mostly start saying Oh my god, whereas they should say slow down, or be gentle or stop. I am one of those people who says oh my god.

He took a deep pleasure in my moaning; it was too much to handle for a while, but I liked it later, it was liberating, losing control, and being pushed to my limits and beyond. He ejaculated, since the condom already broke when he fornicated me first time in the car so this time he didn't bother to put in on and I didn't want him either, he looked clean. After his ejaculation we fell on the bed, he gave me one long kiss, he said " Tonight I had one of the best sexes of my life. "I didn't reply, I kissed him in the middle of his neck, he had neck structure of Aryan, my first love.

Sometimes I wonder why I never stopped searching Aryan or parts of him, his smell, and resemblances of his being. Sometimes I am scared what if I will never be able to stop searching him, what kind of being that will be, and what will be the sense of that being, searching for something I lost or something that I never found, something that was never mine, isn't mine and will never be mine. My mind is a mess, it always runs toward the unfulfilled desires.

I don't remember the time when my mind was not agitated for one reason or another, by one thing or another, I don't remember being in composure from years, sometimes I think my lust and excessive involvement in sexual activities was merely an attempt to peace my agitated mind, but I could be wrong, dam it, why we live through endless dualities.

I didn't like few things about him, my fucker and I liked few things about him, for most of the things I was a neutral, after that night he came to see me twice a week at my apartment in evenings, when he was with me, he always gave me full and undivided attention, he never checked his phone or was distracted by anything else. He was curious in me psychologically as well as physically. Sometimes he came too strong on me in our sexual encounter and sometimes too soft, it was hard to locate the origin of it, the origin of two extreme.

He took me to a whole another adventure , he rented a beach house, we fucked on the beach sand in a doggy style in night, twice he penetrated me inside the water when the beach was crowded with people, standing behind me , penetrating me from back ,we both were little bit more than half inside the water, initially we were just swimming inside the water next to each other, all of the sudden he grabbed me and pulled me towards him , I flew towards him , he started kissing me, I contributed back ,we started kissing each other as if we are in high school.

I pushed my hand in his underwear, he was hard, he grabbed my butt and squished it, he quickly turned me around, and started pulling my beach short down from back, I held both of his hands with my hands and said," Beach is crowded, what if people find out we are having sex?"

He said " Don't worry, even if they find out they will only think and remember two guys having sex in water, they don't know me or you. Please let me do it, I can't control it." and he started kissing back of my neck. He pushed his right hand in my underwear, grabbed my penis and started stroking it. I was aroused, when I was sufficiently aroused, he whispered in my ears, " Can I please". I said " Yes", he pushed his penis inside me, I moaned, turned my head back and started kissing him, it was so easy to guess what we were doing, his moves were strong enough, it brought out the reality over and over from my moves, from his moves, from my moans, from his moans, through my expressions and through his expressions that he was penetrating me. For two days, he penetrated me while we were watching the sunset from the beach house window, twice he asked me to penetrate him, I did it.

A day before end of vacation he asked me " Is there anything you would like to experience or would like me to do?"

I said, " I want to taste your semen, swallow them?"

He said, " Go for it."

We were in the bedroom at that time , the bedroom had lake facing window, his back was facing the lake , I pulled down his short, and started kissing on his white underwear , I used to do it with Yash ,the guy who fornicated me pretty much every day in 11th grade, after school when most of my schoolmates used to go to play one sport or another sport at school playground ,I and Yash used to stay back in hostel, he would come to my room ,each room was shared by four students, most of the time after school my other three roommates were out on the playground either watching one or another sport or playing one or another sport ,Yash used to walk in, he would made me sit on a table and we used to start with lip to lip kissing, him pushing his tongue inside my mouth and I allowing it , in the whole play sometimes I pushed my tongue inside his mouth as well, for a while we used to taste and suck each other's lips and saliva, then he used to pull up my t shirt and suck my nipples, next I used to pull down his lower or pajama and kiss on his underwear while his penis was waiting to be sucked first and penetrate me later. I think I told you about my high school encounters with Yash.

Andrea " Yes, I remember a little bit of it. "

Vivian" Yash was an excellent fucker. Moving back to my adventures on lake shore, I kissed his underwear for a while, then pulled it down, his penis was already hard, first I sucked the upper part of his penis, the glans, he moaned in pleasure, he took off his T shirt, and got fully necked, I don't understand the eagerness to get necked so quickly, so fast. I also have it in myself, and I don't know where it comes from and how it got into me. I don't have much experience with women, that's why I don't know if women carry the same eagerness, but I know for sure men do."

Andrea " We do, now a days we are much more eager into getting male necked as quickly as possible, perhaps we are forgetting the difference between man and instant coffee, perhaps we forgot that man are not instant coffees, although I think men are and have been in assumptions and impressions that women are instant coffees. Instantly take off our panties, instantly push their junk inside us, instantly ejaculate and expect us to be instantly happy and have instant orgasms. I don't know about gay males though but most of the straight males I know are shitholes, mere stinky stools. Their penises are too eager to ejaculate."

Vivan " To me you are equal to me and my competition like any other straight woman and any other gay male. There is a very high possibility that we both will get life sentence or death penalty."

Andrea" What happened next with that guy?"

Vivan " After sucking his top part of penis, I kissed his balls and smelled them."

Vivan stopped speaking, for few minutes silence stood like a gigolo in the streets of Manhattan, then he spoke "You know there is something very strange. Since I remember I have been searching for a home, a place of belonging and I never found it, I found different spaces and different zones. I thought if one space and zone is not comfortable then I should move to another and I did. The painful and disturbing factors, the instabilities, and the struggles they never left me alone, no matter how much I have tried. **Sometimes I wonder why?** with my best efforts I don't find any answer. I can't find any answers. Strange, I can't find answers for what happened to me and why it happened to me. Sometimes, I wonder if I am overly fascinated by home and the idea of home. Sometimes I wish I could ask ants and birds because they make homes and nests, what is their fascination with home, what they search in home. Sometimes I see people who have a sense of belonging, who have found a home, who are not constantly displaced, I wonder what that feeling might be, the feeling of belonging, the feeling of at home.

All these people who allowed me in their lives, in their homes, apartments, hotel rooms and whom I allowed in my apartments, we were seeking pleasures, giving each other pleasures, getting pleasures from each other, I don't think this attitude is a sense of belonging. Anyways, I smelled his balls, I loved their smell, I moved my tongue on them , you know tongue is such a great gift, it not only can be used to create great sexual pleasures and to feel taste but it can hurt in such a way that no other weapon can do , even a thick large unlubricated penis pushed sharply and carelessly inside anal hole can't create hurt as much few inappropriate word can do. I have done it and it works, people did it to me and it worked. Sometimes I feel as if I am a shithole, filled with the smell of stool. I sucked his balls for a while, he moaned " Oh it feels so good". For a while I played with his balls, then moved to sucking his penis again. I sucked him deeply and intensely. I took his penis deeper and deeper inside my mouth, my sucking grew intense and intense. We were fucking several times a day that's why it took him long time to ejaculate, when he ejaculated, he ejaculated enough to feel up my mouth, I swallowed the first ejaculation of semen and later used my tongue to clean his penis like a

mother cow cleans her calf on birth. After ejaculation he walked necked in the kitchen, brought two glasses and a bottle of wine, he opened the bottle, poured the wine in both glasses, handed over one glass to me, I drank it. First few sips created a taste of semen wine mixture in my mouth. Later it was wine only. He jumped in the bed, sneaked his body up to his waist in a blanket, he leaned towards the wall, I followed him. He was necked and I was dressed up in a shorts and T-shirt.

When we were on our second glass of wine, I asked him "Is there any desire of yours you would like me to fulfill? "

I thought there may be none, the way we did things, more specifically the way he did the things.

He said " Yes"

I asked, " What is it?"

He said, " If I tell you, you will think I am a pervert."

I said, " You never know, maybe I won't, maybe I will think it's normal, we all have our own definitions of normal, abnormal and pervert. Please tell me."

He said " I will tell you, but you don't need to do it if it's uncomfortable to you or if

you don't want to do it."

I said " Got it. Now tell me what is your unfulfilled desire? "

He said, " I want you to suck me first, swallow my semen and then I would like to urinate inside your mouth, and you drink it, I mean you swallow my urine as you have swallowed my semen."

I asked, " Why do you desire this from someone? where did you get this idea and what will it do to you if I fulfill this desire of yours?"

He said, " I was molested in my childhood by my babysitter, he used to drag me to bathroom, undress me, touch my penis and balls, then touch my anal area and used masturbate himself saying " Oh it's so soft, someday I want to come inside you, my little slave." He used to bring a small female dog, a bitch with him, whom he would force to sit quietly while he did it. He would put something in bitch's mouth so she couldn't bark, sometimes I got the impression that the dog was struggling to breathe or for life, perhaps during that time. That dog and I both were helpless. He used to force me into blow job , made me drink his semen first, and later he used to urinate into my mouth, most of the urine will flow through my mouth , after that he would give me shower and brush my teeth, as soon as he it done that with me , he would turn into a normal caring babysitter, he would free his dog, but neither I nor his little dog ever turned out into being a normal child or a normal pet, it became an everyday affair. Twice or perhaps four or five times he

penetrated his dog Infront of me in the same bathroom after putting the thing in her mouth so she can't bark or make any noises, his pet was a little female puppy, I vaguely remember him switching between her vagina and he anal area, I remember him ejaculating inside her vagina and his semen popping out of her, I threw up. While I was throwing up, he said " Are you a man or a pussy? we are alphas, we are supposed to fuck the bitches, all bitches. Someday I will make you my bitch too. you are on the way to being my bitch.' He laughed a rascal laugh. After ejaculation he dropped his pet on the floor where it felt to me, she struggled to breath while the asshole was wiping off his penis with toilet paper, he pushed back his dick inside his underwear, flushed the toilet and washed his hands. He washed my mouth, wiped my vomit with paper napkin, and flushed them. In couple weeks he started making me swallow his semen, after that he would urinate in my mouth and make me drink his urine, every time I vomited just after that and felt sick for hours."

I said, " Then why would you like to do the same thing to me or someone else?"

He said, " Because it feels to me if I can do that with someone else it might free me from those bad memories and it will make me feel powerful, strong and it will give me a sense of achievement. "

I asked, " Why do you think it will make you feel strong and powerful?"

He said " Because I felt powerless and miserable when it was being done to me. My molester was feeling immense joy, pleasure, and power. My self-worth and confidence pretty much collapsed. Sometimes I even don't know what I want."

A sorrow filled his face. I didn't allow him to complete his sentence and said " Okay, let's do it in the evening."

He said, " Are you sure?"

I said " Yes, I have tasted semen ejaculated from several penises. I do want to taste urine coming out of penis other than mine. Maybe it will be a new adventure for me in future. People often say perception and reality are two different things, I say perception is what makes reality and reality is what makes perceptions, they both are constantly each other."

We finished the glass of wine and took a long nap. While sleeping he held me in his arms as if I was a delicate newborn baby. While sleeping, I had several dreams about my birthplace, I saw my first penetrator, his face was lit up in joy, I was confused in my feelings, I don't know if I felt violated or felt accepted. In my dream he ejaculated inside me, it felt as if it was real, I woke up, almost four hours passed. I was hard and aroused. He was sleeping, I took off all my clothes, slipped next to him and started kissing him. He woke up.

I said, " Fuck me please. "

He wasn't hard. While kissing me, he jerked him off little bit to get hard. I didn't mind it, sometimes men have to jerkoff physically and sometimes psychologically to get hard, to penetrate, to fuck. He pulled me on him, and pushed his penis inside me, he penetrated me and made me move with intensity as if he wanted to push all of him inside me, his whole existence, his whole being. I have noticed this behavior in a lot of males. Sometimes I have also penetrated and ejaculated with pretty much similar intensities, I don't know what that is, is it the desire to return to mother's womb, back to where we came from?"

Andrea " I can't say why for sure. I have noticed similar behaviors in men who penetrated me. Sometimes it felt to me as if they wanted to push themselves, all of them inside me, inside my vagina. Maybe they want to skip the troubles of the world and want to go back to space where they came from, a womb, or maybe that's just male violence, males are males, gay, straight, bi or celibate, animal, or human. Males are inherently aggressive creatures."

She pushed her right hand into his underwear and started masturbating herself, and told Vivan "Please tell me what happened next?"

Vivan "Even if I was sitting on his penis in top position, he took over the control, he pushed and pulled his penis intensely inside out. I struggled to find balance, in that movement a great realization broke on me, I have always struggle to find a balance and no matter how hard I tried, it was never possible to achieve it, it was never possible to attain it, there on his penis I tried my best to find balance, for few moments I was able to find the balance and in others I lost it. The whole thing was a combination of pain and pleasure, desires, and their consequences, like life, like reality. I moaned loud and heavy, his thick and large penis continued to penetrate me, I got a glimpse of beauty from the window, the clouds were covering and uncovering the moon, I saw moon in decay. He ejaculated inside me, at the same time I ejaculated, few of my semen shot right next to his lips. He touched them with his tongue, pulled me and started kissing me with great intensity, he pushed a lot of his saliva inside my mouth, I swallowed it, all of it. Later we took shower together, we bath each other. He was like reality of the world to me, when it is with me, I got full attention of it, but often I struggled to find a balance in it and with it. When it penetrates me, sometimes it's perplexing and other times it's bewildering but that's not it's all about, there have been many movements where it gave me unbearable pleasures and erections.

Sometimes I fucked the reality and other times it fucked me. It was our last night on the vacation, we went out for dinner, he took me to a very fancy restaurant on the lake shore, the restaurant he liked the most, I didn't like it much, I had some French fries, less than half sandwiches and had two cocktails, sometimes I pronounce it as *cocktale*, the tale of a coke, the tale of a penis. God knows what kind of tale that will be and what will it include and what will it exclude. ``

Andrea " I think at minimum it will include all the spaces it has penetrated or tried to penetrate and fuck."

Vivan" Those will be too many spaces, vagina, anal hole, and mouth. These are not the only spaces cock fucked, cock historically have fucked mind, ego, intellect, society, being, consciousness and existence of less powerful entities, sometimes I wonder what it has not fucked and fucked up."

Andrea" I totally agree with you, the *cocktales* will be long and tedious."

Vivan" Anyways, it might seem from whatever I have told you that I always met good looking , big dick guys who gave me orgasms or who made me come, but that is not true, once I got attracted towards 50 years old white guy, he was average build and bald, when I pulled down his underwear to suck his penis it turned out his hard penis was little big longer than 3 inches, it turned me off but out of politeness or out of some moral obligations I sucked it, then he express his desire to penetrate me , I allowed it with a condom on his penis, I didn't like the overall experience, it turned me off for weeks. I didn't even masturbate for weeks, a strange shame continued to rise inside me in all those weeks, a strange guilt filled me up , I think I am a materialist nonsense that's why it happened or it may be something else that I don't know, sometimes it feels to me, we humans are an extraordinary tragedy ,often we don't know what is in our mind , what is in our heart and what we truly wants or desire , we think we are superior to other living creatures but we are merely an utter confusion, and our confusions are the byproduct of our intelligence, and here is a thing I don't understand if intelligence add confusion what will add clarity. Another time I encountered a thin guy, he was a mixed race, a mixture of Latino and white, his body was as white as white people. His penis was brown, he was thin. I wanted to escape the guilt and shame my encounter with a three-inch-long penis created inside me, to escape it I went to a bar and ran into that mixed race guy, we started talking, he offered to buy me a beer, I agreed, although I don't like beer. While I was sipping the beer, he bought me, he moved his right hands on my thigh, winked his right eye and smiled.

I asked, " What are you planning on doing?"

He whispered in my ears " I want to fuck you?"

I said, " I think you should do it."

We finished our drinks and walked out.

I asked him " Your car or my car?"

He said " Mine"

We walked to his car.

He said " Let's go on the back seat. "

We went on back seat, we kissed, he started kissing me on the neck, then sucked my nipples, pretty much all the males I have been with did it, sometimes I wonder does it have anything to do with their search of their mother's breasts, in childhood which implied food or perhaps survival or maybe it has something to do with deriving the pleasure.

I started undressing him and he started undressing me, I pulled out his penis from underwear and started sucking it, he started moving his hands on my head and started moaning in pleasure. Later I lay down on the seat with my butt facing him, he pulled a condom on his penis spit his Saliva around my anal area, while I felt the stickiness and flow of his saliva on my skin. I heard a man and a woman laughing, the same old fear rose inside me, what if they see us, what if they find out what we are doing in the parking lot of a restaurant, in a public space. While I was in anxiety, the same anxiety I went through at the time of my first penetration, throughout my school years whenever I was being penetrated or was getting fornicated, I had the same anxiety again, I didn't ask any of my fuckers if they got any anxieties while penetrating me in such circumstances and situations, in such a place.

 Being in that mode of anxiety I heard the male telling the female " Do you want to suck it? " they were standing very close to the car I was in , I saw male grabbing one of the hands of the female and moving it on his pant where his penis was hiding inside, she immediately pulled it back, and spoke " Behave yourself , we are in a restaurant parking lot ."I thought she indicated if they would not have been in the restaurant parking lot she would have loved to grab his meat and perhaps have more of it at his apartment or her apartment or home or in a motel room. I didn't see what happened next, but I think the man squeezed one of her breasts and said, "I know you want it."

Meanwhile that guy spit some more saliva on my anal area and pushed his penis inside me, opening up one of my possible space, I wanted to moan but didn't, given the aroused male and female were outside of the car, after two or three moves inside out of me the fucker started saying " It feels so good". I was hoping he doesn't say it loud, he didn't, he moved my head towards one side and started kissing me, he was almost a foot longer than me. It took me a while to participate back, he was persistent in attempts of pushing his tongue, later when I participated back and opened my mouth, he succeeded in his attempt.

At that moment I had too many things to deal with, his penis moving inside out of me, his tongue which he was trying to push into my throat, my anxieties, and memories of the past where I had similar penetrations. The man and woman walked away. I think they were too busy into their lust to notice anything else as most of the human are or perhaps the whole human race is. After sometimes I moved my mouth away, he continued to move inside out of me, he was very light in weight, it felt to me as if there was a penis which was coming from the void and was penetrating me. His lack of weight turned me off, by the time he ejaculated I was completely turned off, I wasn't even hard. After his ejaculation we started dressing up, and walked out, neither he nor I showed any interest in

seeing each other again or asked for each other's contact numbers. In my encounter with several males, not everyone accepted me, it was not that they were the one who made the moves always, a couple of times I made the moves as well, some rejected me saying, " I don't do your type." others rejected me saying " They are not into it. ", couple other rejected me without any reason, others agree reluctantly , someone allowed me to suck them, for few others I was their first same sex encounter so even if they fucked me throughout the act they were sometimes comfortable and other times uncomfortable, couple of them sucked me and left, other asked me to penetrate them , I did , as soon as I ejaculated I was back to being stranger for them .Three times, I ran into males in grocery stores who fucked me in sear joy and were extraordinary appreciative before, during and afterwards , in the grocery store two of them pretended as if I don't exist, one of them came and talked to me, he showed extra care and politeness towards me, and later introduced his fiancé to me. She was very polite, I couldn't make out if she knew about him, about me and him. I don't know why it kept happening to me, people fucked me, most of the time they enjoyed it, but none committed to any serious relationship and several of them were only cheating on their significant other half, man or woman or any other sexual entities. So, if you are having ideas that everyone who fucked me desired me or were good looking or treated me well that's not true. Once a young guy, must be in his early 20s pushed his three fingers inside my anal hole, his nails wounded me, I immediately withdraw and said," Stop it ".

He said " That's how I start baby"

I said " You are a pervert. I don't want to do it, if you further touch me, I will call 911."

He said, " Having penis inside anal hole or having fingers or wood or toys, it's the same thing baby."

I immediately dressed up and rushed out of his apartment, drove my car at the fastest speed possible, his presence on earth, in the city gave me horrors for days. I never ran into him again.

Once I was engaged in sexual encounters with a person who was I think in late forties or early fifties, he had several white hairs in his beer and on his chest, he was good looking, after kissing his clean balls and sucking his penis for a while when I moved up to kiss him, I asked him " Have you started getting gray hairs down there?"

He replied, " I have a couple, I can grow them if you would like to see."

I replied, " I was just curious. I like it clean there."

He replied, " Me too."

He pulled me on his penis and pushed it inside me, the penetration lasted longer than normal, I think it took him around 20 to 25 minutes to ejaculate, in around 15 minutes I started getting tired being on top, jumping up and down on his penis. I

asked him to change the position, he did, I was laying under him, his moves were intense, towards the end we both were showered in the sweat, I felt as if he is struggling to ejaculate, as if he is trying so hard, finally he ejaculated.

He continued to move inside me after ejaculation until his penis was not hard anymore and fell out of my anal hole. He fell next to me, I turned towards him and said, "That was something." I thought to ask him " What did he take ?" or " Say he doesn't need to take any of those things to be with me and to be inside me " but I didn't say it , we have known each other for only couple of days, I thought asking him or telling him this will make him feel uncomfortable or offend him, I have to say we live in a very strange society, we can suck , fuck , leak and ejaculate in couple of hours of meeting , or couple of day or sometimes in only couple of minutes but we can't ask a genuine question or can start a genuine conversation. Rather than asking those two questions, I said " I liked very much what we did, and would he like to see me again?"

He said "Absolutely."

In a couple of days, we saw each other again, meanwhile I jerked myself thinking about him, in those days I used to gather my semen in a glass and used to drink them. Twice I mixed honey in them and swallowed them. It might sound disgusting, but I like semen, I like everything about them, their smell, their touch, their thickness, thinness, and stickiness, if I don't taste semen for a month, I start getting cravings and urges for them.

Andrea" I like semen too but not as much as you do or perhaps, I never inquired and took some time to investigate my interest and relationship with semen. I should do that one of these days. Prison cell seems like the perfect place for such inquiries about self."

Vivan" Sounds like a plan to me. we have plenty of time here whereas outside humans are running like headless chickens for mere survival."

Vivan continued " He was type of a guy who would fuck me anywhere and he wouldn't even worry if someone is watching or not. Couple of times he pushed me into such situations, once we were sleeping in a large hammock which he hung few feet away from a very busy beach on a lake shore, I was fine when he pushed his hands inside my underwear to grab and squeeze my butt and when he pushed my hands in his underwear to grab his penis and touch his balls. I enjoyed doing it under the open sky while I was able to hear the sounds coming from people on the beach, He and I were sleeping sideways. He pulled down my short and underwear together, all the sudden my butt, penis and balls were exposed to light blue sky, it made me very uncomfortable, but before I pull my underwear and short up, he pushed his penis inside me, it was wet and sticky, I think he already applied a lot of his saliva on it or perhaps lubricant. I felt it penetrating straight inside me , till now we fucked with condom, it was first time he pushed it bare inside me, I immediately moved my hands up on his head, he pulled his penis little bit out and pushed it in further, his whole penis was inside me, I moaned " Ah honey, you

should have asked me , we are on a beach, in a public place, people will notice , the way hammock is moving ."

He said, " Fuck them, they don't care about us, why we should care about them. " And he did his classic push and pull, he pulled his penis all the way out and pushed it in, rather than moaning loudly, I turned around, first kissed him and later bit my lips so that I don't moan. Look what presence of others and accepting their presence can do, it forces our moans to be kisses and self-bits. He moved me from side to bottom. He was on top of me, my mouth was pressed on the hammock, he continued to penetrate me, somehow, I adjusted my mouth to breath properly.

I was angry about the whole thing, he pressed both of his hands on the thighs right below my balls and started moving me towards him while moving his penis inside out of me, it intensify his pleasure, my bewilderment and moves of the hammock increased. I felt violated and that incident reminded me of forceful penetration of penis inside my mouth in my high school days. My moans were back " Ah, ah, oh god, oh my god, stop it please, stop it please."

He said, " tell me if you don't like it, tell me you haven't ever desired something like this. "And he continues to fornicate me. When he told me that I got confused, I couldn't draw the clear lines if I am liking it or hating it, if I desired it or it is merely being forced on me, in my confusion, I said " Oh honey, at least please slow down."

He didn't. He continued with same intensity, I pretty much gave up, then he pushed his hands further down and grabbed my penis, moved me and him in such a way that we were pretty much in a doggy position in hammock, he was masturbating me with one hand, moving another hand on my balls, while moving with almost same intensity inside out of me, trying to go deeper and deeper, attempting to derive more and more pleasure for him. His struggle to ejaculate started, when his climax began, he stopped masturbating and touching my balls. He grabbed my waist tight; I felt his penis was hardest and his push inside me was the strongest, he ejaculated inside me.

He moaned " Oh, it feels so good, that's what I needed today. You are amazing."

On ejaculation he lost most of his energy and fell. His weight pushed me down, in anger , bewilderment and agitation , I grabbed my already hard penis and started jerking it off, given what I went through and the sensations in my anal area I ejaculated quickly and deeply, a lot of semen came out of my penis, they left the hammock wet, later I found few drops of my semen made their way to sand below the hammock, my eyes were filled with tears when the whole act was going on ,on my ejaculation tears busted out of them, inside my mind I said "Fucking pig, filthy dog, he fucked me as if I am his slave, asshole , shitty bustard.".

He turned me towards him and started kissing me , the kiss started soothing me, I calm down, then he started kissing me on the neck, he pulled up my T shirt , sucked my nipples, pulled up my underwear and short , along with his own

underwear and short, grabbed me in his arms and said " Today I had one of the best sex of my life but if you didn't like it, I won't do it in such a way ever again. I promise."

I didn't say anything, I fell asleep in his arms. When we woke up, almost three hours passed. I woke up first and then he woke up, when we were walking back to his car, an old white man shouted at us " Perverts, you both will go to hell. "a strange fear arose inside me. My fucker turned around, gave the middle finger to the old man, and said, " Fuck you bastard."

My fucker and I both got into his car. My heart was beating fast. He started driving. I wasn't sure if the old man was upset because we fucked in hammock or because we were homosexuals. I asked my fucker " Was it necessary to shout at the old man? You could have just ignored him."

He said " It was, we live in a free country. He has no right to tell us how to live and what to do and what not to do."

We arrived at my apartment. He said " Hey, can I come inside and take shower. "

I said ' sure, you can. "

The first time he walked into my apartment, he appreciated the simpleness and arrangements of space between the objects. He asked me to join him in shower, I did. He bathed me like a baby and washed each part of my body in detail including the upper most part of my uncircumcised penis. He cleaned my anal area and later cleaned himself in great details as well. He dried him and me with the same towel. He lifted me in his arms and put me on the bed in one of the gentlest ways. Moved his hands in my somehow dried somehow wet hairs and started kissing me. His kiss was soft, gentle, and polite. I kissed back in the same way, he moved all the way down on me and started sucking my penis, I wasn't hard, but he continued, till that moment I was the only one who sucked him, he was the only one to penetrate me, mostly he was the enjoyer, and I was the enjoyed. I didn't get hard. I told him "I came in hammock; you can suck me some other time."

He stopped, dressed up and left. I fell asleep necked.

In my dream I saw Aryan, we were in college, in a classroom on second floor, just me and him, I touched the mark on his forehead, he has a small mark on his left forehead, I kissed him on the mark, his smell filled my nostrils, whenever I was around him, in reality or in dreams, I always felt complete, fulfilled, as if the whole world disappeared, only I and him remained, and my world is complete. It's strange, people move on so quickly and here I am, stuck in past without closure, my agitating past is one of the reasons I picked the gun and pulled its trigger, but you know everything have several reasons, my killing also have several reasons, some of them even I don't know, you might have to ask the supreme, the knower of everything.

I saw him again two days later; he visited my apartment. As soon as he walked in, he grabbed me and started kissing me, while kissing my neck he moaned "Oh baby I missed you, let's finish what we left incomplete last time. 'We both rushed to my bedroom and helped each other in getting necked. I lay down on the bed and started sucking my already hard penis, after a while he started kissing my balls and started sucking them, in pleasure I grabbed the pillow under my head very tight and started moaning. My whole body was filled with great sensations and ecstasy, my nipples got tight. He stopped, pulled me down, told me " I don't want you to come yet. "He pulled me down enough to bring my mouth next to his penis. First, he pushed his right-hand thumb inside my mouth and moved it on my lower lip, then held his penis with same hand and started moving it on my lips, I started sucking it, gradually he started moving it inside my mouth as if my mouth is vagina or anal area, he was gentle and deep in his moves. I surrendered to his gentleness. He continued for a while, then he pulled it out, grabbed both of my lags and put them on his soldiers, touched his penis on my anal area and asked, "May I?"

I said,' Yes'

 He pushed his penis inside me, that was possibly one of the most comfortable and relaxing fornication experiences I had in my life. Things grew intense between us before he ejaculated inside me. I was still unejaculated, when he fell on the bed tired after ejaculation, he grabbed my hand, moved it on his butt and said "You can fuck me if you want, till now I have been penetrating you and never gave you the opportunity. Please go ahead."

I applied some salvia on my penis and pushed it inside his anal area, he moaned " fuck."

I continued; in the first penetration, I came in a couple of minutes. In a couple of hours, I did a second penetration which lasted longer. My complaints against his penetration on the beach disappeared for the moment. He and I slept necked; anxiety free next to each other. Our next encounter was in a shopping mall parking in his car, he was in the driver's seat, and I was in passengers' seat of his car, that area of the parking lot didn't have much visibility and not many people were passing by. We started kissing, while we were kissing, he unzipped his jeans and pulled out his penis from his white semitransparent underwear. When we stopped kissing. He told me "Suck it", I started sucking it, he held the car staring, his penis might have been around 5 or 6 inches long when hard. I started with sucking the top of it as if I am sucking a sugar candy, he moaned in pleasure " Oh sweetheart you know how to do it, suck me deeper."

I took it deeper and deeper; this play went on for several minutes, he several times moved little bit up to push his penis further down in my throat or perhaps to feel more involved, then he ejaculated the same way he always did, I swallowed his cum, all of them, later he gave me a long and deep kiss, a kiss of guilt, I asked him what is it? He told me he has two sons, one of them is in early 20s and

another in late 20s, he has four grand children's three boys and a girl, and he is married, his wife is on a two-month tour to Italy with people from their Church.

I asked him " Does she know you are bisexual? "

He replied " No she doesn't. Even if I tell her she won't understand."

I asked " How do you know?

He said, " Oh believe me, I have lived long enough with her to know."

I said, " Will you never discuss, accept or talk about it?"

He said, " Unfortunately institutes, societies, corporates, cultures and many other fucking things we humans have created stops us from carrying honest conversations, often they stop us from accepting and letting others know who we are, what we are?"

I asked, " Suppose if you tell her, will she leave you? will she divorce you?"

He said, " No she won't because she believes divorce is a sin, second, she worships the institution of marriage, at least superficially, because when we go for vacation, she is not as happy as when she goes to Italy with her all-girl singer choir, sometimes I suspect those bitches may be leaking each other vagina with tongue, and artificial penises."

He continued "Sometimes I suspect she is lesbian, but she won't accept it because it would offend her parents and fucking bullshit church crowd whom we meet every Sunday and don't see till next Sunday. We are not happy in our marriage, but she won't accept or talk. She won't even allow me to bring it up, because the bitch believes it will disrespect our marriage, if being honest is disrespect then what the fuck is respect."

Anger rushed through his blood. He squeezed the car steering wheel. I touched his arm and said," Calm down."

He grabbed me and started kissing. The kiss was intense and lasted very long but at the end his anger was gone.

He complained about her again , the anger resurfaced in a while on his face, he said " In her early 40s she started traveling a lot for church activities living both kids to me, when I asked her to lower down her travel she gave me one line answer "our existence on the earth is a sin , I want to serve god as much as possible so I can go back to heaven." fucking bitch, her service to church is merely an escape, escape from a straight marriage life. Fucking whore, in frustration one day when I was alone at home, I grabbed our dog Latvia and penetrated her in vagina bare and ejaculated inside her, my wife was in Florence at that time singing at a church. I felt a terrible guilt but occasionally I started fucking her every time my wife was out and sometimes, I fucked Latvia when my wife and children were playing in the backyard. I got myself tested for STDs after

my first fornication of any new animal. I fornicated my cat later, again bare. Till now I have fucked seven animals four Cats, one male dog and two female dogs, day before yesterday I fornicated our new dog, her name is filth. It's all because of that bitch I have in my life, the hopeless woman who would neither accept nor talk about the real issues. She will only ignore them or reject them or pretend they don't exist and let the issues grow. It's pretty much impossible to talk to her on any issue, she ignores even genuine issues as byproduct of the sin of disobeying God, she often blames it on Eve who disobeyed God and ate the apple. How can one carry conversations with such an escapist? Do you think I am a bad person?"

A cold chill, fear and strange guilt rushed into my blood when I listened to all of that. I was afraid what if I got some infectious diseases, some STDs, here I was being fornicated and penetrated bare by a man who fucked man, woman, cats, and dogs. By his appearance and behavior, one couldn't even judge that he might be doing something like that.

I replied to his question "No, you are not a bad person."

He continued " I have ejaculated inside you several times bare but don't worry I am all clean. I get myself tested regularly for STDs."

I wasn't convinced. To leave safety I kissed him, said " I am very sorry to hear what you are going through in your marriage. I am always here for you." and stepped out of his car, jumped back into my car, and drove back to my apartment. That night I was thinking about him and his marriage life. There had been movements when I sympathized with him and there have been movements when I felt nothing for him. There have been movements when I hated him. Later I didn't know what to feel or what not to feel for him, for her or for rest of his family.

I jerked off thinking about several males who penetrated me, on my ejaculation I fell asleep.

Next day I went for STD test, until I didn't get the results my mind was very restless, agitated, and afraid, afraid of sickness, afraid of death which is supposed to happen to me and to all other living entities anyways, one day or another. I often worry about the things which are meant to happen one day or another and I often worry about the things which never happened, and I considered myself intelligent. I got the results in two days, I was negative. The same day I invited him to my apartment, as soon as he walked in, I started kissing him, he started kissing me back, he pulled my t shirt up and my lower down with my underwear, in few minutes I was necked and was lying on the living room wall with my back towards him. He was still in his black t shirt and blue jeans, he continued to kiss me, from lips to neck, from neck to all the way down on my back, he kissed both of my hips , spread my legs and pushed his head in between them and started sucking my balls ,it aroused me to a point of ejaculation but I didn't, I held my semen back , then he started kissing, leaking and sucking my anal area , this lasted

for a while. In those movements, I felt loved and desired. He stopped, got necked, rubbed his penis around any anal hole and hit it twice on the hole. Aroused, filled with racing hormones and lust, I requested him " Please push it inside me, I can't wait anymore."

He pushed it inside me , it was unlubricated , the penetration felt raw and intense to me, I moaned " Oh honey, oh baby, you are the best , fuck me , fuck me please.", initially he moved it slow, then pulled his penis pretty much all the way out and pushed it inside, I grabbed his head with both of my hands, and started moving both of my hands on his bald head, he grabbed my hands, moved them down to grab both of his hips, he whispered in my ears , squeeze them, I squeezed them. He moved my head towards him and started kissing me, he put his left hand on belly to control the moves and grabbed my penis with his right hand and started jerking me off, I was engaged and busy at many levels, his penis was thick and large, I didn't measure it with extreme preciseness but it was somewhere around 6 inches long, usually I didn't like bald men but when I saw him for first time in shopping mall I was immediately attracted towards him. I followed him for a while. I don't know if he noticed me or not, then he went to the restroom to urinate and I followed him there, he started urinating and right next to him I started pretending to urinate.

He was done urinating, I quickly zipped myself, when he was washing his hands, I was staring at him from the mirror, when he was about to leave, I asked him " Can I suck you? "I was scared, and my heart was beating very fast, I didn't know how he will respond. He said " Sure, why not ". He checked there was no one else in the restroom throwing out the shit from their anal hole or throwing up what they chewed and swallowed. There was none. We immediately rushed into the handicap restroom. He grabbed me and kissed me, I kissed him back, he made me sit on the toilet, pulled out his penis, I grabbed it and started sucking, in couple of minutes he told me " I can fuck you if you like, I got couple of condoms, I always carry them, not to miss on the opportunities." I pulled his penis out of my mouth, stood up, pulled down my pants and underwear, turned around, my butt was facing his penis, he quickly rolled up the condom and pushed his penis inside me. Someone walked in, we leaned down, that person urinated, washed his hands, and left. We continued our thing. After ejaculation he walked out, he asked me my name and I asked him his name. His name was Jeff. We exchanged each other's numbers and started seeing each other.

In my living room where he was penetrating me, kissing me, leaking me, and jerking me off, things grew intense in time, his penis grew hardest, he pushed it deepest and ejaculated inside me. I ejaculated on the wall; my semen flew all the way on the carpet.

We both were showered in sweat, you might already be aware and have experience, males are hard even after ejaculations, he continued his moves inside me and continued to masturbate me.

He continued both moves until his penis came out naturally and my penis was back to its three-inch size or perhaps a little bit shorter than that. He quickly turned me around and started sucking my nipples with great intensity, another wave of pleasure aroused inside me, I said " Oh honey, you are the best" while moving my hands on his bald head.

Later he lay me down on the carpet, he lay on top of me and started kissing my lips, I kissed him back, we kissed and kissed, until he and I both grew tired of kissing, the kiss was long enough that most of our fuck sweat dried. I and him both fell asleep necked on the necked floor. Next time he fucked me, it was in USPS parking lot, it was not a very busy post office, in several minutes one customer was walk in and out.

We were on back of his car seat, I suggested we should go to my apartment, he said " It's one of his fantasies to fuck me in USPS parking lot. "

He mentioned his original fantasy was to fuck me outside in the parking lot but now a days everywhere cameras are installed, so fucking in car, during daytime will fulfil his fantasy up to most extended, after saying that he unhooked himself and unzipped himself, pulled me on his lap, pulled down my Nike lower and Calvin Klein underwear from the back, pulled out his penis, made me sit on it first and then pushed it inside me. From last several times he started pushing unlubricated penis inside me, he even didn't bother to use his saliva which I always call natural lubricant.

Sometimes I wonder why I didn't ask him to apply some sort of lubricant, maybe I liked the unlubricated, bare, and raw touch of his penis. It was July, the weather was hot outside, on the passenger seat his rubbing penis was creating heat inside my anal hole. The outside heat made its way inside the car, the car pretty much turned into a hot tube, I usual sweat a lot of whiles being fucked, I think I already told you, with July heat I sweated even more, while he was making me jump up and down on his penis I moaned " It's very hot". He said " Yes, it is ", he stopped, he moved my head towards him and started kissing me, he pushed his tongue deep inside my mouth, then he moved his hands into my T shirt and squeezed my nipples, pulled down my lower and underwear little bit more and jerked me off little bit, then he stopped and grabbed me from my waist and again started moving me on his penis.

I stopped kissing him, the way he was pushing his penis inside me and pulling me on it, I started moaning " Ah honey, it's too much, please slowdown. "He didn't slow down, he continued with the same intensity, I was showered in sweat and so was he , my t shirt and lower started getting wet, at the same time when I was

struggling with intense moves of his penis inside out of me , the heat , the sweat, and to find balance, I saw a postman coming out from post office, my fucker already pulled down my lower and underwear to expose my penis and balls when he jerked me off for some time. The postman started walking towards the car, I told my penetrator the postman is walking towards the car, he didn't response and continued his moves, in anger I said "You never listen" , he pushed his penis inside me with higher intensity, I tried to pull up my underwear and lower from front, my fucker didn't allow them to come up to cover my penis and balls, he whispered in my ears" It's getting more exciting and pleasurable, it looks like he is coming closer." and he pushed it penis inside me with higher and higher intensity .

 I moaned " Oh god, oh god, fuck, he will see us.'

I quickly grabbed an empty box of facial tissue and put it on my penis and balls to cover them. The postmaster was deep in thoughts, then his face and body language gave the impression that he forgot something, he turned back and started walking back towards the post office. I end up ejaculating inside that box, when I was ejaculating anxiety, agitation, anger, discomfort and fear all emotions were inside me and perhaps many more. My fucker ejaculated inside me in couple of minutes, by the time he pulled out his penis, all my clothes were wet in sweat. I didn't tell him anything, I was angry at him and very agitated, I felt violated in a very strange way. His face was lit up in joy. He said, "That was fucking awesome ". The whole act reminded me of my first penetration, I was highly agitated and angry after that but my first fucker, my first penetrator was filled with joy, in car his face lit up the same way.

Our next encounter was in my apartment bathroom, he penetrated me Infront of bathroom sink. I was able to see his expressions in the mirror, I noticed his intense attention was on his penetrating penis, where and how it was moving, he took a sear joy in fucking me, he grabbed my waist very tight. I saw my expression while being penetrated; I haven't seen them in a while. It was pretty much seeing oneself in a porn. I have noticed one strange thing about him, he was more intense in public places and soft when he fucked me in private spaces. He pulled his penis pretty much all the way out and pushed it inside, especially in our private space intercourses he did it several times. I loved it when any males I have been with did it. With every intense move he made I moaned " Oh Honey, Oh Sweetheart, oh baby."

When the intensity grew beyond my limit, I moaned "Kiss me, please kiss me. "

I started jerking off. He kissed me. I ejaculated, his ejaculation was yet to happen, whenever I ejaculated first, it was hard to withstand his intensity without total surrender, I surrendered to him. We had our last two encounters before we stopped seeing each other. The second last was in a movie theater. We planned to

go and watch a movie, it turned out in that show the only two people were me and him, initially when movie started, he held my hand in his hand, later when he realized it will be only two of us, he pushed my hands inside his underwear, I started moving my hands on his penis, it was not hard at that time. He asked me to suck it, I was a little bit hesitant, he kissed me and gently convinced me " It's just two of us, enough time has passed in the movie, I don't think anyone else will come."

I pulled his penis out of his underwear and started sucking it ,the soft and little penis started growing large, hard and thick, he stopped me and started kissing me , first on lips , then on neck, he unzipped my jeans , pulled down my underwear ,pulled out my penis and started sucking me , while moaning in pleasure I said " Honey ,I thought we are here to watch movie." , he sucked me for a while and said " That was the original plan but you know things change all the time. "He started sucking my nipples, I was aroused, then he made me seat in a doggy pose on two chairs, he lifted the arms of three chairs, he pulled down my jean and underwear, started kissing my hips, then started moving his tongue on my anal area. I always kept my anal area clean, waxed and washed. For some reason the statement agitated Andrea, annoyed she spoke " Of course you did. "But then her conscience interfered and some level of morality-imposed sophistication and guilt, she said " I am sorry. I don't mean to be rude."

Vivan "Why are you sorry? Did you notice what just happened to you. Your joy, your agitations, your sorrows, and your griefs have nothing to do with others, most of the people are like that. If good things happen to them, they are happy, bad things happen to them, they are sad. Their happiness or sorrow have nothing to do with other people. I am absolutely fine with that but here the tragedy begins, or I should say the disgust and the filth starts , most of the people on earth who are currently may be walking, driving, sleeping , urinating , masturbating , ejaculation or doing other day to day activities like to believe and pretend they are so selfless, that they are happy in others happiness and sad in other's sorrow, if they do the honest observation of their consciousness they will find it have always been me, me , me , I , I ,I , my , my ,my and that's it , degraded filthy hypocrites."

Andrea " I think you are right, similar thoughts crossed my mind several times over years. Most of the people are happy in their joy and sad in their sorrow and we would like to think we are connected, we are related, most of the people I know live in their eggshells, living there, they never hatch, we live in a human society where most of the humans are unhatched. Most of us are too busy with our small eggs, there is no greater disgust than that. My fingers are already moving into my panty, I want to masturbate, please tell me what happened next between you two, did he push his tongue inside your anal hole.?"

Vivan " As I was saying, I always kept my anal area clean, the day I went on shooting and killing people, that morning also I waxed my anal area, I shaved my genitals and arm pits, along with shaving my chest.

In movie theater he started with moving his tongue around my anal area, the pleasure grew intense, my hard penis and lusty mind both desired a space to penetrate, I desired an anal hole or a vagina to be put Infront of my penis, I would have penetrated any anal hole or any vagina at that point of time not just human , from doggy pose I lifted up right hand , delivering my weight on the two legs and left arm , and was about to start jerking me off , he started sucking my anal area like someone sucks melting ice cream bar, it pushed me on whole another level of ecstasy, I moaned " Oh baby , oh honey , it feels so good , please keep on doing it, please suck me more. ", while moaning I was back on both hands. He stopped that action after some time, pulled my underwear and jeans all the way out, pulled out his T shirt, jeans, and underwear, he got fully necked, my pants slipped through my shoes, but he had to take off his shoes first to get necked, the only pieces of clothes he had on were his shocks.

The movie was playing. He started kissing me on the back, the movie theater was mostly dark, here and there few movie scenes filled the theater with light like a temporary hope in eternal bewilderment, rather than providing the entertainment, the movie turned out to be a distraction, from whatever I was able to see in the movie it seems the director, storyteller and the whole cast was trying very hard to be edgy about things and were failing extraordinarily. The movie was turning out to be a fiasco, an utter failure, like modern life. His moves were giving me heavenly joy.

 He pulled my T shirt, I helped him to get it off, apart from socks and shoes I didn't have any other piece of cloth on me. We were in doggy pose , he pushed his penis inside me , he fucked me like a dog fucks a bitch , then lay me down on chairs, I was covering up little bit more than three chairs, while changing the positions he maintained his penis and his moves inside me, him laying up on me and I laying under him in that semi dark movie theater , in the third last row from top, on velvet chairs, he ejaculated inside me in couple of minutes , I ejaculated on one of the chair, the chair my penis was touching, we both fell asleep for a while, we woke up when some screamed in movie , it was a sudden wake for him and me , he said " What the fuck."

I said " Honey, it's in the movie. "With my phone light I started finding my clothes. I helped him find his clothes as well. We dressed up, the movie was 1 hour and 31 minutes, we have 31 more minutes to go. We sat there holding each other's hands, I told him " You are such a great fucker, you know. "

He whispered in my ears and said, " Only for you " and gently bit on my earlobe. Yash one of my penetrators in high school days used to suck and gently bite my

earlobe, in those days that suck used to arouse me to an extended that I would agree to get penetrated by anyone, once he took advantage of the situation, his elder brother who was a third-year college student was visiting him. It was nighttime, Yash and I were in his room, he turned off the lights, outdoor lights made their way inside the room, the room got semi dark. He aroused me, sucked, and bite my earlobe, I asked him to fuck me, he continued to suck my earlobe, I begged him "Fuck me please". His elder brother got out from underneath the Yash' bed, I think Yash and him both planned it, His name was Balvan. Yash whispered in my ear " *Bhaiiya ko bhi leni he teri* (My elder brother wants to fuck you as well), he knows everything about us." While Yash was saying all these, Balvan started kissing my back, Yash started kissing on my neck. Our act was going on standing, I was standing between them, Yash was in front of me and Balvan was in the back. Balvan went all the way down, squeezed both of my hips and kissed both, he moved up, whispered in my ears ``Nice to meet you beautiful, I am Balvan."

I said, "Please penetrate me" As soon as I said it, he pushed his bare penis inside me, when Balvan's penis was inside me, Yash pushed his tongue inside my mouth. Balvan's moves were intense and rough. Later Yash got busy sucking my nipples and kissing on my belly. I somehow controlled my moans. When Balvan pushed his penis inside me, he was fully necked, I think he went hiding under the bed necked, Yash and he planned the whole thing. That night Yash fucked me once and Balvan fucked me twice. We joined two beds, I slept in middle of them, in morning I saw my second fucker Balvan's face, apart from their structure of teeth both brothers don't seem to have much in common. Yash was more inclined towards his mothers' side and Balvan was towards his father, Balvan had a better physique and Yash was more attractive overall. Balvan left next day.

Here and there I complained to Yash that he tricked me into getting fucked by his elder brother. In a couple of weeks Yash visited his family, he invited me, I accepted. We stayed at his parent's house for three days, he and Balvan took me to show their parents' farm, half farm had soya plants and the other half-had corn. Balvan suggested we should take a walk-in corn field, Yash agreed. All three of us started walking inside, when we were almost in middle of corn field , Balram told me sometimes he fantasized about having sex with me in this corn field .

 Yash told me , sometimes he fantasized about having sex with me in the small hut next to the water well , very soon Balvan was sucking and kissing left side of my earlobe and Yash was sucking and kissing my right side of earlobe, both brothers fucked me that day in doggy style in middle of corn field .Next day was time to fulfil Yash's fantasy, Yash pushed his penis inside my anal hole and Balvan pushed it inside my mouth in the small hut next to the well, one brother made my mouth wet another made my anal hole wet on their ejaculations.

Anyways in the movie theater I smiled even if I knew what Jeff said was most probably not true at all. When the movie finished, I knew towards the end why at the beginning of the second week, the movie was running in a pretty much empty theater, the whole movie tried its best to show edge and creative rebel at several levels of life and failed miserably. I think they just mimicked the idea of edge and creativity, the movie makers never understood that edge and creativity both are exceptional original things, the moment they are mimicked, they are neither edgy nor creative, they are a mere mimic. When the movie ended, we tasted some more saliva from each other. I thought things are going well between us, here and there he was edgy, pushing, ignorant and overpowering like in hammocks case and in USPS parking lot but whenever he fucked me, I felt satisfied, at least for a day or two. We humans are morons in that sense, we all search for satisfaction, I think the very desire of satisfaction is the root cause of our several dissatisfactions and agitations. And anyways our satisfactions don't last long. For example, we eat lunch and again are hungry at dinner, we eat dinner, satisfy our hunger and in the morning hungry again for breakfast. He fucked me, I was satisfied for a night, a day or perhaps two, and started longing him or perhaps a good penetration and penetrator again. I wish I would have understood this long time back, my life would have been something else, at least I would have been out of this prison, I would have been in other prisons, in the prison of society, in the prison of corporate, in the prison of institute, I would have been out of this prison into some other prison which very few people call or see as prison. I don't know which one is worse though, this prison or several prisons outside of this one. May be very cage of body is miserable. Anyways, I desired him again or perhaps he desired me again in two days. We went to a park next to a river; it wasn't far from the city and the space seemed mostly quiet. We decided to meet each other there, I drove in my car, and he drove in his car. The main area of park with kids play area etc. was about one mile away from the river access area, we watched the river standing next to each other, the river was neither clear nor muddy, it gave me impression that the river is only couple of feet, may be two feet or three feet at most.

He told me lets go for a walk, I followed him, there was a trail next to the river, he held my hand in his and we walked for a while, while walking he kissed my hand, I turned around and started kissing on his lips, he was around half feet taller than me, so whenever we kissed, he had to lean down, and I had to lean up. He leaned down, I leaned up, we had a long kiss, while kissing he grabbed both of my hips and squeezed them. When we stopped , he grabbed my hands and told me " Let's go "I walked with him , we walked off the trail into an area ,there was a big tree surrounded my small one to provide some extend of privacy, he took off a thin plastic from his jeans pocket and spread it on the grass, it was long and wide enough for both of us, he took off his shoes and shocks first, then took off mine, all other times I was the first one whom he got necked but this time he took off all

his clothes, lay me down with clothes, started kissing me, and gradually as he kissed, he took off my clothes , first T shirt , then my short , then my underwear.

He pulled my underwear down while kissing on my thighs, I bit my lip when he did it. The same anxieties started popping up in my mind, what if someone walks this way and sees us. I mentioned to him " What if someone comes here and sees us like this."

He said, " Before I met you, I used to spend hours here, necked, jerking off, twice I fucked Luthia my little dog, well specifically bitch, she is a female dog, it's pretty isolated and lonely place, don't worry and if someone come here, we will just ask him or her to join us." and he winked at me. He continued, " Don't worry, sometimes I think you think too much and worry too much."

 He stood up and told me " Come on baby, suck me now, bend on your knees. "

I did it, I took his thick and long cock inside my mouth, deeper and deeper. He asked me to stop after a while, stood me up and started kissing every part of my body, he kissed the section between my balls and anal hole for a while, he kind of sucked it. I grabbed my penis and started jerking it off, but decided not to jerk off enough to ejaculate, it would have taken away my interest from whatever was going on. It was evening time, listening to the sound of leaves, seeing the green leaves and sun rays dancing on them, a gaze into blue sky gave me some extra comfort that I never felt while being enjoyed and while enjoying, when he started sucking my penis a butterfly flew, it was blue and black, things were all fine till then. He stopped, grabbed my hand and took me closed to tree, he turned me around, so my ass faces his penis, he moved me closer to tree, and ask me to grab it, I grabbed it.

He started moving his penis around my anal area, and told me "Grab the tree as if you are hugging it" I did as he told me, I don't know why but I kissed the tree and for a moment the tree felt to me as if another partner in that encounter, I kissed it as if it's another male, I was thinking if this tree or any other tree would have had penis , would I have let them penetrate me and ejaculate inside me? . My heart answered yes. He pushed his penis inside me, it felt to me as if this time he used his saliva on it, I moaned. He grabbed my waist and started moving inside out of me, faster and faster. Then the evening mosquitos arrived, they started biting me. I politely told him, " Honey , these mosquitoes are biting me ."He moved my head towards him and started kissing me , it soothe me for a while but the mosquito bites started creating burning sensation , he stopped kissing me in a while and said " No pain , no gain " , pulled his penis all the way out and pushed it inside me harshly, he did it twice , around the same time a large mosquito bite me ,it caused the pain as if someone pushed a large needle inside me .

I said, " Stop please, I don't want to do it, we can finish it at my apartment " and tried to push him back, he intensified his grip, he pushed his body on me hard, I

was pretty much pressed on the tree, he put one of his hands on neck to press my mouth on tree and continued his intense moves. I struggled but with his body pushed on me and with his hand on my neck, he pretty much overpowered me, I got furious and busted into tears, he didn't care, his right hand was pressed on my neck and with his left hand he was still controlling moves of my waist, in tears I spoke " Please stop", three more large mosquitoes bite me. He didn't stop, I moved my hands, grabbed his hips, and pushed my nails in his skin, the act aroused him further, several of his next moves got intense, he pulled his penis almost out of my anal hole and pushed it back, he did it several times, while doing this he said in my ears " Tell me if you didn't desire this, tell me, tell me. "

In tears I told him " I did not. "

He further said, " Tell me if you don't like it, tell me. "

I said, " I don't. Please stop." Several mosquitos continued to bite me. He moaned " Oh it feels so great, push your nails a little more " Strangely enough I did it. I pushed my nails further in his hips, he then said "Let me kiss you, you will feel better. "I was helpless, bewildered and was in pain, I needed some comfort in that horrible situation, I turned my head around, put my lips on his lips, in next steps he pretty much sucked and ate my lips.

I gave up to my exploiter, my abuser, my fucker and started searching comfort in the very abuser for the movement. Isn't so call God is same? The abuser and comforter.

He ejaculated after some time, he continued to move inside out of me until his penis was totally soft and fell out of my anal hole, he turned me around, pushed me on the tree, and started kissing me, this time the kiss was very gentle and comforting, I kissed him back, opened my mouth and let his tongue go inside me, tears were flowing out of my eyes. He continued the kiss for a while, it felt like a high school kiss, in that movement I was searching for a comfort in the exploiter, in the abuser. My observation says that, in general all of us do that a lot, for example we expect respect from someone who insulated or disrespected us or would like to be treated equal by those who look down on us, how about those who are already treating us equal, do we recognize it or appreciate it? He stopped kissing, on separation I started walking towards my clothes, he slapped my left hip hard enough to leave his finger marks on it.

I didn't say anything, I started dressing up quickly, first I pulled up underwear, then short, quickly pulled the T-shirt, and started putting on the shoes. He was still fully necked and told me " Baby what's the rush? Please stay for some time. " And started walking towards me. In anger, I said " don't ", he said " What happened?" He started walking towards me.

I said " Don't, don't come any closer to me, if you ever try to contact me or show up in property, I will call the police, you fucking sick bastard " and I ran as fast as I can to my car, drove very fast, I think I almost broke a signal and got honked twice while driving. On arrival to my apartment, I was shacking in fear, stress, and anxiety, one of the thoughts that crossed my mind was " what happened ? why things went to so bad ?.''because it all started so well, so beautiful, he penetrated me at my will, and he have penetrated me several times in past, what shocked me the most was something that started so well, so beautifully ended up being so bad and nasty.

That night hiding under my blanket a lot of memories popped up in mind, they were all build around the things which started beautifully and ended up being ugly and nasty. Around mid-night I went to urinate. I sat on the toilet seat, urine came out from my penis and his semen pours out from my anal hole, I applied cream on mosquito bites, bruises and on the marks his spank left on my hip.

I came back to my bad from bathroom and fell asleep. I dreamed of the days of my early 20s. I walked into space and time when I saw my first love, his smell filled my nostrils, his smell was very sweet, whenever he was around me I felt as if I am at home , I don't need to be anywhere else, as if I attained my destiny , sometimes fear to lose our desired destiny can be reason not to claim it , I think that's what happened to me, that was one of the reason I never told him ,I like him or I love him and look what happened , I lost him , losing him I lost myself .I allowed the tragedy of being incomplete in my life, if one can find once significant half there is no guarantee he or she will feel complete but if one doesn't find him or her there is surety one will constantly feel incomplete, what an extraordinary creatures we humans are .

Next morning when I showered, the soap created some irritation on bruises, and on bug bites. I was scared that he would show up at my apartment door. I requested transfer to another apartment in the same property, luckily in two weeks another apartment was available. I moved to another apartment in the next building. I didn't block his numbers. He never called me. I never noticed any trace of him in the property I was living in. Sometimes I wondered if he had been abused in childhood and his abuser while forcing a penetration on him would have told him "Tell me if you haven't desired it, tell me if you haven't longed for it, tell me if you haven't wished for it. " And he might have picked the same lines from his abuser and started using it while abusing. If abuse and exploitation are chain reactions it will never end in human society.

I moved to another apartment in same property, just to be safe. The new apartment was exact mimic of the old one, I didn't feel much difference apart from that I need to do several address changes in banks, at secretary of state, at USPS etc. My bruises, bug bites and other hurts on skin healed in couple of weeks, those few weeks I limited myself from home to work and from work to

home schedule, once a week I went for grocery shopping, mostly on my way back from work. I wish I didn't have to do that either. The hurts in my psychological spaces continued from what he did to me, from what happened with me in my childhood, from what was done to me in school and what happened in New York. I had several other hurts, rejections, discriminations, and displacements in so called my pathetic professional life that is one of the reasons I ended up rushing to workplace with gun rather than running to a supermarket or a shopping mall.

Sometimes I feel no regret about killing those rascals because when they were alive, they were doing crimes on behalf of that lunatic immoral corporate and the fools were celebrating it, cherishing it, if they would have continued to live, they would have done the same or worst, its good the rascals are dead. They were going to die anyways as all of us will, I am not sure if I should or even you should be punished for killing those who were going to die anyways, if killing someone who will die anyways is a crime worth of death sentence, does it make us anti existentialist. Perhaps yes, perhaps not, well don't worry, you don't need to answer it, because I know we are born and raised in an era where even questions can create anxieties and worries, so please don't feel any moral obligations to answer this question. Apart from that in general people of this era are unnecessary secretive, for example there was this person whom I shot first, he once brought some blueberries, around one pound at work. He was eating them making sounds like a pig eats stool, he told me and one of my coworkers that he went to a blueberry farm with his girlfriend last evening to pick some blueberries. We asked him name of the farm, he didn't tell us, he told "There are several around the area.", filthy, disgusting, asshole, he was being secretive about the name of a blueberry farm, most of the time the asshole was like that, secretive about things which he should not be. He was the first person I shot; I shot him in his head because his head was filled with filth. I have to say filled with stool, his head was filled with human, pig and dog stool combined. My co-worker with whom he shared the blueberry talk had her own dysfunctionalities, she was in constant anxiety about job security. I think this is one of the dysfunctionalities that most Americans go through, and here we are in a world where most of the countries I know either idealize you guys, let me say more specifically mimic you and there is another set of countries who are too busy hating you guys.

I love those countries who have their own centers, who have their own modernity, originality, who have their own struggles and those who have their own wars, anyways, don't take me too seriously." Andrea didn't respond, she did violence of silence or perhaps played virtue of ignorance or perhaps she fell asleep.

Vivan continued "After my bruises were healed, one of the days I went to get my pickup order from the Cheesecake factory, I saw him, my abuser, with his wife, his children, their wife's, and grandchildren. I don't think he noticed me, all the sudden he got romantic and asked his wife to do a small dance.

I think cheesecake factory played a song which he, I guessed from his lip reading called their song, his and his wife's song, look at human tragedies we want to claim everything, trees, plants, stars, sky, universe, music, songs, land, mind, heart, and books. I don't find any greater filth than that, filth of claim, claim and claim. They did a small dance, right there next to their table. When my abuser and her escapist wife were dancing some women put both of their hands on their heart and showed adoration towards the couple, some of cheesecake factory eaters might have thought what a lovely couple they are ,in their late 40 s or early 50s ,they can maintain such an affection and spark in their relationship , when they were done with their dance people clapped, the whole act created an impression, an advertisement that they are lovely couple or perhaps some of them might have thought they are perfect. We all are running behind perfection, aren't we?

We need perfect life, perfect partner, perfect job, perfect country, perfect society, and perfect death, don't we, so some of them thought them as perfect couple and, here they were, a woman who often skipped to church and sometimes to Italy to not face their marriage issues or to execute her true sexual identity, which is perhaps being lesbian or being bisexual, but she will never talk about it rather she will skip. Here was a man who fucked cats, dogs, guys like me and who will perform several sexual violence to satisfy his psychological and physical sexual needs, and here were people who thought these two entities look perfect together. We love advertisements, phony pretends, and rituals don't me? It gives us a hope, which we use most of the time to skip the reality, now what is reality, what is duality and what is hallucination is a whole another thing. We love ideas as well, that is why we have so many of them, billions of humans have trillions of ideas, what a mess. Anyways in the Cheesecake factory my to go order was ready, around the same time my eye contact happened with him. He winked at me, my heart started beating fast, I left in a hurry. I felt very nervous and agitated that day.

Next day I decide to go out for dinner and to find someone else for sexual pleasures, till then I have just been jerking off on different guys I desired to be penetrated by and never got the opportunity or faced rejections on approaching them, my second choice was Hollywood's hot and sexy actors and models, I looked at their half-necked pics and masturbated. I drank most of the semen I ejaculated, sometimes I collected them in a glass, another time in a coffee cup, sometimes I drank them raw, other times I mixed them in orange juice, apple juice or honey. Couple of times I ejaculated on peeled banana, poured some ice cream, and ate semen banana ice cream Sundance.

In high school one of my classmate told me "To make one drop of semen body uses 40 drops of blood" I believed him, to express my gratitude for the info he provided , I sucked him and drank his semen in middle of the lunch break .When I sucked him I and him were in 11th grade, in 12th grade he realized his desire to penetrate me, when we first started, he penetrated me pretty much every day .

He was my roommate which made things little bit easier for us, although each room was shared by 4 student but as desires always find their ways, we found our own ways to kiss ,to touch, to suck, to fuck and to ejaculate, around mid-night he used to slip into my bed and other times I used to slip into his bed, we always started with a kiss, we got necked only if two of us are in the room otherwise mostly he will pulled down my lower or short to expose my anal area and pull down his lower or short to pull out his penis, often I found his penis lubricated with coconut oil. You know sometimes I see people who truly found their significant half, who are with their significant other half, who live, sleep, wake up and eat with them, sometimes I wonder what they might be feeling smelling each other, touching each other, making love, their life to me seems perfect. I never had someone like that, and perhaps in the middle of the bewilderment of the world and its realities I lost my ways to it forever. Now I even don't know what I truly want, what I truly desire, I have been in that mode from years, I think that's why I pulled down my pant for anyone who came to me with their hard penis, searching for a space to penetrate with their banana and let them ejaculate inside me, saying this Vivan's eyes were filled with tears. In his heavy voice, he asked Andrea " Did you feel your life is perfect when you found your significant other, your husband?"

Andrea" There have been few movements when I felt very safe, at home in his arms laying next to him necked and him laying necked next to me but wounded souls like us never find full satisfaction in and with anyone , with anything, after a while our wounds come back , the same one , the old one and they start leaking and creating mess, otherwise why I will take gun ,and kill people, I have two beautiful children and a loving husband . People who were abused, exploited, raped as I was by my uncle inside my home, finds no home. Apart from that I think you have a lot of romantic ideas about the significant other half, that's what happens for things we long too much and never find, we create unrealistic romantic ideas about them, for them and around them. I think and I have realized humans are incomplete creatures, and two incomplete people or hundreds or millions or billions of incomplete people together can't be perfect, there is no perfection, they can't complete each other, only complete can be perfect, not incompletes."

Andrea Continued " It's not that we only create romantic ideas around significant other half, but we create romantic ideas around everything we desire and don't get or anything which we don't have and whose absence causes pain to us, for example I used to think until few days later if my father and mother wouldn't have separated, I would have been saved from my uncle but was there any guarantee about that? Both of my parents were working. I would have been accessible to mu asshole uncle at some point or another, if that rascal city mayor wouldn't have pushed his penis inside my mouth, is there a guarantee no other man would have pushed it inside me in the same way. I don't know what we should do to make

human society safe for children, for those who can't protect themselves, for those who are innocent and vulnerable."

After saying this she pushed her hand in her underwear and started masturbating herself, she started moaning. Vivan pushed his hands in his underwear and started masturbating himself. She masturbated on Mathew and Vivan masturbated on his several unfulfilled desires, sorrows and on two sparrows he saw in sex when he was around age of 8. He ejaculated on many "what ifs".

He ejaculated, she came, the sticky liquids came out of their genitals remained in their underwear like an unimportant memory of the past, they both fell asleep on the cell floor. Before Vivan fell asleep, he tasted some of his semen, it gave him a feeling of familiarity and comfort. While they were sleeping food was pushed into their cells, the prison food had a lot of smell but very little taste, like promises of a mischievous man. The disgusting smell woke up both. She and him both urinate in the toilet seats of their cells. The flow of each other's urine was audible to both, they swallowed whatever was pushed on them. For some reason from last few days Vivan was eating a lot more than usual, he finished till the last grain of whatever was pushed in the plate. He noticed it and though "He is eating more because he is not being fucked. Am I using food to repress my sexual desires?"

Andrea complained " Oh this disgusting food, look at it, we can't even complain about it because there is a popular belief in society that jails should not have improvements and enhancements which can make them more comfortable. So, the society and government have right to kill us by feeding us bad food and push us into uncomfortable, unhygienic spaces as such and kill us because we are criminals and you know what make me more upset than this, outside , outside of this stupid space food is as shitty as here or may be more shitty most of the time, only thing is that it doesn't look or advertised as shit, all fast food advertisements, they promote the idea that if one get them one will be happy, why the fuck we need so much idea of happiness, I used to see advertisements where everyone is happy , one person walking in the shopping mall is happy , a person shopping is happy , a person walking out of a shopping mall is happy, a person making sandwich is happy, a person who is delivering mails is happy , a person who is packing grocery is happy , a person shopping groceries for another person is happy , if everyone is so happy at their job and in doing their everyday activities then who is buying lottery tickets worth billions of dollars, and why billions of dollars' worth of anti-depressions, anti-anxiety pills get sold every year ,because we are so happy . "

She threw the half-eaten plate on the wall, it hit the wall, food and plate fell on the floor. Her mind and her body were full of agitation.

Vivan " Societies, civilizations, countries, and people who are truly happy don't advertise their happiness. Apart from that, advertisements are mostly what should be, and you know what it should be is, what is not. Your behaviors are still ,as if you are part of the society outside of these walls, I don't think we are part of that society anymore, I feel no obligations and no care for it, look what it did to me ,

look what it did to you and there may be several like us but with that thought, sometimes I wonder are individuals responsible for society or is society is responsible for individuals, if individuals are responsible for society then why we need society ,we should live individually but in that case will there be any individuality or space for it or recognition of it , perhaps not but if the society is responsible then why individuals should be punished ,why and why and why? , Shouldn't society be punished for individuals mistakes? Sometimes I feel these questions and thoughts are killing me. Anyways, walking on the memory lanes of my penetrations is what keeps me alive in this horrible space. Sometimes I wonder when I will be moved to regular male jail, how many males and how many types of males will fuck me and push their penises inside my mouth, inside my anal hole, inside my being and inside my existence. Sometimes that space gives me horrors and other times it gives me ejaculations, sometimes I think of committing suicide, thinking about what is on the way and other times I feel that space will be my liberation but other times I think is liberation possible without death? and if not then is death liberation? Perhaps not."

He started laughing, Andrea joined him. Vivan asked " Why are you laughing?"

She said, " Because you are laughing?"

Vivan " Oh my god, that's what we do as humans, as society, as culture, we mimic each other, we copy each other, and we bully each other. "

Andrea " Did you drink the urine of the guys with whom you stay at the beach house?"

Vivan " Yes, I did. We humans are extraordinary creatures, we love to know who is urinating or on whom he or she urinated .We are very curious in who drank whose urine and who made whom drink whose urine, as humans we love to throw shit on each other as I am doing right now , please don't take my statement personally, I mean to apply it to the whole human race collectively from past to present to future, after dinner we went to the beach house, I had a lot of cocktails, a lot of them, my original plan was to drink his urine that night but my stomach was filled with food and alcohol so I decide to postpone it till next morning , anyways we were not planning on living till noon next day. That night he undressed me and fucked me with me facing the window. I vaguely remember seeing the moon from the window, small clouds covering it and uncovering it when he ejaculated inside me. I jerked off on the beauty of the moon, clouds, sky and ejaculated. We fell asleep just after that, pass midnight I woke up due to thirst, I went to kitchen and had some water, then went to restroom, set on toilet seat, urine flew out from my penis and his semen flew out from my anal hole, I liked the stickiness of them as usual and the way semen lubricate my ass. Just thinking about it I am getting hard, and my nipples are getting tight. Next morning, we woke up, I showered first then he jumped into the shower, I was waiting for him to finish shower, he showered and walked out with white towel wrapped around his waist, necked I walked to him, first kissed him, then said " I

want to drink your Urine, how about first I suck you, you ejaculate, I drink your semen, then you urinate inside my mouth and I drink it."

He was pleased, his face lit up in joy, he said "Let's do it."

He dropped his towel, he was semi hard, I started sucking him, he grew hard, first he stood putting both of his hands on his hips, in that pose to me he felt the sexiest, he moaned .Initially I focused on his glans then took his penis deeper inside my mouth, when pleasure intensified, he moved his hands on my head , started moving his fingers in my hairs, on the picks of his pleasure he took over full control, I surrendered and decided to be his mean of pleasure , and be nothing more or nothing less. He ejaculated moaning " Oh, it feels so good, oh it feels fucking amazing. "Sometimes I wonder why nature have attached such an extra ordinary pleasure with sex, ejaculation , fornication, penetration and masturbation ,is it the selfish mean to continue self or it knew that we are pleasure loving rascals and if pleasure is not attached with such an activities and suppose pain is associated with it , we might not even reproduce and will be happy never reproducing , and will end our species, although I have to admit I continued and allowed couple of anal penetrations which were painful to me, in those I moaned "Oh honey , it's too much, your stick is too large for me , oh it's too big , oh it's too thick and so on." He ejaculated, I swallowed all his semen, I cleaned his penis with my tongue, in couple of seconds I said " I am ready whenever you are " and opened my mouth , he grabbed his semi hard , semi soft penis and started urinating inside my mouth , I drinking it , then I pushed my mouth on his glans, he continued to urinate and I continued to drink , his urine was filled with the tastes of everything he ate and drank last night , it was salty in taste.

In a couple of seconds, he asked me " Can I urinate on you?" I swallowed whatever urine was in my mouth and said, " Go ahead. "

He urinated on my chest first , I liked the Luke-warn touch of it ,I said " Urinate on my face ", I closed my eyes , a urine spring hit middle of my forehead, and flew down, with closed eyes, I asked him to urinate on my head and bow down my head towards his penis , he urinated on my head, by that time his urine was over , he pushed three more springs of urine on my neck, I call them urine quantum. He sat down on his knees, said " Thank you, thank you, you don't know what you have done for me. ", grabbed me and started kissing my lips, I kissed him back, the kiss lasted long. I don't know how long, when it ended, I was on the floor under him, he was laying on me. For a while I didn't say anything, I liked him on me, I liked feeling his weight on me. Later I said, " I think we should leave now. " He said " Let me thank you first" he moved down on me and started sucking me. After my ejaculation we took a power nap in the bedroom, when we woke up, he went to shower again, I decided not to shower. When he walked out of the bathroom I was dressed up and ready to leave. He asked " You don't want to shower? "

I said " No, I want to keep your smell on me as long as possible." He said, " I wish I would have met you years back? "I asked " Why?", He said " I would have

married you instead off." He left the sentence incomplete. That statement told me that he is married and most probably to a woman. I didn't ask or react. I kissed him on his left cheek and started packing the bag. When he and I both were done packing we left in his car. We drove to the beach house in his car, after couple of encounters with him, I knew I could trust him, even after what I went through with that old fifty plus or late forty abusive maniac. I didn't talk much while he drove, the drive was about two hours. I seat relaxed in the passenger seat, gazing outside, I liked the road we were driving on, the same lake on whose shore we stayed followed us for a while then disappeared, the road side trees continue to give us company, few cars drove opposite to us and other few drove in same direction we were going, a thought crossed my mind " We leave ,then we arrive , we leave again , we arrive again, this loop or cycle of arrival and departure seems to never end and if it end, is there continuum ?or continuum have nothing to do with arrival and departure?. And if the continuum is not a cycle, then what is it? Is it the absolute?"

I fell asleep while thinking about it, I had a dream, I saw a place, quite amazing, extraordinarily beautiful, I saw trees, plants, and flowers only, no other creatures were there, that space was glittering.

We arrived at my apartment building I don't know how long I dreamed. He didn't wake me up, when I woke up, he was looking at me. As soon as I woke up, I said " You should have woken me up. "

He said "I didn't want to; you were in deep, and sound sleep. It was good to see you so relaxed. "Did he mean I am not relaxed, did he notice my restlessness, was I not sleeping in peace at the beach house? I didn't ask him, I took a water bottle and started drinking water. Suddenly, he said, " I am sorry. "

I asked, " For what?"

He said, " For not telling you that I am married, I am married to a woman. Her name is…"I put my right-hand fingers on his lips, he stopped.

I said, " It's okay, you don't need to apologize or tell me her name."

I kissed his lips, said thank you for such a nice vacation, took my bags from the trunk and walked inside my apartment building. I had a strong Masala ginger Indian chai, extra strong and sweet. For some reason I didn't feel like complaining that day, I jumped on the bed, pulled a blanket on me, pushed my right hand inside my underwear, moved my fingers on my balls, touched my penis and while doing it, I fell asleep.

It's a bit strange to me that I drank his semen, I drank his urine and still I didn't feel odd. I still believe semen might be the most nutritional liquid or food available. I miss drinking other people's semen, I smelled and drank mine a couple of times since I was pushed in here.

Andrea " Have you ever been with any woman?"

Vivan " I think I have told you a lot about myself, how about you tell me, have you been with any woman, how many men you loved and yes, I have been with women. I want to stop talking and start listening, would you like to share? Would you like to share where it started for you?"

Andrea " A part of me saying maybe I should share, it will take away some unnecessary burden I have been carrying for a while, another part of me is saying I should not, a third part of me is quiet, it does not care if I share or not. I don't know what to do and what not to do?"

Vivan " Humans are endless dualities, our ego and insecurities are so big that they want us to keep secrets even if we are standing right next to annihilation or death. Apart from that I don't know why we don't understand or perhaps don't realize or perhaps don't accept that death and life both possibilities exists on each and every point in the space and in the time we live, anyways ,I told you about one of my co-worker whom I shot right in head who went to pick up blueberries at a farm, he chewed those blueberries like a pig eat stool , he mentioned to us yesterday evening he went to pick blueberries , how much it cost per lb. etc. but when we asked him about name of the farm, he grew unnecessary secretive, it's not first time he behaved as such, he did it on couple of other occasions, he was the first one I shot , second was an Indian woman from northern part of India , the bitch was in constant anxiety for one reason or another, the whore constantly radiated her anxieties and insecurities on others, she constantly seek consolation, she self-pity all the time . She constantly complained about one person or another, she was second one I shot , third was one of the project manager, she was also an insecure whore , she often complained about people , kept unnecessary eye on who is doing what for unnecessary reasons, the company in general exhibited huge discrimination in employee vs consultants, I was a consultant, she took some interest in discriminating me , I shot her in back and on her head , she fell on the floor like stool falls in toilet seat from anal hole , fourth was a manager ,she was an Indian woman, I was planning to shoot her and her husband both, but the rascal was not at his desk, she and her husband both were type of Indian who could lead us back to colonization , in past people like her and her husband were the reason of India's colonization by British, the type of people who are too eager to commit crime on their own people on behalf of white man. There is no lake of such entities, there are plenty such entities crawling in India, let me correct myself, in whole Asia, Europe, Australia, Canada, Mexico, South America, Africa and several other continent's including United States. **The fifth person** I fired shot on was an African American front desk receptionist, she and her own race is highly discriminated in United States and in pretty much every country where unfair people with fair skin lives, but she was too eager to exhibit employee vs contractor discrimination on behalf of that stupid, pathetic, criminal corporate, I had no desire to kill her, I just wanted to hurt her, she was either a fool or had too many insecurities of minority. I didn't want to kill her, so I shot on her shoulder. Having obsessive compulsive disorder has its own advantages, when I went to learn how to use a gun, I was able to play and replay hundreds of times in my

mind how I will shoot whom and where in my mind with an extraordinary accuracy.

In place of my anxieties, I played the instructions, I learned quickly, I played whom I will shoot and how, I didn't achieve the whole plan, but I was able to achieve almost half of it, because the unknown, the unplanned walked in and ruined my plan. If you would have come Infront of me, I would have fired a shot on you, may be on your head, may be on your heart, may be on your stomach, may be on your vagina or may be on your mouth."

All the sudden Andrea said " Yes, I have been with women and men both, yes, I have been with both. "Saying this she busted into tears.

Vivan " Why are you crying? Isn't exploring sexuality a thing of our time, of our age? I think sex and sexuality is a birth right of all living entities including humans."

Andrea " I am not bad enough that you shoot me, especially on my vagina, I love it, it has been a source of pleasure for me, it kept me alive, otherwise I don't find much meaning in living in pathetic human society."

Vivan" Apart from those rascals I told you about, I shot several other people, I don't know who they were, what they do, were they good people or bad people. I think good and bad are foolish measurements of existential reality. Good, bad and neutral are idiot's way of looking at the world, at the existence , at the nature .Tell me your story, I don't want to know if it invade your privacy, there is already a wall between us, I am not sure if court will issue death penalty for you but it will issue death penalty for me , I know it for sure, and I don't know what other suffering I might have to go through before they kill me for killing others. Sometimes I laugh how much and how many anxieties are built around death, hurt, old age and disease, maybe pretty much all of them."

Andrea " After going through exploitation from two males and two heartbreaking break ups ,I lost faith in men being any good, so I started showing interest in women, first one was one of my co-worker, I showed little interest in her, she asked me out for dinner ,I said "yes" , later we went to her apartment, she sucked my vagina like a child sucks Lollipop , she pushed her tongue inside my vagina, she grabbed my boobs , kissed me , I came .Later she expected me to do the same , I did it but gradually I learned I don't have much interest in sucking her vagina, somehow I made her come but as soon as she came , I left. A strange guilt rose inside me, on arrival to my apartment I showered, I cleaned my vaginal area several times .I don't know why , must be some kind of guilt that was pushed inside me forced me to do that, otherwise it wasn't that big of a deal.

I don't think anyone is hundred percent straight or hundred percent gay, we are mixture, at least that's what my realization is, she was couple of years younger to me, we spoke couple of days later at work, till than I and her both, mostly I avoided her, sometimes I think I am an escapist. I said to her I am not into it, she

said " It's fine. " and she told me "She came across many women who realized it after their first encounter." From there on our interactions were as needed by our professional commitments, although sometimes it felt very strange to me being around someone in the office whom I have seen necked, whose body I have explored and whose vagina I have touched. Have you ever slept with someone from work?"

Vivan " No I haven't. I decided to keep it clean there, at least in sexual terms and anyways I didn't like most of the people from my work. They were well behaved, sophisticated, superficial people. I worked as consultant at most of the companies facing one sort of discrimination or another sort of discrimination. I decided never to sleep and socialize as less as possible with any of those entities, although I used to socialize with them on my first job. I got my first job after graduating from university, I was polite, respectful and in a hallucination that all humans are equal and must be respected, the assholes carried whole different ideas, the assholes carried idea of race and racism , While I was respecting them, while I was polite with them , while I was trying to socialize with them, they were too busy discriminating , imposing exclusion , trying to marginalize me, it was an department where all employees were white and all contractors were brown. The department had not a single black person ,since everyone was white in leadership including human resources it was so easy to exhibit systematic and nonsystematic discrimination, all of them were very polite and sophisticated , very superficial and very discriminative , one of the VP was Buddhist , I don't know if she was converted or she was Buddhist by birth but for her also people were white vs nonwhite, she openly called India a third world country, the country where Buddha was born , raised and attained enlightenment, even buddha failed to bring her out of racism. I remember a picture on the wall in the same company, the picture had a white man doing a handshake with black women in an extraordinary gesture of respect and politeness, each of the three floors of company had the same photo hanging in hallways, whereas the black woman or man were missing from the whole company, they were non existing, it's so easy to respect non - existence, isn't it? The pictures were hung to show off that the company believes in equal opportunity, only believes in, not truly exhibits it, I think the leadership loved to have pictures of a black people rather than black people, they confused the picture of a black person with an actual black person.

Later the beasts showed their real faces, the truth beneath the skin-deep sophistication and politeness, I decided never to date, sleep, or fuck or get fucked by anyone from work. I left the company after two and half years, it was very stupid of me to stay there that long, and it was very stupid of me to not take a gun, walk in there and shoot people there. I think I have delayed shooting too much, and my actions took place at a slightly less appropriate place, slightly less deserving place. I wish someone else would grab the gun and do the work I missed. To answer your question, I never slept with anyone from work and now you know why?"

Andrea " I like your lengthy and honest answer. In sophisticated societies, honesty is one of the most missing things, second is courage, third is a genuine desired companionship, that's why I think most of us feel lonely in this part of the world and to mitigate that we have cats and dogs, whom sometimes perverts penetrate and abuse. Second woman I slept with was couple of years older to me and the way she acted gave me impression she have a lot of experience with women and their bodies .The way she moved her tongue on my vagina and the way she sucked my breast made me cum but later without my consent she penetrated me with a fake penis, the penis felt very hard and larger than what I was used to, I came one more time , then with same penis she penetrated me in anal area it pushed the limits for me for some time but later I started feeling violated. I asked her to stop, she did after pushing and pulling it couple of times, she dropped the artificial penis and pushed her vagina on my face, when I wasn't able to suck and create pleasure she was expecting, it made her upset, I think she was expecting same expertise as of hers. I had pretty much none, after being disappointed in me she asked me to masturbate her, I started masturbating her which resulted into even greater disappointment for her. She pushed my hand away and started masturbating herself, then pushed the artificial penis inside her vagina, looked at me upset and said " You straight bitches when not happy with your puppy's penis come to us. Come to us to explore if there is a possibility of more pleasure from lesbian encounter, you bitches want to have everything on your plates don't you, a penis, a vagina, children's born from penetration of penis, respect in society, and even heaven, don't you, don't you. "While saying that she started moaning and she came. By puppy she meant man. She told me to dress up and leave and expressed her desire never to see me again. Thankfully she was from another department in the company I was working at, later I decided to move to another company. I always wanted to ask her question why she want to use artificial penis, why any true lesbian woman would want to use an artificial penis, wouldn't a woman , her breasts and her vagina should be enough but I didn't want to offended her , and I didn't want to offend any other lesbian women I came across, so I never asked.

I have tasted vagina of two women and in total four women tasted my vagina , don't think I always remained in realm of work space, other two girls who leaked my vagina , I met them at a bar, both were partners , they were looking for someone else to join them , I walked in, in that threesome both used my vagina like a shared ice-cream but later, they got busy with each other , I sort of felt lonely, left out ,like an outsider, there had been several movements where they pretty much forgot I exists , it was time when they started tasting each other's saliva saying " I love you, you are so beautiful, you smell so nice and so on" I was laying necked with my boobs exposed and vagina sucked. I wasn't sure what should be my moral position and what should I do, when they were done playing with each other they fell next to me ,each of them sucked one of my boob, when they were done sucking I expressed my desire to leave, none of them expressed any will or desire for me to stay , they immediately said " Thanks for giving us company tonight " among three persons clothes, three set of underwear and bras, I found mine, put them on and left, that was the last female encounter for me, it

took me four woman and three encounters to realize I am not into woman, regardless how much I dislike man and no matter what I think of them , my vagina can be satisfied only by a stick hanging above two balls. As far as man goes, I haven't been with many, if I compare with you my numbers may be less than half, whenever I went to clubs or bars at least couple of guys approached me, when I turned them down, they were shameless enough to tell me " They just want to fuck me." I replied, " I don't want to be fucked by you." Some of them replied " Shoot yourself " other said " Fuck you bitch". Some responded, " bitch or whore or slut or fucking lesbo" and others didn't say anything but looked angry and behaved in anger, I don't know why males react so badly when a woman turns them down, must be male ego."

Vivan " May be , or maybe they had bad relationship with their mothers , sisters , aunts or female supervisors etc., that's one of the excuse some men come up justifying their aggression, although does bad experience with one woman or few women give rights to treat all women bad I don't think so but there are several aspects about everything, one of the time years back one of my Indian friend in a gym in the Hollywood area of Los Angeles started casual conversation with a white woman , she asked "Are you Pakistani? ", he said, "No I am not, I am Indian", in arrogance she said " You all are same, Indian, Pakistani, Nepali, all of you. " It hurt his feelings, people often intentionally generalize to hurt, apart from it I think males are inherently aggressive, and I don't know where this aggression comes from , there are different theories about it , one of them is, in the evolution process man used to go for hunting and woman used to stay home that's where man derived their aggression from , from hunting but this theory doesn't appeal to me.

If this theory is correct than man is a predator and woman or anything famine is merely a prey and the whole act of violence towards woman is merely a response of predator towards the prey. Other theory is the way males are biologically built, that's saying we are not responsible for anything, nature is responsible, although I don't know if gay man vs straight vs bisexual who is aggressive compared to each other and if there is any theory about them, is it correct or incorrect? Apart from that, the theory that women are less aggressive than men are also incorrect. Women when given opportunity show a lot of passive aggression. How many males have you been with?"

Andrea " Male is a very broad statement, I have been with couple of man , some good , some bad and some I don't know where to put .Among those ,one of them is my husband Mathew, I met him at a club, there was something about him, I don't know what, perhaps discontent or agitation in his eyes and being which attracted me, what I went through in my childhood made me little bit uncomfortable and insecure around man in general, seeing groups of male sometimes gave me a strange anxiety, which further worsen when mayor of the city where I was doing internship forcefully pushed his penis inside my mouth, forced me into oral sex ,tried to ejaculate inside my mouth, when he pulled out ,I was about to threw up, he ejaculated on my head , pervert, bastard. You know not

having something in life or part of our life creates romantic ideas about them, and those missing things start seeming more beautiful than their actual beauty. My mother and father separated because he cheated on her once with another woman. My mother didn't know about it , there was no way she would have known but my father believed that the institution of marriage is based on honesty, he told her, his expectations were she will forgive him, and will cherish him as honest, loyal husband , I think his root desire in sharing was to be seen as great human being , or perhaps above human beings, like an angle , an honest angel, there is something extra-ordinary foolish and stupid about human in general trying to be great , or an angel or godlike figure, it's actually ugly and pathetic, it's just expansion of the sick ego. My mother ended up filing for divorce and kicked him out of the home. It bewildered him, he bagged, she didn't listen, person who said honesty is the best policy is the greatest fool, my stupid father thought honesty is the base of marriage, his marriage broke because he was being too honest or I should say he was being unnecessary honest, these general moral principles are merely garbage, a filth, a nonsense, some sort of disgust, they treat individuals as masses. I have seen them fighting for hours on a spoon, on a cup, on a two dollars plate, bastards, seeing those fights I realized even a person in high school will behave better, later when I grew up, I realized most of the grownups or so called grownups are no different than bunch of high schoolers .

Especially when they are angry or their ego is hurt, these are the people who are running the world, no wonder it's a pathetic mess, an utter nonsense. My parents separated, my uncle raped me several times, after penetrating me and abusing me for couple of weeks he died in a car accident, the whole pain of seeing my parents bickering over pity and insignificant things and the pain of sexual abuse I went through which I couldn't share with anyone because my uncle threatened me if I share it with anyone, he will first rape my mother then kill her. Later he will kill me and then will kill my father. I was horrified, at that age I felt I need to protect my parents, his threat worked on me. My mother thought my uncle was a man of values and morals, he kept saying to her that he is seeking for a woman to whom he can commit his whole life and until marriage he is following celibacy. He often used to say her "I am a one-woman man." My mother used to think "The woman who marries him will be one of the luckiest women on the earth." She felt lucky to have such a moral and well-behaved cousin. The rascal was not only fucking me but sometimes he pulled out photos on his phone and showed me pictures of girls and used to tell me " Last night I fucked this bitch and before last night he fucked that bitch and, on another photo, he told me this bitch swallowed my cum, I pushed my penis deep into her throat etc.". One of the days while showing me photos he forced me to drink his cum, I felt terribly sick. There are few memories from which it's pretty much impossible to grow out, they pretty much destroy our life, the sexual assault by two males did the same to me. When my parents divorced my life was a constant displacement, from one home to another, my father rented an apartment, sometimes in middle of night I woke up and didn't know where I am, a constant displacement between two places pretty much destroyed idea of home for me, none of the place felt like a home, it felt to me as if I am merely a guest, a temporary entity at both places, the very feeling was dark

and ugly. It filled me with strange insecurities, and horrors, you lost your home in one way, I lost my home in another. We both lost it my friend."

Vivan " When I think back it feels that I never had a home, and I kept on searching for it, one of the reasons I came to United States was to find a home, coming here further destroyed my idea of home, in future perhaps displacement is the only home most of us will find, we the people of modern age."

Andrea " As it happens with most of the things we desire and don't find, the same thing happened with me, kids whose parents didn't divorce seemed luckiest creatures on planet to me. My father took the divorce too serious; he was first one in last four generations to get divorced, my grandparents were high school sweethearts, they stayed with each other till end of their last breath, my great great grandparents and great great great grandparents didn't divorce.

I don't think divorce was that popular in those days and maybe people had slightly different ideas of the self and life. The divorce, his expectations from the institute of marriage and his ideas of the world all lead my father to severe depression and anxiety, apart from his job, he was eating and sleeping most of the time, he was taking the anxiety and depression treatment but was irregular in taking his medicines. Sometimes in both spaces it felt as if I am growing up without grownups, my dad was filled with guilt and shame, my mother was filled ego, hate, distrust, or over- trust. Sometimes both forgot, there is a child who might need them or who might need their care. I hope Mathew doesn't take kids to my mother's home. She was too busy hating my dad after divorce. He died from heart attack caused by excessive eating, anxiety, high cholesterol, and obesity. He died within a year of divorce, by that time I was already molested, the molester already died in a car accident, after my father's death my mother shifted her hate for my father to his memories, when he was alive, she hated him, when he was dead, she hated him, our mind has extraordinary capacities of never letting go, amazing, isn't it? We can hate the dead, we can hate the living, we can love the dead and we can love the living. "

Vivan " Most of the time, do we love and hate people or their memories, I think memories. What are memories? Something which is gone, the past, and what is past something that can't be changed, so we are too busy hating and loving something which can't be changed."

Andrea "Very true, and in our killing perhaps that's what we did? We killed people for the memories created by those people. My father gained 150 pounds from the day of divorce to the day of his death. He had a heart attack; I was at my mom's house at that time. My first molester was dead, she was still grieving his death. I guess I can't blame her, I never told her what he did to me, I don't know why and when I lost trust in her. Perhaps her too much trust in my molester or her too much distrust in my father caused it, I don't know, it's a bit strange that I do the things and I don't know why I did it, have I divided myself so much that I don't know what state of consciousness or what consciousness causes my actions and what were the reasons behind them, strange. Isn't it?"

Vivan " That's not just mine or your state of mind, it's the state of pretty much the whole human race collectively and individually, no one can find true reasons for their actions and reasonings anymore."

Andrea" My father couldn't call 911 when he got a heart attack, he was found dead, he died lonely, feeling lonely, struggling with loneliness in a country where almost 300 million people live. " Tears burst out of her eyes.

Vivan " I am sorry to hear that. Loneliness is one of greatest problem most of the people in the first world are facing. I think the feeling of loneliness was one of the reasons which led me to such and so many sexual encounters, loneliness was one of the reason I kept on going back to my abusers and exploiters, to not feel lonely , to feel up the void of loneliness by gaining and giving pleasure, did it solve the problem of loneliness , no it did not, it further wounded me , distracted me from real issues and helped me to avoid them and as escaping issues never solve them, the issues continued within me , they grew more and more and I picked the gun."

Andrea " Sometimes I used to feel a terrible loneliness in the crowd and even with the people I know. Have you ever felt that? "

Vivan " Yes, I used to have the same feeling pretty much every day for years, in India, here and pretty much everywhere. I guess the absence of one can't be fulfilled by many. I will always feel incomplete and lonely without him, without Aryan."

Andrea " Maybe you should call him. Do you think, what you did, made news in India?"

Vivan " Yes, perhaps on most of the news channels. Sometimes my heart sinks when I think about the pain and suffering my parents would have been going through. I feel shame, guilt, horror and want to kill myself, but suicide doesn't offer the escape I am looking for, because there is an understanding and a realization in *Sanatana-dharma,* in which I was born and raise, at the time of death body is the only thing which decay and die. Mind, ego, intelligence, and consciousness all goes with the soul, and in next birth or whenever and wherever we start next, it's always from the point we left. To escape this cage of birth and death, one must purify oneself. In general, what is pure? what is impure? Is a bit vague and controversial or perhaps my mind wants to define the definition of purity according to its own comfort? Sometimes no escape seems the greatest tragedy and another time it seems the greatest justice. The stories of *Sanatana-dharma* told me to escape, one need to take the shelter of the absolute and the cause of all causes. I don't want to take His shelter; I want to make love to Him."

Andrea " Morality, purity, hell, heaven, *karma* (actions), *vikarma* (ill actions), *sukarma* (good actions), akarma (actions without reactions), meditation, prayers, enlightenment, justice, fairness, and any actions opposite to them, all sometimes seems a hallucination to me and now from here, from this prison cell, none of those seems to hold any value.

Anyways I don't think you and other people should agree with me on these, I think vagueness in these areas helped me to get a gun in my hand and pull the trigger.

If I would have had clarities and precise understanding. I think I won't have pulled the trigger.

When my father died ,my mother went to his funeral with me ,rather than speaking of his good memories she spoke about why it's very important to be loyal in the institute of marriage, and what are the punishments for those who are not, in her speech not for a single time my father or my grandparents or any sweet memories she , him or they had together was mentioned, wounded ego can let us do reckless things, it can help us to hate those who are alive and it can help us to hate those who are dead. After his death, she hated him, sometimes she got so busy hating him that she forgot to bath, to cook, to date and to fuck. I think she loved him along the same lines when they were married. Anyways so coming back to my husband, I saw him in a club, his discontent, agitation, and restlessness attracted me, there was something in him and still I don't know what it is that attracts me so much, although his presence in my life didn't stop me from killing and didn't bring me out from the horrors of molestations. In the club, I walked to him, and said, " Hi I am Andrea ", he told me his name. He was silent and reserved and offered me the beer from which he was drinking, I said " okay " and I took a sip, and was planning to walk away, the very moment he grabbed my face and kissed me, I kissed him back, on third date I was in his apartment, and he was on me, more precisely inside me. There was a part of me which wanted to give him contentment ,I forgot I don't have much of it myself, I have to admit he have always been a great love maker, first time he fucked me , he pushed me to limits of pleasure and joy, it was intense, I came way ahead of him , when he came I thought his discontent, agitation and discomfort he seems to be in will be gone at least temporarily for few moments but that didn't happen, when he fell next to me he kissed me, the kiss was deep and intense, it gave impression he is still in search of some more comfort , something more, he loved me and he still love me. I have no doubt about it, but for some reason his discontentment, his agitation, his discomfort perhaps in his own skin or body never left him and it seems will never do, I don't know what caused it, and why he is that way. There are several layers of him I never got access to even after having two children with him. I don't blame him, there are several layers of me he never got access to, I guess we can never know any other person completely. Sometimes it feels I don't know myself either, I am a stranger to self. "

Vivan " If he knows you completely, will he be able to love you? If you know him completely, will you be able to love him? If any other human being knows me completely, will he or she be able to love me? perhaps not.

That's the story of all of us, if we know everything about someone or if someone knows everything about us, I don't think we will be able to love each other, apart from that, to know everything about just one person is also too much information, Isn't it?"

Andrea " I think you are right. I didn't tell him several things about me, I don't know why? Does it make our love false, does that mean no one truly loves each other?"

Vivan " I don't think love has an obligation to share everything or tell everything. Perhaps love is being together, caring for each other, compromising for one another, enjoying each other and each other's company but what do I know about love? I fell in love but never attained my love, what do I know about it, perhaps you are right, none of us love each other truly and fully, no wonder in this world most of the people feel incomplete and lonely."

Andrea " He proposed to me within six months of dating, by then I remembered his smell, taste of his mouth, taste of his semen and his boy from head to toe. I think he remembered me along the same line. I am deriving the conclusion from his statements, as I never stated directly how I remember him being my male, he never stated directly how he remembered me being his female, of course that's not all how I remember him. He is very sweet and gentle, I don't remember him ever disrespecting any woman, he always loved me with great intensity, sometimes he fucked me long enough to give my vagina a hot burning sensation. I miss it, I miss him being on me, inside me, I miss those burning sensations, I miss his weight on me, I miss sucking him and I miss stickiness of him semen."

Her nipples got tight, she pushed her right hand inside her underwear, started masturbating her, then pulled her hand out without complete, she left her masturbation like an unconcluded conversation.

She continued " Two children, a loving husband, and great sex, none of them were able to stop me from taking a gun and pulling the trigger, sometimes I wonder why? were they not sufficient? Were they not enough? Perhaps not or perhaps yes. Sometimes I wonder why it was not sufficient for me?"

Vivan" There is nothing in this world which can ever be sufficient for human mind ,human ego, human lust and human intelligence, and without any of these we won't even be human, that means to be human means to be constantly dissatisfied, to be constantly dissatisfied means to be in constant anxiety, to be in constant anxiety means to be in constant discontent and discontent is the one which lead me to pick up the gun and pull the trigger .

So, if opportunity is given, each and every human will pull a trigger if not on other, may be on self, and we do pull triggers on each other, sometimes that trigger through a bullet of violent body language, sometimes of ignorance, sometimes of discrimination, another time of biased attitude and so on. I and you might have a few bullets in our guns, people crawling outside, outside of these cells have hundreds, thousands, millions or perhaps billions of bullets in their mind, in their ego, and in their intelligence. Anyways, why did you do it? Why did you kill people? What did they do to you? What happened?"

Andrea " I intended to kill only three people, the ex-city mayor who forcefully pushed his penis inside my mouth while I was doing an unpaid internship at his

office. Outside of his office, the media, his followers, churches to which he was making a lot of donations, all projected him as a man of family, a person who cherish love, and respect the institute of marriage and who love God. Another was a manipulative whore, a nun. She was the one who referred me there, I was a fool then, my parents' divorce and then my father's death, my mother's hate towards my dead father, all these put me into strange situations, in varieties of pains, horrors, and uncertainties. I started comparing my life with those whose parents are not divorced, their life seemed perfect to me and any famous person who was projected as a man of family, or any family who is projected as ideal, loving, sticking together in tough times etc. fascinated me. One of the Hollywood celebrities who found her husband cheating on her with another woman forgave him, she was nothing less than an angel to me, growing up when I had no one to talk to, I found sister Nancy in the church my mother and father used to go before they got married, after they got married and when they got divorced. In the moment of weaknesses, when we feel lonely, we tend to lean on someone, we search for a shelter, and I don't think we have built a society where right guidance and shelter is easily available, most of the time people who seek the shelter, the comfort, the protection is either manipulated or people take their advantage, innocence is always exploited and that's what happened with me as well, Sister Nancy consoled me. Now I think consolation is a shit, consolation is as degraded as human stool, at that time Nancy was young and thin, average looking. She gave me some consolation and comfort, in search of leaning on to someone I found her. I used to think she is angel send by God, but I was only someone through which she was looking to fulfill her desire, desire to go to heaven by helping those who need help, the bitch was thin but over the time her overeating to repress urges created by her vagina got her fat, she was almost two hundred fifty pounds when I shot her dead. "

Vivan " What did she do to you?"

Andrea " Well it's more what I allowed her to do to me, when the asshole pushed his penis inside my mouth and ejaculated rather than calling 911, and reporting him , giving his semen samples to laboratory and sending the pervert into jail , I rushed to sister Nancy, she consoled me, preached on forgiveness, she convinced me to clean myself, and assured me that God loves me more than him, and that he will suffer in hell for eternity for what he did to me and if I forgive him ,eternal heaven is assured for me. I followed whatever she said, I tried my best to forgive and sort of moved on after Mathew walked into my life. Kyle and Kylie were born, one day I turned on the local news, and the fucking whore was glorifying the rascal as great human being, a man of morality, a man who has committed his life to one woman , a man who live his life through great values and a man who hold extraordinary respect for the institute of marriage .I started my investigation, I found out he has been pouring a lot of money as donation to that church and sister Nancy had been a key point of contact for him from years. I was not the first girl he has molested , she have send couple of other girls , few of them he fucked, with other few he did what he did to me , among those girls couple of them surrendered to him, others were cleaned up and moralized by sister Nancy to not

protest or report the issue , she had been a pimp and took advantage of children who came from broken families like me, on TV she urged people of the State should vote him in congress, and she can see anyone who is alike him leading this great nation United States , indirectly she was recommending the pervert to the white house, I can't believe it. I felt a strange insecurity not just for me but for my children, the episodes of being forcefully penetrated, of being molested by mayor, betrayal of a nun and pretty much all bad experiences of life started playing and replaying in my mind, up to the extended that sometimes I forgot where I am, what am I doing, what am I supposed to do and so on. I started taking Lexapro, it didn't help much, my PCP prescribed another medicine it didn't help much, a constant anxiety continued in my mind. As if someone or something was forcing me and was telling me that this world and this society won't be safe if the bastard and the bitch continued to live, I found their being, them being alive a threat for Kylie and for me, and for many other women like me and many other children like Kyle and Kylie."

Vivan " Do you think you were doing greater common good by killing those entities?"

Andrea " That's one of the justifications that helps me with my shame and guilt otherwise it's rare to act in selfless ways, I shot them dead because their presence made world feel little bit less safe for me and my loved ones, so it was about me, I and mine.

Apart from that even those who portray that they are selfless, most of the time they are utterly selfish, perhaps most selfish, for example that disgusting bitch Nancy she was portraying as if she is helping me or even if any other nun who is not degraded as Nancy what she is doing by helping others and by being selfless. She is only securing heaven for herself, that's it and that's all. So those who come out as selfless, celibate is far more selfish, greedy, and full of lust, my behavior is not as degraded as them or maybe I am wrong, I don't know, there could be other reasons, reasons I even don't know why I did it, but I like to believe I did it in search of safety for me and my loved one, is that wrong? Is that right? I don't know. While I was investigating the truth about the asshole and the bitch I came to know the asshole was doing physical violence and was sexually abusive on his wife as well, but when they were on camera or in any public gathering they both pretended as if they are perfect , in his words he described as if he worship her like an angel, as if she is a guiding Goddess in his life, in reality he never respected her, I don't think he respected any woman or ever considered them equal, when he was pushing his penis inside my mouth, he was shouting you fucking bone , you fucking bone, woman like Nancy who believe their existence degraded and who believed woman is merely a bone, an inferior entity, they all loved him. I think she believed woman deserve to be punished. God knows from where she did get such ideas, maybe she has very bad relationships with her mother or stepmother, or aunt or female teachers or grandmother or perhaps with herself. You know asshole's wife was a very well-educated woman, in her speeches she often quoted empowerment of woman, more strict punishment on

domestic violence. The whore never protested or reported the abuse and the violence she was going through, she wanted other to protest it and report it."

Vivan" Is dualities in this world not enough that people started duplicities as well?"

Andrea" Mayor's wife was third person I shot. I have no regrets. Nancy was the first one I killed, the bitch would have polluted the society a lot more if she would have been allowed to live any longer, when I met her first time, she weights around 90 lbs. when I shot her dead, she weighs more than 250 lbs. the whore was eating a lot of food which was purchased by the donation money. The sexually repressed whore was constantly eating. She loved potatoes, cheese, ice cream, I shot two extra shots to make sure she dies. I also killed a nun standing next to her because she reminded me of young Nancy but sometimes, I think what I have done to kill the perverts. I destroyed my family. I am separated from my husband and pretty much destroyed childhood of both of my children or perhaps their life, what would happen to them now?

I should have been with them protecting them, loving them, caring about them, what if Mathew marries a bad woman, what if Kyle and Kylie need to face the world same way I did, how can I be such an idiot, there could have been other ways to revenge, other ways to get justice."

Vivan " Every child is born with their destiny. We did as well and that's what we attained and that's what we will attain. Nature does not give options to selfish people and it's the truth."

Andrea " Your philosophy sometimes makes me feel sick and most of the time it's out of context. "

Vivan " I think, that's the job of the philosophy, to be out of context and to make people sick. "

He laughed loudly, very loud for a long time and then he started crying. she started crying as well.

When his tears dried, he said "You know sometimes I feel no woman is responsible for anything bad, unfortunately we have created a society where either woman must take off their own panties, or someone else will take it off. Now, in this era the expectations are that they should not even put on the panties and keep their vaginas always ready, waxed and hairless."

He wiped his tears, stood up and started urinating, the sound of urination was audible to Andrea.

She asked, " How long is your penis?"

Vivan " Around five inches erect. Why would you ask that?"

Andrea " I am just curious. Have you ever fornicated any woman?"

Vivan" I don't think a male should feel obligation to fornicate a female just because he has a penis and two balls, and a female should never feel obligation to get fucked or fuck just because she has a vagina, but to answer your question yes, I have been with two girls. I won't call them woman; I was too young to be man at that age and they were too young to be woman. I was only a boy; a guy and they were girls. I was in my early 20s and they were in their early 20s , after completing my masters , I got my first contracting job in Wisconsin ,fucking Wisconsin winters, they always enhanced my desires to be loved by Aryan .Aryan my love, whose absence I can't feel up even with thousands of other males, I rented a room in a house on second floor, a girl named Julia moved to first floor room .

She started fucking the landlord within a couple of days of moving. It seemed to me as if she moved in to fuck him. She often used to say to me " You know I can't say no to you for anything." So, I decided to test it. I told her that I have never been with any woman, I am woman virgin and if she really meant what she kept on saying, I would like to fuck her, strangely enough she agreed to fuck me. I like the fact that now woman started saying that they also fuck, and can fuck, in past only males were the fuckers, at least that idea was famous. Her fucker, the house landlord went to visit his divorced mother, after divorcing his mother married a guy who was almost 30 years older than her. I think she related wisdom with age. I think age can only give experiences if we allow ourselves to that and there are no guarantee experiences converts into knowledge. Sometimes experiences just give us information and lamentations. Useless information and bad experiences turn into horrors. When we started kissing, a strange discomfort raised inside me. Somehow, I continued the kiss, somehow, I sucked her nipples, the most discomforting act was kissing and sucking her vagina which she absolutely wanted me to do, and I did it. Then she started her work, she moved all the way down to my penis and ball, and started sucking them, I couldn't get hard, I closed my eyes and imagined I am being sucked by a male, I got harder, she rolled condom on my penis, and pushed it inside her vagina, she was on top, I opened my eyes, and pushed my middle finger, the fuck finger inside her mouth, she started sucking it and took off her bra , I grabbed her boobs and squeezed them, I sensed my penis is getting softer , I closed my eyes and imagined I am fucking a male, a hot guy, I am inside his anal hole . I got harder, she came in couple of minutes, I didn't come ,she intensified her moves and I tried my best to imagine that I am inside a guy rather than a girl to ejaculate , it didn't work out, she tried her best , one of her move end up hurting my penis, I said " It's hurting me , please stop" She immediately stopped, pulled up her vagina, my penis was out of it , still hard , thick and unejaculated,. She said " Are you all, right? ", in pain I said " I think it's hurt; my penis is hurt. Let me check."

I walked necked to the restroom, pulled out the condom. I noticed some blood, my uncircumcised penis was hurt, I applied some coconut oil on it and came outside. It was painful, I walked inside the room and said, " my penis is hurt, will it be fine if we stop here?"

Even if I didn't desire, I said " Maybe we can do it some other time. "I started dressing up and she started dressing up.

She said " Anytime, you know where to find me."

I felt a guilt, a terrible shame because I didn't come. I don't know why I felt it.

 I said " I am so sorry. "

She smiled and said " Why? because you didn't come. I don't mind, I came, I didn't come in last 3 months, our landlord, my fucker he ejaculates when I am not even halfway, after ejaculation he falls on me as if I am a mattress. I often push him on the side and masturbate myself to come. He is not the only one , most the men on the earth are struggling to make a woman come now a days, most of us have to rely on our hands, vibrators and gay men to come because straight men have so much shit in their mind , too much of it because assholes want to run, control , manipulate and fuck the world .The assholes who can't even control their erections and who even don't know when to ejaculate and when not, want to run the world , no wonder, the whole world is a mess .Women , gays, bisexuals and transgenders are the only hope because so called straight shits are ejaculating very fast and urinating too slow. " By that time both of us were dressed up.

Vivan " Sometimes when I hear you and him, it sounds like you enjoy it a lot."

Julia" As most of the woman in this country pretend , I do it as well, we like to believe we live in a free country and women are in better situation than the most parts of the world but we feel extraordinary obligations to make and feel man happy, and we try our best to pretend that man can give us the highest pleasures because they got a penis, after pushing him to side after his ejaculation first thing I do is to run to restroom, let his semen flow out of my vagina, then masturbate myself, come, wipe off my vagina and go lay down next to him. You wouldn't have guessed it if I wouldn't have told you, correct?"

Vivan " Correct?"

Julia " See, I can act, he can act, we all are such extraordinary actors, pretenders, and hypocrites, don't be like me don't be like him, never lose your honesty and never compromise your individuality. "

She walked out saying that. The hurt on my penis was not huge but it was painful. I went to see my primary care provider, to check my hurt he held my penis with gloves on his hands, while he was inspecting the hurt, I got hard, I felt terrible, I apologized, He said "Don't worry about it." He prescribed a cream which healed the hurt in two weeks. He was good looking, very handsome but I never desired him that way, long time back in one of my visits he mentioned he is married and told little bit about his wife, she is also a doctor, maybe that's why I never desired him consciously, never pleasured myself on him or jerked off on him, I don't

know why I got hard when he touched me. Maybe I desired him in my unconscious mind, see mind is a mere mess, it has too many splits, divisions, and dualities.

In couple of months when I visited his office again for fever, it was very strange for me to see him because I got hard on him, strangely enough he was fine, maybe he forgot, or maybe it was not as unusual as I thought to get hard on your primary care provider for a gay man like me. Does the idea of respect make us nervous? Perhaps it does, doesn't it? Second time didn't happen with Julia, my landlord and she broke up, my initial thought was maybe it was because of me, and I will be asked to leave but it turned out they were falling apart or maybe they were never truly together. Second and last woman I have been with was Julia's friend, she was a virgin, she had her own versions and ideas about things, her parents separated, she never told why, or maybe she was never told why, she has seen her brother being hit by her stepfather, she mentioned " He never hit me, sometimes he was even loving and caring towards me". She had this idea that her real father would have never hit her brother, I don't think that's a correct idea, even biological parents hit their children, most of the time to correct them and it should not be misunderstood as abuse or exploitation. My father used to hit me; I am pretty sure parents in United States do it as well. You are correct, absence of something we desire creates unnecessary romantic ideas about them and around them. She continued to believe that her life would have been perfect if her parents would have remained married, as if everyone whose parents doesn't divorce live a perfect life. There is no possibility of a perfect life, people even don't get the minimal required, look at me and my life. I desired a good place to live, just good not extraordinary or exceptional, did I find it, even with best attempts. One circumstances or another popped up to disturb it, none of them were in my control. In my childhood my grandpa never allowed us to feel at home, I left for boarding house at age of 14, it was a horrible place, I was bullied ,discriminated , ill-treated ,and was sexually abused, who can feel at home at such a pathetic place , was it mine fault that I end up meeting such assholes I don't think so , then Bachelors , Masters and constantly displacing contracting jobs where sometimes I was discriminated because I have brown skin and other times because I was a contractor , the constant displacement never allowed me to realize or feel what and how a space called home feels like.

Here in United States, I came across couple of people who were too eager to make me feel I don't belong here, this is not my country then whose country is this, this country used to belong to native Americans where are they, what was done to them in this country, in their native country, if I don't belong here then why this country is called the country of immigrants. I know I talk the same shit over and over but we are in *Saṃsāra* which means cycle, oneself is trapped into a cycle, or perhaps into numerous cycles , from one cycle we jump into another cycle, and from another to another to another, that's all we have, cycles, you know there is a novella by Franz Kafka named The Metamorphosis , in it the lead character sleeps

as human and wakes up a worm , that's what happening to most of the human on the earth, or that's what they allows to happen to themselves, they sleep human and wake up a worm, worms who are too eager to commit crime on behalf of corporates and Institutes on individuals and individuality , assholes , rascals, it's good that someday all of us will die in one way or another ,under the pressure and influence of energy of time. Death is the most beautiful and the fairest, it creates possibilities through which weak people like me can live in the stool of the world with a hope that when I can't stand up the shit and its smell, I have an option, someday it will all be over, anyways Julia's friend was virgin. Displaced between two homes, constantly projecting her step father as bad guy because he was not perfect , she never asked if her biological father is perfect or not, that's what I call biased observation, to see whatever one wants to see .I do that as well and I do it even if I know I am doing it, this is the consciousness of modern man, we know and yet we do. I love beauty of solitude and bewilderment of reality, but I hate those who impose it on me, I absolutely hate them, and I know I am trapped in cycle of desire and hate, yet I never jumped out of it, why? I don't know. So, this girl, named Angelina, white, blued eyed , black haired, her hairs were not natural black , she painted them black just to annoy her mother, her mother was blond, she was blond , her grandmother was blond, she often said to her mother " I like black hairs and people with black hairs", she got engaged to a guy who was blue eye , blond hair , a white guy because she like people with black hairs. She wanted to keep her virginity till marriage, when they got engaged, he was fine, a year passed, here and there she sucked him but as it happens with desires one is fulfilled other popes up, higher, and bigger. He started desiring to spread her legs, first push his tongue inside her vagina and later his penis, she expressed her disagreement, that's what she told to me, he was not a virgin, he started fucking at age of 14, she told me to keep him without sex was getting as hard as keeping a lion on water who tasted blood, they started falling apart.

One day he announced that he can't live on blowjobs and on jerking off, his statement was "Maybe we should take our relationship to next level or take a break.", by next level he meant start fucking. It broke her heart, she disagreed to fuck before marriage. He broke the engagement. Her idea was she will be worshiped like an angel for keeping her virginity and who ever marry her will commit his life to her because she was virgin until marriage, when her fiancé broke the engagement with her and didn't appreciated her virginity at all, her heart broke, she saw it as failure , it pushed her to depression .For being virgin, for maintaining it she was expecting several guys will tell her " Someday I want to marry you or marry a girl like you who maintained her purity and holiness.", it did not happen , even few guys joked on her that even their grandmas was not virgin at age of 23. She wanted to lose her virginity desperately, but she put a prerequisite she needed a virgin guy, so she communicated it to Julia. Julia told Angelina that I am a virgin, it was an intentional miscommunication from her, in depressed and hopeless state Angelina bought it, when we fucked, she pulled off condom from my penis, and expressed her desire we should do is bare, I went for it, I used to be in the mode of not saying no for any sexual adventures in those days. I pushed my penis inside her, continued my moves in and out of her, she

came first time, I did not come, I continued, by the time she came second time my penis was hard, but I wasn't able to feel anything, I pulled out my penis on her second orgasm, my penis had blood on it, she asked " What happened? Did you come?"

I said " No, I need to use the bathroom. "

She pointed me to the bathroom. I went inside the bathroom, wiped off the blood and the liquid that came from her vagina on my penis. I set down on the toilet seat to urinate but wasn't able to, I got trapped into neither nor cycle, neither I was able to ejaculate, nor was I able to urinate, I thought to jerk off but didn't do it, thinking that a girl is laying necked in the bed, whose vagina I have just penetrated , I can't jerk off, it would be a disrespect to her but is not coming for so long is also a disrespect. I don't know. I walked back and said, " Can we stop here, and I am sorry?"

She said " It's alright, the first time is always hard for male and female? Will you remember me for your whole life because I am your first?"

I said " I am not virgin; Julia was the first girl I had sex and I have been with several men; I didn't know you are looking for a virgin? Did Julia not tell you about me, about me and her?"

She got upset, her eyes turned red, she said " That fucking bitch, I asked for virgin guy and she send me a sick bisexual gigolo."

All the sudden, her politeness, care and sophistication disappeared.

I said, " Excuse me, I am not sick, nor am I a gigolo, I am all clean."

She busted into tears " I asked God if you are right for me. He said yes, how He can be wrong. "

Vivan to Andrea " Look what we do to God and idea of God, we want him to be correct in our own ways, he should meet our definitions rather than we meet His, we humans are excellent creatures, aren't we? She got very upset and asked me to leave."

I said, "I am so sorry, I didn't know anything, I only knew what Julia told me."

She warned me if I am not out of her apartment in 5 minutes, she will call 911.I rushed to put on clothes, in the rush I wasn't able to find my underwear and socks, I left them unfound. I got rest of the things. I put on my shoes and rushed out of Angelina's the apartment building.

Julia already moved out from the home I was living in; I didn't call her or text her about what happened. I never heard from Julia or Angelina. Sometimes I thought about them, sometimes I thought why Julia will lie to Angelina, was she helping her or was she jealous of her. I never found my answer. It's a bit strange, in my life I have more unanswered questions than answered one. I have more questions than answers, that's my consciousness, both girls I have been with I wasn't able to

ejaculate, I never tried for third, I knew I am not meant for women and women are not meant for me. When I think about the whole thing, I feel a shame that I couldn't come, that I didn't ejaculate, it's a bad feeling, actually a horrible one."

Andrea" I think you are overthinking, it's not as bad as you think, you know what would have been horrible if you would have come too soon as it happens with several men, several times and worst would have can't get you hard. Apart from that most of the men are shameless enough to never apologize for coming so early, so why should you feel guilty about never ejaculating inside their vagina."

Vivan" Sometimes I can't make sense about several things I did and why I did them, it's strange, very strange. I did something, and I don't know why I did it. Look at me, at age of 33 most of the people of my age have some sort of stable career, stable relationships and perhaps know the path where life is going. I killed people, I am in jail, I lost my path or perhaps never had one.

 I can't make any sense of what happened to me, what I did, why I met the type of people I did, what went wrong and what went right, my whole existence to me is a mere confusion, a mere distress, a mere anxiety."

Andrea didn't say anything, Vivan assumed she fell asleep. He also went to sleep.

Chapter 13

He woke up past midnight, urinated, and washed his hands. When he was about to go back to sleep, the officer who arrested him, the officer who dropped him from the airport to apartment and whom he sucked in his apartment parking lot came to see him. His name was Liam. Seeing him made Vivan sad, very sad, his eyes were filled with tears.

He reached the cell bars and asked, " It's late officer, what are you doing here?"

He said, " I came to see you, to check on you if you are happy after whatever you did."

Tears busted out Vivan eyes, he said "I am very sorry for what I did, and how I have treated you. I don't know what happened to me and why I picked the gun and killed people. How many I killed and injured?"

Liam "You have killed eight people, seven are seriously injured, they will never return to their normal life, only four will return to their normal life but might never overcome the trauma they have been to, so congratulations you achieved something. You successfully spoiled nineteen people and their families."

Vivan " Please don't hate me, I did it because I was unhappy and lost, and after doing it I am very sad, guilt and shame are the only emotions I feel most of the time."

He said, " If you feel so much shame and guilt, then why did you do it?"

Vivan " Some of us are damaged up to an extent that there is no recovery for us, that's all I can say?"

Liam didn't like the answer, he kind of got upset but somehow managed his emotions and said, " In a couple of days you will be transferred to another prison, I thought you should know in advance."

Vivan " I knew you won't come without any professional reason."

Liam "It's not listed anywhere in my professional obligations and if I would have followed the professional protocol, I would have shot you dead instead of arresting you."

Vivan " I want to take shower and change my clothes. Can you please take me to the bathroom? I didn't shower, it has been more than 10 days, people come and push the food inside my cell and that's it. I am stuck in this space, if I don't shower and change my clothes, I won't be able to withstand my own smell, please take me to the bathroom, please."

He lets Vivan out and takes him to the bathroom.

On the way Vivan said " I want to brush my teeth as well. I haven't brushed them since I got here."

In the bathroom Liam provided him a new toothbrush, new toothpaste, and a new pair of prison clothes, he pointed" There is the bathroom, I will stay here, you can shower as long as you want, here is your towel."

Vivan " Thank You "

Vivan brushed his teeth, cleaned his tongue with the brush , got undressed and jumped into the shower, he shower for a while , opened his uncircumcised penis and cleaned it , he was extraordinary detailed in cleaning his anal area, as soon as he was done , he opened the shower curtain, he was necked ,the water drops were flowing off of his body, Liam looked at him, Vivan stretched his right hand calling Liam near him ,Liam walked closed to him , Vivan started kissing him ,he kissed Vivan back then stopped saying " We need to remain in our professional boundaries. "

Vivan" You and I both know what will be done to me for what I did, in these circumstances professionalism and unprofessionalism doesn't matter, have you not desired what I am asking from you."

 Liam got hard, aroused, agitated and restless, he said " Yes, very much, since the movement I saw you in the flight from New York."

Vivan " I thought about it several times in the last couple of days. Can we please forget where we are, what rules and regulations want us to do, and be what we are, do what we want, please? "

Listening all these Liam grabbed Vivan and started kissing him, he undressed himself and jumped into shower with him, pulled the curtains, in couple of minutes he pushed his bare penis inside Vivan.

Vivan moaned and for the first time he felt loved while being fucked, all other times he felt penetrated, fornicated, fucked, ejaculated inside etc. In that moment he forgot Aryan and fell in love with Liam. He remembered Liam 's touch, smell of his breath, taste of his mouth and texture of his existence, the shape of his lips, the shape of his hips, his touch, his structure and his moves, their love making lasted a while, Liam switches his poses couple of times. His ejaculation, his moves before ejaculation were intense. Vivan ejaculated effortlessly around the same time when Liam ejaculated inside him. While putting on the clothes on completion Vivan said "I want to take this shower every night, with you."

Liam while dressing back in his police dress said, "Will you need anything tomorrow?"

Vivan "I want to shave."

Liam "I will bring the supplies you need."

Liam walked him back to his cell, locked Vivan back and said, "I never thought I would meet you in such circumstances, I thought about you so many times, I wished to run into you in a shopping mall or in a restaurant or in a park or in an airport not here."

Vivan cried and cried and cried. That's all he did.

Chapter 14

Next night Vivan clean shaved his beer, armpits, genital area, and his chest. Several nights they showered with each other the same way. Somedays they lay necked in each other's arms for hours, for most of the days Liam brought food from outside and they ate together, once, or twice he lit candles, and they had candlelight dinner, twice he brought him red roses. Gradually Aryan's remembrance, touch, smell, texture, desire, and longing were replaced by Liam 's remembrance, touch, smell, texture, desire, and longing, in that prison cell Vivan found something to look forward to, conversations with Andrea in day and till some part of night, and love making with Liam in late nights. More he explored Liam s psychological spaces and physical beings Vivan's complains against self, against the world, against the society he was born in, against the society he was living in, against his penetrators, fornicators, fuckers, relatives, friends, co-workers, parents, and to those whom he fucked and sucked started disappearing. In years for the first time, he felt content and relaxed.

One of those days, Andrea said to Vivan "There is something very special about you, someday I want to find out what it is?"

Vivan replied, "I am just an ordinary man, bound by space, time, relativity and material desires."

Andrea "That's what I am talking about, an ordinary man can never give such an answer and your descriptions about any events are so detailed."

Vivan "I write, I have written short stories, Novellas, Novels, and poetry. I never published any of them."

Andrea "You should ask him, what's his name? You know he loves you, I can see it, the way he acts around you, the way he walks with you, the way he looks at you. I have been seeing both of you walking back and forth from days."

Vivan" Liam, his name is Liam. He is the one who arrested me, he was the one who helped me when I was flying back bewildered and heartbroken from Manhattan, I sucked him in the parking of my apartment complex, and I was very rude to him after drinking his semen."

Andrea "I remember, you told me about him. Where is the literature you have written? "

Vivan "All of it was in my apartment; I think it should still be there untouched, I have paid the whole months' rent, what day of month is it? Do you know?"

Andrea "I think today should be 27 or 26th, something around that. I kind of lost count or perhaps I lost the sense of time."

Vivan "Count is perhaps our sense of time and time is perhaps our sense of count. I think time is the nonsense which gives us all sort of nonsenses such as stress, anxiety, and depression. Sometimes it feels to me as if time is the one which give us all desires. You know if ever time come Infront of me as a person, I want to grab him and kiss him so hard that his lips bleed, I want to suck him long, long enough that his penis starts hurting, I want to fuck him long enough that his anal bleed and when he fucks me, I hope he suffer erection dysfunction. You know sometimes in my masturbations I imagined time to manifest into a man, dark, mysterious, necked and very handsome, I desired to kiss him, I desired to suck him and swallow his semen, I desired him to fuck me, penetrate me, ejaculate inside me and I desired his semen to be a mixture of white and gray with a hint of blue shade, like shades of bluesish white marble with some nature gray textures in it.

Sometimes in my masturbations, I desire to expand myself into one more of me, suck one more of me, fuck one more me and get fucked by one more of me. Sometimes I desired to time travel and lose my virginity to myself, have sex with my younger version, protect him from the world, love him, feel warmth of his body, lips, and existence, is the desire to make love to self is creepy?"

Andrea "I don't think so. I think it's natural. I think masturbations are expansions and realizations of such desire."

Vivan " Sometimes I have masturbated on memories of arrival of new leaves on plants and trees , sometimes I have masturbated on memories of growing baby sparrows, sometimes I have masturbated on a fish swimming in the lake, sometimes I have masturbated on ants dissecting a dead insect, sometimes I have masturbated on thinking about male pig fornicating female pig , and several of my masturbation were on memories of my childhood when I have seen a bitch being fucked by a dog , and other dogs were just wandering around both, the fucker and the fucked, the penetrator and the penetrated .Most of my masturbations have been on my first penetration and on my first penetrator. Sometimes I wonder why most of them were not on Aryan, perhaps because I loved Aryan and have never seen him as object of sex, I have always seen him as an object of love. Sometimes I think if I would have had a twins' brother, I would have made love to him and would have allowed him to make love to me. I would have masturbated him, I would have sucked him, I would have let him penetrated me. Sorry I got distracted, what were you saying about my literature?"

Andrea "I think you should ask Liam to bring your literature to you. It seems he likes you a lot, maybe he is in love with you. He might be able to do this favor to you. These walls, this cell, this stinky prison is killing me. I am getting constant anxiety attacks about Kyle and Kylie security , about their future, what if they get the same experience or worst then what I did, what if Mathew is not able take care

of them, what if he remarry and his new wife hate my children, when I was outside of this prison I was in constant anxiety for them, when I am in prison I am in constant anxiety for them. Sometimes it feels to me being parents is to be in constant and endless axialities all the time."

Vivan "I am not a parent so I won't be able to understand your emotions fully, but with whatever I have been through I can never imagine bringing any progeny of mine in this world, if I ever do or ever adopt a child I will be in horrible anxieties and will end up being an extremely protective parent, may be spying psycho parent. Those little innocent creatures need to be protected, this fucked up world of ours, which we have created is not safe for innocents and delicate.

Wow, look how much I am wounded and fucked up; I fear having any progeny of mine. Tonight, I will ask Liam to bring my literature. "

Andrea "How much is it? I meant how many pages. "

Vivan "Around 300 or 400 pages, most of it is handwritten."

Andrea "Once you get your work. I want to hear what you have written."

Vivan "What if you don't like what I have written, what if it's just crappy shit."

Andrea "We are so close to death, sometimes I can smell its presence, in these moments, good, bad, right, wrong, like, dislike, we should drop these dualities and all duplicities if we can, at least we should try. Most of the humans live in endless dualities and duplicities, at least we can try to die without them."

Vivan" I think you are right, sometimes I also have sensed as if she (the death) is on her way for me."

***

Same night when Vivan was laying in Liam 's arms after their love making, he asked Liam if he could bring his work, his literature to the prison cell. Liam said, "I can bring it."

Vivan told him "All of my literature is in a black plastic bag, it's in the bedroom closet."

Next day Liam handed Vivan all his literature in the same black bag. It was afternoon when he got it. He pulled out all the pages. Only few stories were complete, rest were incomplete, those which he completed were not organized, here and there when he turned the pages he noticed a constant theme of displacements, distress, anxieties around existence and non-existence, there were several pages in which he captured an extraordinary sense of beauty, existentialism, and sensuality. Going through them he realized his lamentations and his hankerings, both have been the same from years because most of the time he never got what he desired, when he didn't, he never dropped the desires, on several pages a loop or loops of desires and hate were dancing. All those pages accumulated several genres. He organized three stories The Glass of Wine, The

Face, and The Son of Music, along with couple of other pages, re-reading of those pages mesmerized him.

He moved close to the wall and said "Andrea, I got my literature." At that time, she was moving her right hand on her vagina, she stopped and said, "Please read me something."

Vivan read "His eyes had the colors of the unknown. His hairs were energies of time."

Andrea "I sensed several times while you were speaking from the other side, something is in you, something very special. Whom are you describing here?"

Vivan "Perhaps something that I want to be, perhaps something I wanted to be, or perhaps something which will solve all my problems or perhaps I am describing the cause of all causes. Sometimes it feels to me that preciseness, accuracy, measurements all are mere tragedies."

Andrea "What type of work have you written, poetry, short stories, Novel, Novella, nonfiction?"

Vivan "Apart from nonfiction, everything else?"

Andrea "Read me something, read me a short story."

Vivan read Andrea "The Glass of Wine", one of his short stories.

***

That night when Liam came to take Vivan to shower room, he asked Vivan to take some of his literature and expressed his desire to listen to it. Vivan took the whole bag with him. When they arrived in the shower room, Liam asked him not to take off clothes and not to shower, he asked Vivan to read something. Vivan picked a short story "The Face "and read it.

He read "His eyes were deeper than the ocean and the bluest. "

Men, women, animals, birds, trees, and plants fell in the spell of his charisma and beauty. As he grew, his charisma and physical beauty grew every day. Anyone who saw him, remembered him forever.

He used to wander alone in the gardens and in the woods.

Often trees bent their fruit-laden branches down to him as he passed. Sometimes he noticed and other times he didn't.

His looks and eyes were perfect for every season, but he had never seen his own beauty, charisma, good looks, and appearance. He had never seen his face in a mirror or in a lake or in a river or in someone's eyes.

Others remembered his face and were able to recognize it, not him.

With such an immense beauty, there was a constant indifference in him and many thoughts in his mind which he was unable to stop. Discomposure and restlessness often appeared in his eyes.

One day when he was wandering in the woods, a sparrow looked into his eyes. She saw the discomposure, the restlessness, the reflection of the questions in his mind and agitation of his being.

The sparrow picked up a seed from the ground, flew toward the lake and dropped the seed on its bank.

As time passed, his beauty, his indifference, his restlessness, his discomposure, his agitation, and many thoughts in his mind grew, as did his fame.

Princes and princesses came to visit him.

In time, the seed grew into a beautiful plant, a blue flower blossomed on it, as blue as his eyes. The flower attained its peak, that day he was walking along the bank of the lake.

He saw the flower. It was leaning toward the lake. He sat down on the bank and started looking at it. In some time, he saw his reflection in the lake, for the first time he saw his eyes, the structure of his face, a reflection of his charisma, and himself.

He thought "Oh, this beautiful face."

He kept staring at his face. Evening arrived, and later night. The moon appeared in the sky. He kept staring at his blurry reflection. Morning arrived. He continues to stare at his reflection. He fell under the spell of his own beauty, his own charisma, his own face, his own being, his own existence, and his own sight. He kept looking at his reflection for many days and died of starvation and thirst.

The blue flower wilted, and the sparrow flew toward the cold mountains in the north."

Vivan "That's the end of story."

Liam "It's amazing. Is he you?"

Vivan "No, I think it's the human race or perhaps he is him, and there is no one like him."

That night when they showered together, when Liam made love to Vivan, it was on whole another level of intensity, desire, and beauty.

Laying down necked next to Vivan, Liam said "I want my every night to be like this, next to you. I think I fell in love with you when I saw you first time in the flight when I am around you something happens to me. Something that I can't describe."

Vivan's eyes filled with tears, he said "You know what I did and what will be done to me, most probably I will get death penalty or life sentence for hundreds of years. Most probably I will be moved to another jail. I might not have access of you, and you might not have access to me. You know one of the greatest regrets of my life is, I didn't invite you to my apartment when you came to drop me from the airport that night. If I would have invited you to my apartment, you would have been in my life a long time back and I would have never done what I did. You know I allowed many in my apartment and many in my life but the one I should have allowed, I didn't. Decades ago, I made the same mistake and again decades later I did exactly same mistake. I am a disgusting filth. I keep on repeating the same mistakes over and over."

Liam "Anything you did, whatever happened and will happen can't change the fact that I love you and I will always love you. Even if I desire and try, I can't alter the feelings I have for you."

Vivan " You know, you are my liberation, if I wouldn't have found you, my life would have remained incomplete."

Liam " I don't want to be your liberation; I want to be your attachment."

Vivan kissed Liam and said, "I love you too and I hope all my remembrance be around you and be about you."

Liam" I want you to meet my mother, I spoke with jail authorities, they are fine, I don't want to force it on you, only if you want."

Vivan whispered in his ears "I will love to meet your mother, my boyfriend." And sucked his right earlobe. In a couple of minutes Liam was inside him in doggy pose, it was their second penetration of the night. Vivan ejaculated jerking off in that pose.

***

It was almost 4 am when Vivan returned to his cell, Liam left him with a kiss. Vivan sat down with the cell wall being his back support and started crying.

His heavy cry woke Andrea up, she walked to the wall and said "What happened Vivan? Are you all, right?"

Vivan "Liam is in love with me."

Andrea "I knew it when I saw him walking next to you, I saw little bit of how he acts around you, from that time I knew his heart was falling for you. Why are you crying? Do you not love him?"

Vivan "I do, I love him as much as I used to love Aryan or perhaps a little bit more than that. But I can't do this to him?"

Andrea: ``What you can't do to him?"

Vivan "I want him to fall in love with someone whom he can take on thanksgiving dinners, whose hands he can hold and walk on lakeshores and beaches, with whom he can go on vacations and for whom he returns to his home. For me he walks into prison, into a prison shower room, he is a nice soul, he does not deserve this, he deserves better, he deserves someone with whom he can plan vacations, he deserves someone with whom he can make love in open sky when beauty of moon and stars dances hands on hands with darkness. I can't give him any of those, I can't even give him the most common things which are available to any human being. With me he will be stuck and will never be able to have and realize a family he deserves; I want him to have several children and raise them because I know he will be such a loving and caring father. I want to see his children, hold their hands, kiss their foreheads, and love them as if they are mine. I hope I get the death sentence so he can move on. I don't know how many people's lives I have messed up and destroyed, I don't want to destroy his life. If I don't get the death sentence, I hope I die in some prison accident or get a chronic disease which kills within one month. I don't want to live. Maybe I should break up with him."

Andrea "When you walked on lake shores or in art galleries or in beautiful streets without Aryan, how did you feel?"

Vivan "Discontent, incomplete, as if a major part of me is missing."

Andrea "If you break up with him or if you kill yourself that's what will happen to Liam, would you like him to go through it? Would you like him to feel what you felt without Aryan?"

Vivan "No, I don't want him or anyone in this world to feel that way? I don't want anyone's love story to be incomplete."

Andrea" Then let life happen and accept whatever is on the way. If you think your death will help him to get over you, it won't happen.

We humans are creatures of memories, we live in memories, we live through memories and sometimes we kill because of memories, as I did. We are creatures of memories, Vivan. Apart from that as much as I have known you, falling for you is easy, very easy but getting over you is pretty much impossible. In the last few days, sometimes even I have desired you, inside me, I desired to taste your mouth, smell your breath and body. Don't worry too much Vivan, don't even bother to fix anything. I can sense our ends are on the way and very soon they will reach us."

Vivan "You know I can't come inside a woman; I told you about two girls I have been with."

Andrea "You know males who ejaculate are like fulfilled desires, males who made a woman come and can't come themselves are like incomplete desires, one can never stop desiring them. Both of those girls who let you go are idiots. Tomorrow Mathew is coming to visit me; it will break my heart to see hate and dislike in his eyes."

Vivan "We never know what we will find in someone's eyes, this world is a fucking mystery."

Andrea didn't say anything else. On both sides of the wall silence fell, later both fell asleep.

***

Next day Liam 's mother came to see Vivan. Liam came to pick Vivan from his cell.

While walking.

Vivan "How do I look? Do I look alright?"

Liam "You look fine."

Vivan "I am nervous."

Liam "You will be fine, don't worry."

Vivan" What should I call her?"

Liam "You can call her Mary or Mrs. Smith or." he whispered in Vivian's ears "You can call her mother-in-law."

Vivan whispered back "I will love to call her mother-in-law."

Liam "I will love to make you her son in law."

By that time, they had arrived in the visitor's area. Mrs. Smith was waiting, before Liam left, he whispered in Vivian's ears "Don't be nervous, you will be fine."

Vivan picked the phone and said "Hello Mrs. Smith "

Mrs. Smith "Hello Vivan, it's so good to meet you, my son talks a lot about you, you know when he talks about you, he is so happy, I don't remember seeing him so happy speaking about anyone else."

Vivan's eye were filled with tears and his throat got heavy, he said "You know what I did? "

Mrs. Smith "I know it, the whole city knows it and it also made news into international media but that doesn't change the fact that my son loves you and since when love understands reasoning, if reasoning can dominate love, it's not love. You know my son if it's true love then it can overpower anything, that's the strength of love."

Vivan "I want Liam to be happy, I want him to have several children of his own because I know he will be such an amazing and loving father, with me I can see grief and sorrow on the way for him. I don't know how many days I have in this prison; will I get life sentence or death penalty? Which prison will I be moved to next; will Liam have access to me or not? There are so many unknown. "

Mrs. Smith "Unknown is always more than known and most of the time life doesn't work as we plan. Liam, I, and his father were a happy family, one day Mr. Smith was driving back from work, he had an accident, after suffering for a week in hospital he died. Our happy life turned upside down, there had been several moments where I felt I can't go on like this, but look what it turned out to be, Liam is grown up, we were able to find moments of happiness in our life. One can never know what the next moment is holding for us."

Vivan "I think you are right Mrs. Smith."

Mrs. Smith "Where are your parents? Did you speak to them after your arrest?"

Vivan "They are in India. I didn't speak to them in a while."

Mrs. Smith "As nothing can change the fact that Liam is in love with you, nothing can change the fact that you are their baby, I think you should talk to your parents. "

Vivan "What will I say to them?"

Mrs. Smith "Don't plan too much. Speak whatever comes in the moment."

Vivan "Now I know from where Liam got all kindness, good heart, and care. I promise, I will love him till the last movement of my life."

***

When Mrs. Smith was about to leave, Andrea was brought to the next talking booth. Mrs. Smith left. Vivan stood up and was about to leave, he saw Mathew walking in, Mathew looked at Andrea first, then his sight fell on Vivan. His eyes filled with tears seeing both, at the same moment Andrea looked at Mathew, she saw how Mathew looked at her and how Mathew looked at Vivan. Vivan looked at Andrea and Liam. Liam saw how Mathew looked at Vivan, how Vivan looked at Mathew, how Vivan looked at Andrea and how Andrea looked at both Mathew and Vivan. Vivan looked at Liam. Liam s' eyes were filled with tears. In those few moments they all realized, they might be more connected to each other then they thought , that their lives somehow cross each other, the lips Liam is kissing was kissed by Mathew on the lakeshore, the body Andrea smelled was also smelled by Vivan, the mouth which sucked her vagina also sucked Vivan's penis , the space Liam was penetrating was penetrated by Mathew as well, the semen which helped Andrea to make her babies were swallowed by Vivan on the lakeshore before drinking Mathews urine, that there is a common connection between Liam , Andrea and Mathew who was just standing next to Andrea. Vivan's heart started beating fast, a shame, a guilt, a discontent, and a strange depression rose inside him. He walked to Liam and told him "I am ready to go back. "While walking back he said "Your mother is an angel. She is very wise."

Liam said, "I am glad you liked her."

By that time, they arrived at Vivan's cell, Liam grabbed Vivan and started kissing him. The kiss was intense, toward the end, he ends up biting Vivan's lower right lip. When the kiss was over, Vivan looked at the camera in the walkway.

Liam "Don't worry about them. They know about us. I love you okay, I love you so much."

Vivan "I love you too."

He walked in the cell; Liam locked the cell. Vivan lay down on the bed, tears started flowing out of his eyes, at that moment he thought he lost his love Liam, and his friend Andrea. He fell asleep, he had a dream in which he was climbing steps in the darkness and all the sudden the stairs disappeared, he had a steep fall, it woke him up. He heard Andrea crying. He stood up and sat down next to the wall. His eyes filled with tears and throat got heavy, he said "Andrea, I am so sorry. My life and mind are a mess, and I keep creating mess in other people's life.

Mathew is the guy with whom I spend vacation on the lakeshore, he is the guy whose urine I drank."

Andrea "Today, he told me everything, about you and him, about his childhood, about his affair with his secretary. I don't think you should feel any guilt or shame, you didn't do anything wrong, you didn't even know he is married. You know what hurt me the most, he never told me what he went through in his childhood, the abuse, the exploitation, we have been married for years, we have two children together, yet I didn't know a major part of his life, why he never told me, why he never trusted me?"

Vivan "There are several things' a man feel comfortable sharing with other man instead of a woman. Most people have this idea that someone who resembles them biologically will understand them better, although this idea results in gender and racial biases most of the time. Did you tell him what you have been through in your childhood, about the sexual abuses you went through?"

Andrea "Yes, I told him today. I guess we both are at fault, he never shared a painful part of his life with me, and I never shared a major pain of my life with him, we both were hiding something from each other, something which we should have shared with each other a long time back. We were two wounded souls raising children, making love to each other, fucking, and fornicating each other hiding our leaking wound from each other, what a tragedy our life has been together. We both, Mathew and I realized something very strange, even if we would have shared our suffering and exposed all our wounds to each other we wouldn't have been sufficient for each other, we wouldn't have completed each other as significant another half."

Vivan "Why not?"

Andrea "For all these years we have known each other incompletely, hiding things from each other. Today we realized if you would have been part of us, part

of our marriage, it would have completed us and if Liam would also have been part of us, if we would have been part of each other's life, if all four of us would have been married to each other, I think we would have been perfect. Suppose if all four of us would have been married to each other, would you have accepted Kyle and Kylie?"

Vivan "I would have loved them as if they were mine."

Andrea "That's what I thought. They would have been lucky to have you in their life and I would have been the luckiest bitch in the whole neighborhood, surrounded by three very handsome and good-looking guys. "

Vivan" I think we would have spoiled Kyle and Kylie well. Three fathers and a mother. I think we would have never felt lonely, life would have been amazing. I might have turned into an overprotective asshole father. Oh, this mind, it's a fucking asshole, a bastard and we are day dreamers. Aren't we?"

Andrea "What's wrong in being a daydreamer, don't we have the right to be happy before we die? Even if that happiness is only in dreams."

Vivan "Yes, we do. Look what a great tragedy humans live in, we need death, its idea, and its remembrance to be happy, what a marvelous by product we are after millions of years of existence."

Andrea and Vivan both started crying, they cried for a while. Andrea slapped herself twice, pulled her hairs and pressed nails on her skin to hurt herself. Vivan pulled out his penis and started jerking off.

***

Mathew went back home. Kyle and Kylie were at their grandma's home. He had already seen news about Vivan and Andrea several times on local news, in national news and in international newspapers but seeing them together, next to each other, in the same prison bewildered him. While he was driving back from prison, he felt his male significant half Vivan and his female significant half Andrea are locked down, both were caged into the same prison. They are inaccessible to him and without them the world seemed absurd, a hopeless existence. He was agitated, angry, frustrated, and depressed. By the time he walked into his home, his mind was filled with several racing thoughts. He fell on the living room sofa. Their pet ragdoll cat jumped next to him, he started moving his hands on her soft and silky coat, a desire of pleasure started inside him. He unzipped his pants, pulled out his penis from underwear, started moving his right hand on it. He got hard, thick, and long. He grabbed the cat and pushed her vagina on his penis, it penetrates her. She yowled, turned around and bit his hand, he lost the grip on her, and she jumped off, ran away with the highest speed possible to the basement. Seeing her running as such created a terrible guilt, distress, shame, and disgust inside him, his eyes filled with tears, he grabbed his penis with both of his hands and continued jerking off.

Chapter 15

That night in the shower room, sitting next to Vivan, Liam pulled out an album from his backpack, he handed it over to Vivan and said, "My mother wants me to show you my childhood album."

Vivan "That's what your mother wants, what do you want Liam?"

Liam "I want you to always love me. I wish I should have been your first kiss; I wish I should have been your first."

Vivan put his right-hand finger on Liam 's mouth. Liam stopped speaking. Vivan kissed him and said "I will always love you, and after you I don't think I will be able to love anyone else. You should not feel any insecurities, no one else has access to me apart from you."

Liam "You tell me, can one truly be free from insecurities?"

Vivan "I don't know about others, but I don't remember ever being out of insecurities, being without them but there are stories about people who freed themselves from all insecurities and fears, I never came across any such person. "

Liam "Because they only exist in stories."

Vivan "Possibly. "

Liam "Did you fall in love with someone else in the past?"

Vivan "Why you want to know? Does it matter? Will it change anything?"

Liam "It won't, it won't change anything. I answer all your questions, correct?"

Vivan "yes you do."

Liam "Have I ever said no to you for anything?"

Vivan "No you never did."

Liam "Then "

Vivan "Then?"

Liam "I ask you a few questions and you don't want to answer them."

Vivan's heart sank in fear and started beating fast, for the first time he sensed an anger in Liam, at the time of shooting when Vivan and Liam came across each other, rather than anger Vivan saw sympathy and compassion in Liam 's eyes.

Vivan "I fell in love with someone in the past, I was around 18 or 19 years old. He was my classmate in my bachelors, he was a year older to me. His name is Aryan."

Liam "Where is he? I mean Where does he live?"

Vivan "I think he is in India, I haven't spoken to him in years, so I don't know for sure."

Liam "How long were you in relationship with him?"

Vivan "It never started. I didn't allow him to express his feelings and I never expressed mine. "

Liam "Why not?"

Vivan "I don't know. I think it was my ego and insecurities which stopped me from expressing my feelings. I don't know why I never allowed him to express his feelings, I think he tried several times. I used to like him a lot, yet I don't know why I pushed him away every time he tried to be closer to me. Why did I do it? I don't know. I think I am sick; I think I have always been sick. You know pushing him away, not loving him and not allowing him to love me later became one of the greatest regrets of my life. His absence created the void which no matter what I did was impossible to fill in until you walked in. The moment you walked into my life that void disappeared. I have never know him as I have known you, I have never touched him as I touched you, I don't know how his lips feel, I know how yours do, I don't know what's the smell of his breath , I know the smell of your breath .I don't know the warmth of his body, I know yours, I never heard his heart beats, I did yours, I have never known what his arms feel like, what does being in them feels like , I know how yours do. You know there is something very strange about my life, I have never achieved the most basic human relationships. I had several guys who wanted to fuck me and who fucked me in my high school, in university and in later life but I never had a friend, I don't know how a normal family looks like, and feels like. When I was growing up my parents used to live with my grandparents, there was constant bickering in the house, most of it caused by my grandparents and their two lovely daughters my paternal aunts, who used to live in the same street of my grandparents. My grandpa often, pretty much every day mentioned that the house doesn't belong to my parents or to me, that he can kick us out whenever he wants and very soon, he will.

You know pretty much every day he announced the house we are living doesn't belong to us, everything that was going on, the bickering, the disputes, the restless environment pretty much destroyed the idea of home and the idea of family for me. Then I was sent to boarding school at the age of fourteen.

I was bullied and discriminated. Many people were eager to fuck me, but I never had a single friend. I was forced into sex and was molested.

At the age of 14, the story of my displacement started, sometimes I wonder, can people like me, who never found home, who never had a home, can be called displaced, and do people like me have a home country in true sense? Do homeless people like me have a home country or idea of it in a true sense? perhaps not. By the time I graduated from high school I was exhausted and discontented. I was praying for the high school nightmare to be over, two of my classmates were

fornicating me towards the end of my high school, they turned into assholes and rascals. They double penetrated me several times against my will, with both it was always threesome, they fucked me mercilessly, one used to push his penis inside my anal and another inside my mouth, as one use to increase the intensity rather than consoling or comforting, the other used to increase the intensity as well, couple of times they end up hurting me. I had no choice if I disagreed, they forced me, they overpowered me. It was horrible. If a thought about it crosses my mind it gives me horrors. On graduation I was displaced from a town to a city, there whole another story started, again I had no friend, one night my anal pretty much bleed after four guys penetrated me, in four year of period one circumstances, or another led me to change four places of residence. Once I rented a room with tin roof, on the third floor of a house, at that time it was the only option I could afford, the room used to be a heater in summers, used to flood when rains and used to be as cold as outside in winters. "

Liam "Is Aryan on Facebook? I want to see what he looks like."

Vivan felt strange when Liam didn't respond to anything Vivan talked about his family, childhood, boarding house, and college days.

Vivan said "Why? Why do you want to see him? Are you upset? Are you angry? Do you not like me anymore?"

Liam didn't reply. He handed his phone.

Vivan "He is not my Facebook friend. "

Liam took back his phone, logged into his Facebook and handed it over to Vivan saying "Here, search him."

Vivan searched for Aryan, it was not hard to find him. He pulled up his profile and handed the phone to Liam.

Liam scrolled through some of Aryan's photos.

Liam "Is that why you love me? Is that why you are allowing me to fuck you? because my neck, my shoulders and my nose have resemblance with him? Because I remind you of him, because you were never able to have him, so you want to have something that resembles him. I don't love you because you remind me of someone or you resemble someone else, I love you because you are you, I never searched someone else in you."

Liam 's eyes filled with tears and anger.

Vivan "He is not you and you are not him. He is he and you are you. I don't love you because you remind me of him, I don't search him for you. I love you for being you. If you would have looked totally different from what you look now, even then I would have fallen in love with you. I love your psychology and being, far more than your biology, that's why I will always love you, even when you grow old, 90 years old or 100 years old, I will love you even if you lose all your physical beauty. In one way or another, we all to an extent resemble each other,

you are my sense of beauty, my sense of being and my sense of creativity, you are my sense of being, please don't doubt my love. I don't love you because you are someone else, I love you because you are you." Saying this one tear dripped down from his right eye and another dripped down his left eye.

Liam "You know maybe I should have born in your neighborhood, then I would have been able to protect you. I would have been your first crush, I would have been your first kiss, I would have been your first sexual encounter and I would have been your first love."

Vivan "Sometimes I wish the same thing, maybe I should have been born next door to you and everything would have been perfect. I would have loved you to be my first and I wish you to be my last. Suppose if I would have been born in your neighborhood or next door and we have dated, do you think we would have been married by now?"

Liam" I think I would have married you in my early 20s, I wouldn't have waited for both of us to be in our thirties and then get married. I think by now we would have been raising our children, maybe our first born would have been ten or eleven."

Vivan "How many children do you want to have?"

Liam "With you, may be three or four. Without you none."

Vivan" Four sounds great. "As soon as Vivan said this he burst into tears and said "We are dreamers, aren't we? We like to imagine the possibilities which comfort us, don't we? We are dreaming the impossible."

Liam "What's wrong in being a dreamer?"

Vivan "Nothing, it's good to dream. I want you to have four children without me. I want you to live a normal life. I want you to marry someone whose hands you can hold and walk on beach hearing sounds of waves , whom you can take on thanksgiving lunch , with whom you can see stars , moon and the darkness of midnight sky, with whom you can walk outside in the world, with whom you can go for shopping and with whom you can cook in your kitchen and eat on dinner table. I want you to have someone in your life with whom you can go for vacations you deserve. I want you to hold his hand and watch a romantic movie in a theater."

Liam "I don't want any of that, I just want you."

Vivan "What if I get the death sentence?"

Liam "Then I will live with your memories."

Vivan "Why you love me so much? How can you love me so much? How can someone love someone else up to this extent?"

Liam "I don't know why and how. I only know I do. When I saw you first time in the flight from New York, I felt something inside me, something inside me

moved, it felt as if I have been looking for you from years, when you set down next to me it felt to me as if I don't want to be anywhere else and when you touched my forehead it filled my whole body and mind with ecstasy. When you kissed me and sucked me in your apartment parking lot, for weeks I was only thinking about that and about you, since then all my masturbations and pleasures have been on you and about you. Love doesn't walk on the ground of reasons, love doesn't dance on the platforms of reasons, love doesn't understand reasons and maybe love is the reason of all reasons, but love is not a reason. So why I love you, why I love you how I love you, I don't know, I don't know the reasons of it, maybe there are no reasons. Sometimes I tried to find the reasons for my love for you and I found none. I think the love which can be reasoned out is not true love."

Vivan turned around, pushed his nose and mouth inside the right armpit of Liam, first he smelled it, then moved his tongue on that area and kissed it.

Vivan "I love your smell."

Liam moved his mouth closer to Vivian's and kissed him. After tasting each other's saliva for some time Vivan said" I want to see your childhood and high school photos."

They both started going through the photo album. They arrived at a photo where Liam was standing with his father, Vivan "You got your nose and neck from your dad." They continued to flip the pages. Liam s high school day photos popped up, Vivan "Wow look at you, so handsome, I am sure most of the girls in your high school desired you, did they just used to throw themselves on you?"

Liam smiled "Kind of."

Vivan "I know what your kind of means."

Liam smiled and said, "Are you jealous?"

Vivan "Very jealous, specially of those who were your first, first kiss, first masturbation, first blow job, first sex, first night together and first love because I should have been all of that."

Liam "Even if you are not my first kiss, my first masturbation, first blowjob, first sex and first night together, you are my first love, and I don't think I will ever be able to love anyone else as I love you. "Saying this Liam gently bit Vivan's left earlobe and said, "You know I want you to be necked and I want me to be necked and I want to be on you necked and I want to be inside you necked."

Vivan smiled and said, "I like the idea, let's do it."

They both quickly helped each other get necked. Vivan kissed an inch below Liam 's belly, kissed his balls and sucked his penis. Liam moaned in pleasure. Liam explored and kissed every part of Vivan's body. Later he pulled Vivan on him and pushed his penis inside. Liam 's bare, unlubricated penis started moving inside out of Vivan. Vivan started moaning, Liam pushed his right-hand middle finger in Vivan's mouth, Vivan started sucking it as if it was Liam 's penis. In

couple of minutes Liam ejaculated inside Vivan. Liam 's penis was thickest, hardest, and longest just before ejaculation. While ejaculating Liam pushed his penis deepest as if he wants to be completely inside Vivan, as if he wants to be one with Vivan. On ejaculation Liam asked Vivan to penetrate him. Vivan penetrated Liam in doggy pose.

When they were done, they lay down in each other's arms. Liam kissed Vivan and said, "I love you."

Vivan "I love you too."

Liam "Can I tell you something?"

Vivan "You don't need my permission. You can tell me anything you like."

Liam" I think you should call Aryan."

Vivan "I don't think he will talk to me after what I have done. I don't think he will pick up."

Liam "I think you should still call him. He deserves to get the closure. You should tell him that you loved him. Life without closures leave endless open questions."

Liam handed Vivan his phone and asked him to dial Aryan's number.

Vivan "I will dial the number I remember; I don't know if he still has the same number."

He dialed the number; the phone rang half earth away and it was picked.

Vivan "Hello, can I talk to Aryan?"

Other side "This is Aryan "

Vivan "Aryan, this is Vivan. I am calling from America; I mean from the United States. We were classmates in bachelors. "Saying all these his throat got heavy, his eyes filled with tears, the tears dripped from his chick on the floor.

Aryan" Vivan, you don't need to tell me who you are? I never forgot you. Are you alright?"

Vivan "I am alright. You?"

Aryan "I am as good as I can be without you, and I am as bad as I can be without you. Your absence is my incompleteness. I miss you every day."

Vivan" I am calling to let you know that I have loved you, I have loved you with my whole heart and being, and I am sorry, I never allowed you to express your feelings, your thoughts, your emotions, I know you have tried so many times. I just want to let you know, you are my first love and look what absence of you did to me, look without you how lost I felt."

Aryan "I still love you Vivan, I will always do, and I always did."

Vivan "You know what I did. You know I killed so many people. I am a beast; I am a murderer."

Aryan "What you did, what you are doing and what you will do can't change the fact that I love you and that I will never be able to love anyone else." Saying all this, Aryan's throat got heavy, and tears filled his eyes.

Vivan "How can you love me so much? You never touched me, you never kissed me, you never hugged me."

Aryan "I have loved you, hundreds of times in my imaginations and in my dreams, that is more than enough for me in this lifetime. I just want you to know, I will always love you."

Vivan "There is a part of me which will always belong to you, there is a part of me which will always be about you. Good by Aryan."

Aryan "Goodbye Vivan. I love, I love you so much. I am very happy, you called."

Vivan disconnected. In Liam 's arms he cried and cried.

Liam "You did the right thing."

Vivan "Will it do anything bad for him? Me telling him that I used to love him, that I loved him for years."

Liam "I don't think so. Maybe it will do something good to him, knowing that the person he loved, the person he loves also loved him. I don't mind if you love him and love me. I don't mind if you love us both."

Listening to this Vivan closed his eyes and asked himself "Am I still in love with Aryan?", the answer came from within him, he didn't understand the answer. He asked, "Do I love Liam and Aryan both?", the answer came from within him, he didn't understand the answer. He asked, "Can I love Liam and Aryan both?" the answer came from within him, he didn't understand the answer. He left the questions and answers in the void. The vagueness of existential realities continued.

Liam moved his right hand in Vivian's hairs, he felt the softness of his hairs, kissed his right chick, Vivan smiled with his eyes closed, Liam said "Maybe you should talk to your parents. Don't you think they deserve to hear your voice?"

Vivan opened his eyes and said, "Why are you so nice?"

Liam" Because I love you."

Vivan "I think you love me because you are nice." Saying this Vivan dialed his father's number, almost half earth away, the call was picked by his father, his father "Hello ". Vivan's throat got heavy, tears burst out of his eyes, it grew impossible for him to speak, he started crying.

His father said "Vivan *betaa,* are you alright?"

Vivan "I am not, I miss you and mom. "

His father said, "We miss you too. Talk to your mom, she is here."

His mom's throat got very heavy, she somehow managed to say "Vivan *betaa*" and tears flooded out of her eyes.

Vivan "I love you mom and dad; I love you both so much. I am very sorry for what I did. I should have never done it. I should have come back to you long time back or maybe I should have never left you."

His mom and dad both said, "We love you too *Betaa,* we will always love you and we have always loved you."

For some time on both sides of the phone, on both sides of the earth a lot of tears flew from the eyes, the emotions were dense, and their existence was bewildered, seeing all these Liam s eyes filled with tears. That night Liam held Vivan in his arms as if Vivan was a newborn baby. The same night Vivan decided not to live anymore.

Early morning when Liam brought him back to his cell, they came to know Andrea committed suicide. She ended up cutting her blood vans with her teeth, whole night blood flew out from her body. She died couple of minutes back. Liam walked Vivan back into the cell and started helping the team with Andrea's dead body. Her suicide broke Vivan's heart, that day he felt terrible loneliness.

He picked up a paper from his literary work and wrote "Loneliness is my most frequent companion. I don't think it will ever leave me.", then he flipped through pages , here and there he read them, a constant theme of loneliness , displacement , homelessness , search for a home , a comfortable space and longing of a suitable companion were on those pages, reading through those pages he realized till now most of the time the same themes have occupied his psychological and physical spaces and he have frequently written about what he desires and less frequently written about what he have.

Vivan wept for hours thinking about his parents, Aryan, Andrea, about what he has done and about what was done to him. That day he felt unexplained horrors along with a terrible loneliness. When he fell asleep, he had the same dream, he is climbing stairs in an unknown space in the dark and suddenly the stairs disappeared, he started falling, it woke him up, he was horrified. He urinated. The jail food was pushed into his cell, he didn't eat. His whole body was agitated and distressed. Every bad moment, experience, and treatment he has received started flooding through his memories.

He remembered last conversation with Andrea where she expressed her desire to not go through the whole legal process, court, hearing, questions from attorneys and judgment from jury.

She said " She have no desire to tell her story to those who wouldn't even genuinely try to understand it , to those who might have already concluded her act without understanding the reasons behind what she did and even if she tell they won't get it because most of the time the jury and the judge both are creatures who have been raised with a predefined idea of good and bad , whose imaginations are stuck on dualities like good and bad , right and wrong , who most of the time might not even be able to capture and calculate the significance of individuality and insignificance of what they are trying to stand up for. "

She told Vivan along with firing shots on James and Nancy she also fired several shots on Lucas, he is founder and CEO of a multinational corporate. She said "The asshole (Lucas) was the one who poured a lot of money in James's political campaign. He also poured a lot of money in Mary's church. In my search I found out both assholes and the bitch have been watching each other's back from years, manipulating people on behalf of each other, hiding each other's crimes. Asshole's (Lucas's) company owns a blueberry farm in Brazil whose blueberries are not available to the citizens of the country where the farm stand. The extracts of blueberries are pushed into the company's multi vitamin bottles. The asshole and his company are and have been committing several crimes and have been manipulating the governments across the world and in United States to sell its products for very high prices, fucking asshole, the owner of a shampoo, lipstick, and multivitamin selling company. I shot him right in his forehead, the asshole fell on the ground like stool from dogs anal. The stinky, filthy rascal, the representation of corporates crimes on individuals, individuality, and countries. In my investigation I came across this girl who used to work at James's office, she told me when she was doing her internship at the mayor's office as I was, Lucas and James, both forcefully double penetrated her. Lucas penetrated her in anal area, he was very rough, her anal bleed, when he saw blood on penis he shouted in joy "yes, yes, I made her ass bleed, I won James, I won." when he was shouting in joy. James was still inside her vagina. Lucas shouted, "Make the bitch bleed from front and I will give five million more for your election campaign." She told me listening this James turned into a fucking monster, several times he pulled his penis all the way out and pushed in, rather than penetrating her, his whole goal switched to make her vagina bleed, he stopped for a moment pushed his two fingers inside her vagina, the sharp nails went inside her vagina and it bleed, he pushed the penis back inside her vagina and continued to penetrated her .He showed his fingers with blood to Lucas and spoke " Here, here is the blood from her pussy."

Lucas said, "That's not fair, I thought you would bleed her with your penis."

James "You were not specific, you told me to bleed her vagina and I did. I won my friend." Pushing his penis deep inside her, he shouted "Five million are mine."

Lucas joyfully said "That's my man. Let me smell your fingers." James moved those two fingers next to Lucas's nose, he smelled them and said, "Smell so nice." Later James pushed those two fingers inside her mouth, he ejaculated inside her while those fingers pushed inside her mouth. Later they both threatened her if she goes to police or talk about it to anyone, anything could happen to her and her family. James grabbed her hairs and said, "Police work for people like me and Lucas. You, common people are fools who think police are there to serve you. All systems are meant to serve rich, there is nothing for poor and middle-class people like you. Later he spit into her mouth and made her swallow the spit. Vivan, while she was saying this to me, she was trembling in fear, she reminded me of me at age of six, I used to be the same way around Jack. I don't think she will ever be out of those memories and fears. I don't know how many other women both assholes have molested, and I don't know how many children and women Nancy manipulated and I don't know how many James, Lucas and Nancy exist on the earth. I wish to kill them all, I wish to kill them all." Saying this Andrea busted into tears.

Vivan "I know what you mean. Do you think if we would have put some efforts, it would have been possible for us to heal our wounds, to grow out of our experience and to not kill people?"

Andrea "I think in the vast existence, all possibilities exist all the time and they can be realized but I don't think all wounds can be healed. Sometimes there is a possibility to be wounded but no possibility to heal."

Finally, Andrea concluded she doesn't want to live because she is sick and tired of masturbations, she would rather commit suicide than live on masturbations.

Vivan "Perhaps you are right, human race who is being fucked by corporates and institutes only have two choices, either to masturbate or to commit suicide, later seems a better option. Sometimes it feels to me as if corporates and institutes joined their hands together and cut the penises, balls, boobs, have sealed the vaginas and anal holes. The crimes of institutes and corporates are far bigger than yours and mine, but they will never be jailed or sentenced for life or will get death penalty, its only individuals who get such punishments. Our disgusting societies, too eager to criminalize individuals and individualities. I lied to you about Aryan, he was in love with me, but I never allowed him to express his emotions and feelings, I don't know why it did it and you know not allowing him to express his emotions, not telling him what I felt towards him, not holding his hands, kissing him, and making love to him became one of the greatest regrets of my life."

Andrea "We all are a bunch of liars in one way or another Vivan. You are honest enough to accept your lie. Most of the people lie to themselves and lie to others

and they even don't recognize the fact. Some of them even need lies to live, without those lies they will commit suicide, and these are the entities labeled as grownups. I am very grateful that I have known you. I want to remember you and your stories forever. I hope Kyle and Kylie never go through what I have been through, what Mathew has been through and what you have been through. You know sometimes I wish I would have told Mathew what I have been through in my childhood, I wish I should have allowed him to see my wounds and I wish he should have allowed me to see his, perhaps then we would have been able to take care of each other, perhaps then I would not have done what I have done, perhaps there was a possibility or a choice or a free will not to do it . I hope I should have used it. I don't know why I am lamenting so much; I know lamentations won't change anything."

Vivan "I hope no children on the earth ever go through what I have been through, what you have been through and what Mathew have been through."

Later Andrea pushed her hands in her underwear and masturbated herself.

She did the same thing from which she was getting tired off.

***

Kyle and Kylie were bullied by couple of their classmates as "Children of a monster", listening these words broke their heart. When they got back from school, they shared what happened with them and they asked their grandma "Is mom a bad person? is she a monster? Why did she kill so many people?"

Their Grandma with tears in her eyes said "She is one of the nicest souls I have ever known, sometimes even good people lose their paths. She is not a bad person, she only lost her way for few hours, that's all. She loves you both a lot and I want you both to always remember that." saying this she hugged them both. Tears dropped from her eyes, from Kyle's eyes and from Kylie's eyes. Kyle was in her left arm and Kylie was in her right arm. All three creatures cried and cried and cried.

***

On his first visit to Andrea in prison, when Mathew saw Vivan and Andrea in the same prison, few feet apart from each other, his eyes filled with tears, heart with multiple intense emotions and mind with agitation and anger. He sat down and picked the phone. First question Andrea asked, "Why him? was I not enough?" by him she meant Vivan.

Mathew "It's never about what is enough or not. Was I not enough for you that you picked the gun?"

Andrea "Sometimes things are about what one had been through, it has nothing to do with anyone else, whatever I did, for that you are not responsible at all."

They continued their conversation, they talked about Kyle and Kylie, they opened their wounds to each other, they realized several things, regretted several other things, longed, and desired many other things.

In their conversation they realized they can't complete each other, they need a third or perhaps fourth person to complete them, Vivan and Liam were needed to complete them and to complete their marriage. They realized perhaps all four of them should have been married to each other.

Chapter 16

The night arrived as it always does, Liam picked Vivan. As soon as they reached the bathroom, Vivan immediately kissed Liam, he unzipped Liam 's pants, pulled down his underwear, bent on his knees and pushed Liam 's semi hard penis inside his mouth and started sucking it. Liam 's penis got hard; he started moving his hands in Vivian's hairs moaning in pleasure. Vivan continued to take his penis deeper and deeper into his mouth. Liam ejaculated inside Vivan's mouth. Vivan swallowed the ejaculated semen.

Liam" That was one of the best blowjobs I ever got. "

Liam sat down on his knees and kissed Vivan. Vivan's saliva mixed with Liam 's semen got into Liam 's mouth. When their kiss was over Liam said, "Taste of my sperms aren't that bad."

Vivan said "They taste pretty amazing." and he winked at Liam.

Liam ``Let me taste your."

He made Vivan lay down on the floor, pulled down his pajama, kissed his balls and took Vivan's hard penis inside his mouth. He sucked his glans first for a while then took his penis deep inside his mouth. Vivan loved the warmth of Liam 's mouth on his penis. He ejaculated inside Liam 's mouth. Vivan's lukewarm semen filled Liam 's mouth, he swallowed them, moved on to Vivan, kissed him and said, "Yours taste far better than mine."

They fell a sleep for a while in each other's arms. Later in the night around 4 am Liam penetrated Vivan in doggy pose, after that he dropped Vivan back to his cell. He didn't notice that Vivan had picked some shaving blades and pushed them into his pajama pockets.

Vivan walked back into his cell, he grabbed one of Liam 's hands and said, "I love you, and I will always love you, I just want you to know."

Liam "I know that. I love you too." Saying this he walked away.

Vivan's eyes got filled with tears. His throat got heavy.

He sat down next to the same wall through which Andrea, and he used to talk. He pulled out all his written work from the bag. He set it down next to him on the right side, he picked up a short story he has written "The Son of Music". He set pages of that story in his lap, pulled out the shaving blade from the pocket and cut his blood vein, the blood started flowing out of his body. The jail hallway was empty. He started reading the story. It read as "

He was sleeping under the blanket of dew drops. The blanket was protecting him against the sunrays. In a few moments a beautiful woman walked to him and pulled off the blanket, all the rays blocked by that blanket started falling on him.

His body started glittering. That woman kissed on his right cheek and said, "My lovely son". He opened his deep blue eyes. In that moment his face contained in half sleep, half awake-ness, a hint of laziness and immense beauty. His hairs were dark and had the mysterious of blackholes. That woman picked him and said, "It's time to wake up, my lovely son."

After some time, he went to a garden to play. He was necked and all other children playing there were necked as well. All those children had equality of beauty, uniqueness, and transcendence. The name of that son of music was Hymn. For some time, he played in that garden with other children, then he sat down under a tree.

After some time, a butterfly flew to him, she was holding a small violin, she asked Hymn "Would you like to listen to my song?"

Hymn nodded his head in yes. The butterfly started playing her song on the violin. When she was playing her song, several butterflies gathered around him, each of them was holding a musical instrument, someone was holding a harp, someone was holding a violin, someone was holding a viola, someone was holding a cello, a flute, a trumpet, and a saxophone. When that butterfly was done, all the butterflies said "Goodbye "to Hymn. They flew far away towards the section of the garden which was filled with the red flowers.

After that a golden squirrel passed by.

She asked him "Would you like to have a piano fruit?"

Hymn nodded yes.

The tree under which he set down was filled with piano fruits. The squirrel climbed up the tree and dropped two piano fruits. When they fell on the ground, sound of a piano sonata emerged from them. Hymn and the squirrel both ate the piano fruits together. After finishing the piano fruit, the golden squirrel said "Goodbye "and went towards the dense plants. Hymn set down under that tree for a while, then started walking towards the part of the garden which was filled with blue flowers. On the way he came across a fawn. The fawn walked to him. Hymn hugged the fawn, and both walked together for a while. The fawn saw his mother and ran towards her.

Hymn spent the whole day in that garden. He saw many creatures playing musical instruments. He spent a considerable amount of time on the lake shore seeing the lake getting wrinkled with small waves. Here and there colorful fishes swim up to the surface of that crystal clear lake. Their colors were the colors of music.

The garden was filled with music, beauty, and comfort. The garden had several eternal elements which never decayed. In the evening Hymn returned home.

His whole day and his whole life were filled with music, peace, beauty, comfort and belonging. He went to his bed and lay down on it. The same beautiful woman kissed his forehead and said, "My lovely son."

She put the dew drop blanket on him. His Sleep was filled with composure, comfort, beauty, and beautiful dreams.

Around midnight that garden filled with the dense moonlight.

He wrote "I hope someday I can have that sleep and that existence. "

The story had a completion date written at the end; it was almost a decade old. Vivan realized he never found that sleep and that existence. A page was attached to the same story. The title on the page says, "A Sense of Beauty". It read as "A world was there with its sense and senselessness, significance, and insignificance. A world is here as well, with desires and pains. A space between word and wordlessness stood. He moved his fingers on piano, later he picked the wine glass and swallowed couple of sips of the wine. The world was there with its stability and perplexity, there were not only questions, but answers as well and the questions born out of those answers and answers born out of those questions. The endless cycles and repetitions never seemed to end. Was it a tragedy or mere the sense of being?"

Few moments passed as they always do, enough blood flowed from Vivan's body, he lost the consciousness.

A page from his literature written in his handwriting was laying down on the prison cell, his blood was about to reach it. It read –

He knocked on the door.

The other side asked, "What are you looking for?"

He said "Past."

Other side replied, "Take a walk into the memory lanes."

Later that day Vivan was found dead in his prison cell. Most of the pages of his literature were soaked in his blood by then.

Ingram Content Group UK Ltd.
Milton Keynes UK
UKHW021810030723
424469UK00017B/853